Consider
THE
Lilies

Prov. 10:28

Lynnette

THE WYLDHAVEN SERIES
by Lynnette Bonner

Not a Sparrow Falls – BOOK ONE
On Eagles' Wings – BOOK TWO
Beauty from Ashes – BOOK THREE
Consider the Lilies – BOOK FOUR

CHRISTMAS NOVELLAS
Sheriff Reagan's Christmas Boots – BOOK FIVE (Novella)
Doc Griffin's Christmas Sleigh – BOOK SIX (Novella)
Deputy Joe's Christmas Saddle – BOOK SEVEN (Novella)
Marshal Zane's Christmas Horse – BOOK EIGHT (Novella)
Washington Nolan's Christmas Watch – BOOK NINE (Novella)
Parson Clay's Christmas Pup – BOOK TEN (Novella)
Kin Davis' Christmas Send-Off – BOOK ELEVEN (Novella)

Songs in the Night – BOOK TWELVE
Honey from the Rock – BOOK THIRTEEN – Coming soon!
Beside Still Waters – BOOK FOURTEEN – Coming Soon!

OTHER BOOKS BY LYNNETTE BONNER

THE SHEPHERD'S HEART SERIES
Historical

Rocky Mountain Oasis – BOOK ONE
High Desert Haven – BOOK TWO
Fair Valley Refuge – BOOK THREE
Spring Meadow Sanctuary – BOOK FOUR

SONNETS OF THE SPICE ISLE SERIES
Historical

On the Wings of a Whisper - BOOK ONE

Find all other books by Lynnette Bonner at:
www.lynnettebonner.com

Consider the Lilies

Wyldhaven 4

Lynnette BONNER

Pacific Lights

Consider the Lilies
WYLDHAVEN, Book 4

Published by Pacific Lights Publishing
Copyright © 2019 by Lynnette Bonner. All rights reserved.

Cover design by Lynnette Bonner of Indie Cover Design, images ©
   www.depositphotos.com, File: # 151222162
   www.depositphotos.com, File: # 148003883
   www.istockphoto.com, File: # 499778671
Book interior design by Jon Stewart of Stewart Design

Scripture taken from the New King James Version®. Copyright © 1982 by
Thomas Nelson, Inc. Used by permission. All rights reserved.

ISBN: 978-1-942982-13-5

To Those Prone to Worry:

Worry can sneak up on the best of us.
A lost job, lost child, lost marriage, lost friendship,
and suddenly worry becomes a constant companion,
robbing tranquility, contentment, and rest.
God longs to take the worry and give peace in its place.
But we have to let go of the tendency to try and fix everything,
and learn to trust that God sees all, knows all, is all.
Do you know Him?

If not, but you would like to know more
please visit:
www.peacewithgod.net

Luke 12:27

"Consider the lilies, how they grow: they neither toil nor spin; and yet I say to you, even Solomon in all his glory was not arrayed like one of these."

Chapter One

Jacinda Callahan stood next to Marshal Zane Holloway on the train depot platform with a smile fixed on her face as she waved goodbye to her son, Reagan, and his wife Charlotte. Their train had been late. But it hadn't dampened their enthusiasm. They had boarded only a few minutes ago and were even now grinning at her from behind the grimy window of their boxcar.

"Goodbye! Have a lovely time! Don't worry about a thing!" Jacinda blew a few kisses their way, truly hoping Reagan would be able to leave the pressures and concerns of his job as sheriff behind.

Charlotte flapped her hanky in response and literally bounced up and down from what Jacinda could see through the dingy glass.

Jacinda saw Reagan say something to Charlotte and they both laughed, then leaned close to relish in a lingering kiss.

Jacinda kept her smile in place, but as the train belched a column of steam and chuffed a slow exit, she couldn't keep up pretenses any longer.

Her shoulders slumped as she watched the train shrink into a small speck on the horizon.

Lord, keep them safe. Bring them back to me all in one piece.

Something tightened in her chest. What would she do if something happened to them? And there were certainly any number of things that could happen!

There were outlaws and gangsters and train robbers. Murderers and thieves.

And that was just the beginning of the list!

Not to mention that Reagan and Charlotte were headed right into the heart of godless San Francisco. Oh, why had she ever agreed with them that this trip was a good idea?

When they'd gotten married late last year, they'd planned to take a wedding trip within a couple weeks of the ceremony— after Charlotte's parents returned to Boston. However, one delay had led to another and now here it was early March and they were just setting off.

Jacinda would have preferred if they'd never gotten around to the trip.

Beside her, Zane cleared his throat. "Ready to head back? Or shall we stand here staring at the tracks until they return next month?"

Jacinda gave him a deprecating look. She'd almost forgotten that he was beside her. Almost. But not quite. Because it was nearly impossible to forget about the handsome Zane Holloway, even if he was only a friend.

She looked down and fiddled with the lace at her cuffs, willing herself not to give in to the tears that suddenly begged for release. "Yes. I suppose we should get going. It will already be near dark by the time we arrive back in Wyldhaven. I wouldn't want us to be caught out on the road after dark, especially since that new gang of outlaws has been raising such a ruckus in the area." Her heart rate increased merely at the thought. "I'm just not certain it's a good time for Reagan to be away. On the other hand, maybe it's the best time for him to be away—for his own protection. With the new bank being built in town..."

Zane settled a hand at her back and gave her a nudge down

the platform. At the same time, he gave her a sympathetic look that was almost her undoing.

The look told her to buck up, but it also said she could confide in him.

Was there any other man who could say so much without speaking a word? She felt thankful that he'd come with her, because he was such a good listener and she really needed someone to spill her concerns to.

Jacinda stepped out at a smart pace. "Of course, I'm not doubting that you and Joe can protect Wyldhaven, you understand? But do you think the outlaws might try something?"

Zane's only answer was a bit of a squint around his eyes and the uptick of one corner of his mouth.

Jacinda released a huff. "I know what you're going to say. You're going to say that I shouldn't worry. That I should trust that the good Lord has good plans for everyone. Even better plans than I could ever hope for."

She glanced over her shoulder.

Zane said not a word, but there was a glint of humor in his blue-gray eyes as he followed in her wake.

"The problem is—"

"Mind the steps," Zane said.

Jacinda faced forward, lifted her skirts and took the stairs down to the flat area. Then she turned to look at him again. There was something comforting about the man's soulful eyes. "The problem is that one can never know if God is done with a person on this earth. I understand that—"

"Look out for the wagon."

Jacinda spun just in time to avoid crashing into the tailgate of a farm wagon.

With that hurdle cleared, she twisted to face Zane again, but before she could resume her speech, he lifted a hand.

"I think things will be safer if you come here." He reached out and wrapped the warmth of his fingers around her own, then tucked her hand into the crook of his arm. He glanced down at her with a smile. "Now...you were saying?"

But the impact of that smile, combined with the knee-weakening assault of his long-lashed blue eyes, knocked Jacinda's thoughts six ways from Sunday.

She pressed her lips together. Tore her attention to the path before them. "It doesn't matter, I suppose."

Zane rubbed the back of her hand where it rested on his arm. "Matters to me."

She swallowed. And how well she knew it. His affection for her was part of her current barrage of worry. Always in the past, she'd been able to put off his attentions with excuses of being busy helping Charlotte or Reagan with this or that. But now that they were going to be out of town for a month, what excuse was she going to offer?

She gave a flap of her free hand and then settled it over the crimp in her middle. "I know it does. And I appreciate that. You've been a good friend, Zane." She layered a little extra emphasis onto the word "friend," hoping he would hear it.

Needing him to hear it. Because, heaven help her, the man was a temptation. She'd known from the moment he walked into her dining room just over two years ago now, asking for information about a couple of murderers he was tracking, that if ever there was a man who could make her forget her promise never to love again, it would be Zane Holloway.

After she'd lost Wade to that outlaw's bullet, she never wanted to go through the pain of something like that again! It was better not to love at all, and certainly loving another lawman was out of the question! So far out of the question that it shouldn't even be a consideration.

The last time Parson Clay had preached about worry, he'd said it was a sin because it was a lack of trust in God.

Jacinda would be the first to agree with that. But how did one get back to a place of trusting a Being who'd had the power to save the man she loved, but had chosen not to do so?

She only realized they had reached their wagon when Zane stopped next to it. "Oh, and here we are." She forced a smile and made to climb aboard, but Zane's hand on her arm stopped her.

"You know you don't have to pretend to be strong with me, right?"

Jacinda blinked at him. Something inside her curled up a little.

"Pretend?" Did he think she was weak?

Zane grimaced. "I didn't mean it like that. Trust me, Jac, you are one of the strongest women I know. I just meant…you don't have to hide your real feelings and struggles from me."

Jac. Everything in her stilled. Zane had never called her that before. But "Jac" had been Wade's affectionate name for her. And Zane had said it with a hard C just as Wade always had. If she didn't know better, she would swear the two men were conspiring against her. But Zane had never had the opportunity to meet Wade. Nor had Jacinda been afforded the opportunity to meet Zane's first wife, who had died in childbirth when he was just a young man.

Jacinda hoisted herself up onto the wagon seat without even waiting for Zane's help. "I don't have anything I need to confide. We'd best get going if we're to beat the dark."

Zane pressed his lips together, traversed the back of the wagon, and swung up onto the driver's seat. With a click of his tongue and a snap of the reins, he set the team to trotting down the road.

He'd been patient with Jacinda Callahan for several years. Especially since he'd been attracted to her from the moment he'd first laid eyes on her in her dining room all those months ago.

At first, he'd flirted with her a little, but it had been clear from the start that she wasn't interested in jumping into a courtship with an old codger like him. He'd thought maybe she had another beau in the wings, because surely a single woman as attractive as her would have men buzzing around like bees to clover. And a few had tried. But Jacinda had always put them firmly in their place—which was anywhere other than in her life.

Zane had proceeded with caution after that, never wanting to make her take enough offense that she might put him out on his ear also. But in the past few months since Reagan had married, Zane had found his patience with the whole tiptoeing around their feelings growing thin. He wasn't getting any younger, and neither was she.

And there were times when he could sense that she was attracted to him.

There would be a softening of the cornflower blue of her eyes. Or a little release of breath which reminded him of the way that Daniella used to respond when he took her hand. But then Jacinda would give herself a little shake and in a blink, it was as though she had dropped a mask back into place and reconstructed a wall between them.

Zane canted her a look. He shouldn't have let that endearment slip out. But Reagan had mentioned it to him not long ago—how his father had always called her "my Jac"—and ever since then he'd not been able to think of her as anything else. It was diminutive, just like her, but also implied the strength that embodied her.

Even now he could tell from the pinched pucker of her lips that she was fretting about something, but he knew she wouldn't say anything. She would battle through her fears alone and with a smile and a word of dismissal for anyone who questioned if she was all right.

So he simply wouldn't ask. "The trains are quite well protected these days. I'm sure Reagan and Charlotte will be fine."

She straightened and dusted at her skirt. "Yes. I know. I'm certain you are right."

"And that gang of outlaws has been quiet for several weeks. Joe and I think they must have moved on to a more lucrative area. The bank will be fine."

He swallowed. Had she heard the hesitation in his voice? Because the truth was more like *hoped*. Hoped they had moved on. Hoped the bank would be fine. They shouldn't have any trouble there for a while anyhow, because it was still being built and had no money or even a vault yet.

She fidgeted and glanced toward the rapidly setting sun. "That's good."

He felt her worry as palpably as if she had screamed it aloud. And if he was honest, the concern echoed in his own heart. It was why he'd urged her back to the wagon so quickly after the delayed departure of the train.

It would be dark inside five minutes, and they still had a good thirty minutes till they arrived back in town.

Maybe he could take both their minds off it with conversation. "So, what do you plan to do with your time while Reagan and Charlotte are away?"

Jacinda smiled at him and he knew she had immediately perceived what he was up to. "Charlotte's material that she ordered for their drapes arrived just the other day. I suppose some of my time will be spent in getting those sewn up for them."

"And how are they settling in at old man Jonas's place?"

She tipped her head. "Well, I think. His son was relieved to sell it to someone who would care for it after Mr. Jonas's funeral."

"I'm sure your house seems empty now that they've moved out?"

Jacinda cleared her throat. "Yes. But I don't mind being alone so much."

Ah, yes. He'd wandered too close to the taboo. "I suppose it is easier to keep everyone at arm's length when you can keep your distance from them."

He jutted his jaw to one side. He hadn't meant to say that.

Her mouth dropped open. "Zane Holloway! Whatever you might—"

A puff of gray dust kicked up in the roadbed before them. The horse neighed and reared. The echoing sound of a rifle shot bounced along the steep hills on both sides of the road.

Someone was shooting at them!

"Jac! Get down!" Zane grabbed her arm and urged her to the floorboards at his feet all while trying to maintain his grip on the reins and get the horse back in line. They were going to have to make a run for it!

But just as the horse's hooves hit the road once more, another bullet slammed into the ground.

"Whoa!" Zane tried to keep his voice steady to calm the panicked horse.

Jacinda cowered next to his leg, but when he glanced down, he did a double take. She had a pistol held at the ready in her hand and was searching the surrounding hills with a practiced eye.

"Don't move!" A voice called out of the darkness on the hillside to their right.

Jacinda pointed her gun in that direction and Zane reached down to slowly cover her hand.

She looked up.

He shook his head.

They couldn't just go shooting at voices in the dark until they learned more.

She gave him a nod of understanding.

"We don't want any trouble!" Zane called.

"Well ain't that just dandy? 'Cause we don't want no trouble neither...just your money!"

Several voices laughed, each coming from a different direction.

Zane swallowed. They were surrounded.

"Zane?" Jacinda whispered. "What are we going to do?"

Chapter Two

✦❖✦

Zoe Kastain hurried along the rapidly darkening road with a bit of trepidation. Ma was going to be so worried until she got back home, but how were they to have known this morning when Ma sent her in to Wyldhaven to fetch Pa some more medicine that Doc had ridden out to Camp Sixty-Five today to attend to a birthing? Zoe had walked the miles to the camp as quickly as she could, but it had taken her some time to find Doc, and then she'd needed to wait for him to mix Pa's powders. Since the baby he was waiting on still hadn't arrived, Doc had tried to get her to delay and travel back with him, but Zoe had been too concerned over Pa by that time to take him up on the offer. Now, with darkness coming on, she was second guessing her choice to hurry home on her own. She still had a good ways to go.

She kept her focus on the rocky roadbed so she wouldn't turn an ankle and be in an even worse fix.

Off to her right, she heard the crackle of breaking branches and the crunch of footsteps. She froze and felt her eyes widen and her breathing hitch as she turned to see what might be lurking just behind the concealing curtain of foliage at the forest's edge. Her gaze darted first right then left.

Where would she hide, if she needed to? But she was out in the open with nothing to conceal her except the falling darkness. And there wasn't much comfort in that thought.

A horse lurched from the tree line just a few paces ahead. "Zoe!"

She jolted, gave a little screech, and then laid a hand over her pounding heart.

It was just Washington Nolan yelling her name. He was obviously searching for her.

"Washington Nolan, you about sent me into an apoplectic fit! What are you doing way out here?!"

"There you are! Thank God!" He swung down and strode toward her. "I'm so glad I finally found you. Your mother sent your little sister, Sharon, to get me. Asked me to try and find you. She was worried because you'd been gone so long." He scanned her from head to toe. "You all right?"

Zoe waved a hand, then tucked it away behind her before he could see it trembling. He'd given her quite a fright. "Doc had a birthing. I had to go out to the camp to find him."

"Well, come on." He gestured to his horse. "Let's get you home."

Zoe accepted his offer without thought, but as the warmth of his hands settled around her waist to boost her into the saddle, and then he swung up behind her, she certainly had plenty of thoughts flitting through her head. Most of which were causing a heat in her face that she knew would make her almost as red as her detestable hair. Thank goodness for the darkness and the fact that Washington was behind her now.

Washington's arms brushed hers on either side as he took up the reins and clucked to the horse. "Glad you are alive and well, Zo. Was starting to get worried. Been looking for you for hours."

Zoe swallowed, willing down the additional wave of warmth that swept over her with his use of the short version of her name. No one but Washington ever called her Zo. When they were younger, she had chastised him for it plenty. But now she could admit, if only to herself, that she liked it. Too much. She fisted one hand tight enough to dig her nails into her palm and ground herself in reality. Wash was just a friend. "I'm sorry to have caused everyone concern."

A shot rang out, followed by several more.

Zoe stiffened. "Why that's—"

"Gunshots!"

One moment Zoe was on the horse in front of Wash, and then next moment they were on the ground and Wash was pushing her into the covering shelter of the forest's edge. "Get down. Get down." He urged her behind a tree and pressed himself up against her so the tree protected her from the front and he protected her from behind.

"Wash, what is it?" She didn't even bother to try to disguise the tremor in her voice.

"Shh." His breath warmed her ear. "Let me listen."

Zoe shivered. And whether it had to do with Wash's proximity in the dark, or with the fact that strangers were shooting at who knew what, she couldn't have said.

"We don't want any trouble!"

That was Marshal Zane's voice! Zoe tilted Wash a look over her shoulder.

He laid a finger over his lips, listening intently.

"Well ain't that just dandy? 'Cause we don't want no trouble neither...just your money!"

That voice wasn't one she recognized.

But she felt Wash stiffen behind her.

"Do you know him?" she whispered.

"Zoe, now ain't the time for questions. Hush up."

She clenched her teeth, more than a little hurt by his clipped command.

Sure, he'd always teased her about being a chatterbox, but she'd never taken him seriously. Did he really think she talked too much? She opened her mouth to ask him, but then thought better of it and clamped her lips tight.

Wash pushed away from her suddenly. "Zane's in trouble. Come on. But you have to promise to do exactly as I say." His hand wrapped around hers and he didn't give her a choice but to stumble after him in the dark. She crashed into several bushes and tromped on a branch that cracked loudly beneath her weight.

Wash spun back to face her so suddenly that she collided into his chest.

Darkness had settled all around them now. She could barely make out Wash, and he was right before her.

"Quiet." He pressed the word against her ear so silently that she never would have heard it if his mouth hadn't been so close.

She trembled, but this time she knew it had nothing to do with Wash's closeness and everything to do with the other sets of footsteps she could now hear crunching through the brush.

"What is it?" a voice called.

"Not sure. Thought I heard something over this way," another responded.

Motioning for her to remain quiet, Wash eased to his haunches and if she hadn't known so well that he wouldn't leave her, she might have thought he'd melted away into the forest, so quiet were his movements and so dark was the forest. Only a moment later, she felt him stand once more. A flick of sound and a soft puff of his breath were her only indications that he'd moved, but then something crashed into the brush several feet off to her right.

"This way!" the second voice called.

She felt the air stir as Wash threw something else and the sound crashed even farther into the woods.

"After them!"

The sound of bushes crackling as the two men careened in the opposite direction, brought relief. Or maybe that was from the fact that her hand was once more firmly ensconced in the comfort of Wash's as he tugged her forward.

Zoe held her breath, and tried to sense bushes and branches before she crashed into them or stepped on them, but for the moment it didn't matter.

The two men were making so much noise of their own what with their running and hollering that she didn't suppose they would hear a small snap of a twig beneath her boot.

Wash led her through the trees as surely as if he could see, and moments later the brush parted and Zoe realized they were on a narrow game trail. She was thankful for the easier going, but even so, she tripped on bulged-up roots a couple times and only the strength of Wash's grip kept her from sprawling headlong.

After they had jogged for a couple minutes, Wash paused and Zoe propped one hand against a tree, glad for the break. Her breaths beat a tattoo against her teeth. When had Wash grown such long legs? She used to be able to at least keep up with him. Mostly.

Beside her, the shrill whistle of a bird rose into the night. She startled, then realized Wash was making the sound.

"My horse will make his way home now. We're going to have to keep walking. You doing all right?"

Zoe nodded, rubbing her hands up and down her arms.

"Zo?"

She realized he hadn't seen her nod. "Yes," she whispered. "I'm fine."

Wash reached out and squeezed her hand. "Thank God I found you when I did. You could have walked right into the middle of all this."

Zoe shuddered at the thought.

~~~⁂~~~

Terror pumped through Jacinda like it hadn't in a very long time. The very substance of her fears had materialized! Who were these ruffians to think they could accost citizens right out in the open on the roads?! She was so thankful that she was here with Zane, because she hated to think what he might try if he didn't have her safety to think of. Knowing him, he would have set to shooting without thought to his personal safety and then where would he have been? Shot dead, that's where!

"We don't want any trouble. Just tell us what to do," she called.

Zane hissed at her to be quiet, but she didn't care. She'd be hanged if she stood by while another man she loved was shot down by an outlaw.

The thought froze her. Loved? No! Dear Father in heaven, please no. But there was no denying that the thought had lodged itself in her mind and seemed like it planned to settle in and stay for a while.

"You got money?" The voice in the darkness was a low growl. Somewhat scratchy.

She considered. Why did it sound familiar?

Zane grumbled something under his breath. The horses bobbed their heads, setting the trace chains to jangling.

He scanned the surrounding hills. His voice was pitched for her ears alone when he spoke. "It's dark enough that they can't have good sight. You just stay down and keep your head below the footrail there." Louder, he called. "I've got a dollar and maybe a couple bits in my pocket is all."

Zane reached into the back of the wagon and hefted an empty wooden crate from the wagon bed. He motioned for Jacinda to scoot closer to his legs, then set the crate between her and the empty side of the wagon where she was exposed. Next, he started shrugging out of his long heavy leather coat.

"What you doing down there?" the voice whined.

"Just taking off my coat is all, gentlemen! Seems getting shot at warms a fellow right up." Zane's casual words held a bit of bite. "How would you like me to give you this dollar and change?"

Jacinda's confusion was growing by the minute. What exactly was Zane up to?

"My man will be right there for it. You just put your guns down and stay put."

"I'm not likely to go anywhere with all your weapons trained on me." Zane leaned past her and put his coat into the crate. "Help me, Jac," he whispered. "Stuff it in good and tight."

It hit her then what he was planning! And Jacinda felt a jolt of fear crash through her. He was thinking of making a run for it!

She shot out a hand and gripped his arm.

He glanced down, jaw clamped tight.

She shook her head.

A hard glint lit his eyes. "You stay down. They aren't just going to take our money and walk away. Understand?" He wrapped the reins more tightly around his hands.

Panic nipped at Jacinda's pulse. If they simply sat here and waited for the outlaws to come take their money, they were dead. If they made a run for it, they might be dead. She'd take the better odds any day. Still...

Her eyes closed for the briefest of seconds. *Jesus please...*

There was no time for more of a prayer than that. She double checked the rounds in her pistol. "Well, I'm not just going to sit here and watch a man I care about get shot. On three. One."

Zane stiffened. "What?"

"Two."

He hissed. "Jacinda—no!"

"Three." She rose to her feet and fired three shots into areas she remembered voices coming from.

"Ha!" Zane slapped the reins down on the horse's rumps. "Ha!"

The wagon lurched into motion and Jacinda crashed against the seat.

"What the—"

"They's makin' a run fer it!"

Rifles blasted. Flashes of light revealed the positions of two of the outlaws to the south and to the east.

Jacinda gripped the back of the wagon bench to keep her balance as she fired off the remainder of her bullets in those respective directions.

A man loomed up beside the road ahead, leaning out to try and grab the reins.

Zane shot him.

The man clutched at his torso with a cry.

And then they were past and galloping down the road.

Zane reached over and yanked her down. "Get down, woman! Ha!" He slapped the horses again.

Jacinda didn't have any trouble obeying his command. Her legs were suddenly just about as strong as a newborn colt's. She collapsed onto the seat beside him.

But Zane wasn't content with that. He took her arm and

urged her to return to the floorboards where she'd have more cover.

And she was happy to sink down there and wrap her arms around her knees.

She trembled from head to toe.

Chapter Three

Washington Nolan had never been so scared in his entire life. He only hoped Zoe couldn't feel the quaking of his hand as he tugged her along the deer path behind him.

He peered through the brush, willing all his senses to the fore. Looking for any aberrant shadow that seemed out of place. Listening for any snap of a twig or rustle of leaves that clashed with the symphony of a nighttime forest. Sniffing the air for the scents of tobacco or body odor that might alert him to someone's presence before he saw them.

Ahead of them, Jacinda Callahan's voice called, "We don't want any trouble. Just tell us what to do."

Wash cringed. So the marshal wasn't alone.

A moment later, the familiar voice called out that they shouldn't move. A man was heading down to collect the money. Who did that voice belong to? He couldn't quite pin it down. So familiar and yet...not someone he'd known recently.

But he didn't have time to figure it out right now. Wash felt his gut churn. Was he going to be too late to help the marshal and Mrs. Callahan? The outlaws surely wouldn't leave them alive, would they?

He quickened his steps, mindful that Zoe was no forest woman. He had to balance speed with silence. Thankfully, the deer trail helped some with that. Zoe had been doing an admirable job of keeping up with him for the past several minutes.

The thought of Zoe crimped his gut even tighter. What if he hadn't found her in time? What if she'd innocently wandered into the middle of the hold-up? He shuddered to think what might have happened to her. Even now he was worried about taking her nearer, but he couldn't leave Zane to fight the battle alone, nor could he leave Zoe by herself in the dark woods when there were outlaws creeping all around.

By his calculations, they were close to the road now. He motioned for Zoe to halt and pressed his mouth close to her ear. "Wait here. Be right back." She gave him a nod and he had to admire her gumption. Most girls would be a heap of sobbing uselessness by now.

He eased silently up the embankment to peer from beneath a small maple into the moonlight that washed the roadbed. Zane's wagon was just ahead, the pine boards standing out against the darker trees and grass of the hill on the other side of the road.

A shadow leapt up above the wagon's bench and Wash only had a moment to realize it was Mrs. Callahan before Zane yelled "Ha!" and slapped the reins down hard. The wagon lurched forward as Mrs. Callahan squeezed off three quick shots.

On instinct, Wash flattened himself against the bank.

Then all sorts of ruckus broke loose. Bullets and curses were flying every which direction.

A missile zinged through the leaves just above his head.

"Get down!" Wash dove to the path, dragging Zoe with him.

He curled his body around hers, pressing her tight against the thick grass of the embankment. They cowered there for a span that seemed all at once forever and only a moment. Thankfully, the earthwork of the roadbed acted as a shield.

The clatter of the wagon wheels faded into the distance and the shooting stopped.

Thick ringing silence fell.

And then a curse. Footsteps crunched as the outlaws must have converged on the crushed rock of the wagon road.

Wash figured, hidden as he and Zoe were in the shadows of several bushes, this was the safest place for them right now. Zoe stirred and he was suddenly aware of how small her body felt snugged up against his side beneath his arm. The soft floral and citrus scent she always wore drifted up to tantalize him. He rolled his eyes and forced himself to ignore the feel of her delicate hand resting against his chest. He needed to concentrate on what was going on above their heads.

"Blasted uppity high falutin'—" A boot scuffed sharply against the ground and then a rock clattered away down the roadbed.

Another voice spoke with a laugh. "That marshal's got sand, I'll give him that." Sharp metallic snicks indicated that speaker was reloading his rifle.

"I think I winged him," commented another with a deeper timbre. "Saw him flinch."

"Serves him right if you did," said the voice that continued to strike a familiar chord with Wash.

Again, he searched his memory, but couldn't come up with where he'd heard it before.

"Roddy! Aw no! They shot Roddy! You okay, man?"

Wash did a quick calculation of the voices he'd heard. So far, counting this Roddy just mentioned, there'd been six of them.

A yowl preceded a curse. "No! I'm not all right." More cursing. "Burns like a branding iron's stuck in my gullet. I almost had the traces. Could have had that wagon stopped." More curses rained down on Zane's head for having the audacity to shoot him.

Wash smirked.

Another voice out of the dark, this one he'd not heard yet. A bit high pitched. Whiny. Nervous. "He-he-he needs a doc."

There was the sharp sound of flesh connecting with flesh.

"Ow! Wh-what was th-that for, Jim?"

Footsteps crunched as a man stalked away.

Another voice spoke in a kinder tone to the simpleton. "We can't go to the doctor, Tommy. Roddy will be fine."

Roddy yowled and cursed again. "I won't be fine!"

"We can't go to the doctor. But we can bring the doctor to him." The familiar voice again nudged at the back of Wash's mind. He should know this man.

"Bring the doctor into camp? Yeah, that would be brilliant!" Heavy sarcasm was evident in the words.

A pistol cocked and feet scuffled. Several gasped.

The familiar voice spoke again. "Who's in charge here, Jim?"

"You are, Lenny." Jim's words were hard. They held no resignation. Only challenge.

Lenny! Wash felt a wave of realization course through him. That was why the voice sounded so familiar. Lenny Smith had run with the infamous Waddell Gang until their leader had been killed by Sheriff Reagan a few years back.

Wash angled a look toward Zoe. Yes. She'd heard the name too. Her lips were pinched in that certain way she had when she was just about to let someone have the whole of her mind.

Wash laid a restraining hand on her shoulder and felt her relax a little.

Though Lenny hadn't shot her pa, he *had* captured Zoe and used her to lure Mrs. Reagan Callahan—Miss Brindle back then—into captivity. Sheriff Reagan had rescued her only a little while later, but...

Wash grimaced as he remembered stepping into the

classroom to find Zoe strapped to a toppled chair, her arm broken and her face pale with the pain of it. He'd never been so scared before or since. Maybe that was the day he'd fallen—

He frowned. Pushed thoughts of his feelings for Zoe aside. Forced his focus back to the situation at hand.

For his part in the whole affair, Lenny had been arrested and sentenced to life in prison. So what was he doing here?

"You want to imply that I don't know what I'm doing again, Jim?" Lenny's voice grated like the bedrock beneath his boots.

"You don't want to be thought of as incompetent? Then don't be! I told you before we came here tonight that this was a bad location. But you didn't listen. Now either shoot me, or get your gun out of my face."

A long silence stretched.

Feet scuffled and one of the men loosed a string of nervous laughter.

But he must have decided against shooting the man named Jim, because a moment later, Lenny snapped, "Shut up, Jango! Get him up. Don't worry, Roddy, we'll get you taken care of."

"I-I-I'm hun-hungry." The simpleton was sounding more distressed by the minute. Wash felt his sympathies rise. How had someone like that ended up with a gang of outlaws?

Wash tossed a glance at Zoe. She had her arms folded and her jaw thrust out to one side, but she seemed to be keeping herself in check.

Lenny's voice sounded weary when he spoke this time. "I know, Tommy. I know. Come on. We'll go back to our cave and see if any of our snares caught us a rabbit, huh? How will that be?"

"See if our snares caught us a rabbit. I-I-I like ra-rabbit."

"I know you do. Come on now. Don't dawdle."

The footsteps faded into the brush on the opposite side of the road.

Wash tipped his head against the embankment. He was torn. He should follow them. Figure out where their lair was so he could let Deputy Joe and the marshal know, but he had Zoe to think of. He needed to get her home. And what about Doc? He needed to let him know he could be in danger. But Zoe had said he was out at the camps, so he should be safe for now. He clenched his jaw. Maybe he could come back here in the morning and follow the men's trail. If he could figure out where their hideout was and let Joe and Zane know, maybe they could have the whole lot of them rounded up by tomorrow night.

Zoe rolled away from him and scrambled to her feet. "We should follow them."

Wash shook his head as he stood. "What about your pa's medicine?"

She hesitated only a moment. "Fine. Right. *You* should follow them. I can make it home from here on my own. Just be careful." She took a step toward the road.

Wash shot out a hand and gripped her arm. He looked down at her. A shaft of moonlight spilled through the branches of the maple to dance in the flames of her tresses that had come loose and tumbled about her shoulders. He swallowed, wishing his fingers had the freedom to do the same. He sealed his lips before he blurted something he might later regret. Zoe was nothing if not practical.

She would tell him to take his foolish sentiments and stuff them.

Realizing she was still looking at him, he shook his head and released her. "No. I'm taking you home. Deputy Joe, Marshal Zane, and I can try to follow their trail in the morning."

Zoe stabbed a finger in the direction of the outlaws. "Did you hear the name Lenny? You know who he is! He must have escaped from jail! We can't let them get away!"

"Zoe, this is too big for you and me. We have to let the law handle it. Besides, I'm not going to leave you. Your ma asked me to make sure you got home safe, and that's what I intend to do."

"But Wash—"

"Zoe, no. I mean it, it's too dangerous. Let's get you home." He reached out to help her through the brush and back onto the game trail they'd been following. It paralleled the road for at least another mile. After that, it would likely be safe enough to use the road again.

Still, she hesitated. But she pulled a vial from her skirt pocket. She studied it, turning it over a few times. "You're right..." She thrust it back into her pocket, took his hand and clambered over a half-buried log and onto the trail, then stepped away to brush some bits of grass from her skirts. "My pa really does need to get this medicine. I have to go home, but if Lenny Smith gets away, I may never forgive myself."

"Their trail will still be there come morning. Let's go."

✦～◗✦❦✦◖～✦

Zane kept his left arm pinned to his side as tightly as he could while reining the wagon to a stop behind Jacinda's house. So far, he'd been able to keep Jacinda from realizing he'd been shot. Which was good. She worried about everything too much. Maybe he could drop her off and then get Doc to sew him up with her none-the-wiser. It was dark enough that he might be able to get away with it even though he could feel blood soaking his shirt all the way down to his waist. He wished he could put his long duster back on, but he didn't think he'd be able to move his arm through the sleeve. Judging from the center of the pain, the bullet had taken him through the fleshy part on top of his shoulder. Might have busted his collarbone, he couldn't quite tell. What he could tell was that likely the bullet was still in there.

He wrapped the reins around the brake handle and lowered himself gingerly from the seat, reaching up his good hand to help her.

She took it and jumped down.

He gritted his teeth against the pain. Willed away the lightheadedness.

Jacinda started up her back steps. "I'm sure you'll need to go tell Joe—"

She froze and then spun back to face him. With her up two steps she was looking down on him now. "Did you just gasp? What happened?" Her focus dipped and her eyes widened. "Zane Holloway! What is that?!"

Zane felt defeat wash over him. Had he made a sound? He hadn't thought he had. But the truth was he might need her to go fetch Doc. "I think I was shot."

She took hold of the stair rail. "You think!" She assessed him again. "You've got blood everywhere!"

He shook his head. "I know." He gave a lame gesture toward his shoulder.

Jac stamped one foot and turned for the door. "Zane Holloway, are you addlepated? We've been out of danger for a good twenty minutes. And you kept quiet this whole time? Get in here!"

She was right. He needed to move. But right now, he was doing good just to keep to his feet.

She glanced back, saw he wasn't moving, and returned to

his side. "Come on." Her tone softened. "Can you make it up the stairs? I've got a chair just inside the door."

To keep her from worrying, he would make it. He offered her the best smile he could muster. "I'm not dying. Just hurt a little."

Her lips pinched together tightly and she slipped beneath his good arm. "Lean on me and I'll help you."

He felt her trembling as they made their way up the stairs, and he couldn't deny that he was thankful to collapse into the chair by her kitchen door. He wanted to ease her worry. He grinned up at her when she bent over him. "If I'd have known it would allow me to put my arm around you, I'd have gotten shot a long time ago."

"Hush up, Zane. You're talking nonsense." Her hands fluttered over him. "Just stay with me. I need to get some light." She was back in only a moment with the lantern. "Now, where were you shot? Hmmm?"

He'd gone and worried her even more than she already would have with the attack. And he was sorry about that. He tipped his head back against the wall and caught her hand as she bent to examine his shoulder. "Jac, I'm going to be fine."

"Not if you keep bleeding, you're not." She tugged her hand from his and when she set the lantern on the table, her face was so pale he wondered if she might faint.

But she was already rolling up her sleeves. "Off with your shirt and let me take a look."

He couldn't seem to find the energy to move. "Don't you think you should just get Doc?"

"Shirt." She snapped her fingers at him. "I'm not walking away from you while you are still bleeding." She kicked the door with her toe to send it shut while she yanked a handful of cotton scraps from a drawer and spun to face him.

Zane still hadn't moved. So like a man to wait so long before he asked for help. Her gaze drifted down, and she felt shock drop her jaw as, with the aid of the lantern light, the full amount of blood he'd lost—was losing—finally registered. Her stomach took a dive and her heart pounded so hard she could feel the knock of it inside her chest.

His head was still tipped against the wall, and his eyes were a bit glassy. "You are mighty beautiful, you know that, Jac? Mighty beautiful. I'm sorry to have worried you."

Jacinda took herself in hand and didn't allow herself to relish his compliments. Situations like this were the very reason she'd never allowed herself to love another man. Except, well, maybe she hadn't done such a good job of guarding her heart when it came to this one.

She strode purposefully toward him. One thing was certain. There was no time to wait for Doc. She had to get this bleeding stopped. And now.

She swiftly undid several of the buttons and pushed the shirt off his shoulder. Part of the material stuck. She dampened the material until she could loosen it from the wound.

"Ow, that hurts."

He was woozy from blood loss then, because the Zane she knew would never admit to pain of any sort.

The wound was in his shoulder, and still oozing. She used one of the cloths to clean the area as much as she could so she could see the wound better. Thankfully, during Wade's time in the law, she'd dealt with a fair share of bullet wounds. This bullet seemed to have entered his shoulder from the front. "Lean forward."

He complied.

No exit wound. Her hands turned clammy. "Okay, the bullet is still inside. Doc's going to have to get it out, but we have to try to stop as much of your blood loss as possible. This is going to hurt. I'm sorry." She pressed a wad of the cotton scraps against the wound.

Zane hissed through gritted teeth.

She moved his good hand up to hold the wadding. "Hold that. Good and tight." She took another strip of cloth and tied it at an angle across his body to hold the compress in place. "All right. Up. I need to get you onto a bed, then I'm going for Doc." His gray pallor made her stomach pitch. "Stay with me, Zane. Don't you pass out on me, or Doc will have to do your surgery right here on my kitchen floor."

"I'm not going to pass out," he grumbled.

Jacinda led him to the downstairs bedroom closest to the kitchen. She mostly used it for her sewing projects, but had never taken the bed out of the room. And now she was ever so thankful for that fact because she didn't think Zane would have made it up the stairs to the second floor.

Once she had him situated on the bed, she hoisted her skirts and ran down the alley to where Doc lived with his wife Dixie above their boardinghouse. She pounded on the back door. "Dixie? Doc?!" She banged again, her worry making her impatient.

Only a moment later, Dixie opened the door, alarm showing on her face. "Jacinda, whatever is the matter?"

"Zane's been shot. I need Doc. Is he here?"

Dixie shook her head. "He had a birthing out to Camp Sixty-Five. He's not home yet."

Jacinda's hopes crashed into a heap at her feet. "Zane's bleeding bad." She scrambled to think what to do, one hand pressed to her forehead. "We are going to have to do this ourselves. I need your help. Carbolic acid and some sutures. Does Doc have extras of those here?"

"Yes. Yes. Go. I'll grab what we need and meet you back at your place. Flynn leaves a surgical knife here too. But he always says it should be boiled. Put some water on."

Jacinda waved her acknowledgement and ran back to her house. She built up the fire as high as she could and put the kettle on the hottest part of the stove, then dashed to the bedroom with a glass of water. With so much blood loss, Zane needed to drink plenty of liquids.

But when she got to the room, Zane was sound asleep.

She thunked the glass onto the end table and gritted out quietly, "Zane Holloway, if you don't survive this, I'm going to kill you myself."

Chapter Four

Zoe had never before felt more thankful to see the golden glow of the cabin windows. Jinx set to barking the minute they stepped into the clearing.

"Hush up, Jinx."

At the sound of her voice, he gave a welcoming bay and loped toward them.

She bent and gave his ears a friendly scratch, but she couldn't give him much time. Ma was already tugging open the door, her hands wringing in worry.

Zoe took the steps in one bound and threw her arms around Ma's shoulders. "I'm here, Ma. Sorry it took me so long."

She heard Wash's more sedate footsteps on the porch behind her.

Ma set Zoe from her and skimmed her from head to toe. "Goodness, what happened to you? You look like you've been rolling in grass... Oh my! Dear Lord." Her gaze landed with blatant accusation on Wash.

Sudden understanding hit Zoe. Heat flashed through her face. "Ma! No! Goodness, no!" She hurriedly gathered her hair and twisted it into a bun, using the few pins left to hold it in place.

Wash looked down, scuffing the toe of one boot against the porch while one hand scrubbed at the back of his neck. With the brim of his hat casting a shadow over his face, Zoe couldn't quite catch his expression, but she could imagine it was plenty aghast.

A perfect match to her own feelings. Zoe flapped a hand to cool her face. Surely her cheeks were as rosy as an evening sunset and her freckles likely standing out like splatters of brown paint! She spun back to face Ma. "Doc had a birthing out at the camps. I had to go out there to get Pa's medicine. Wash found me only a bit ago, but then there was a ruckus with"—she thought better than to name Lenny and give Ma yet one more thing to fret over—"some outlaws and we had to hide and…"

She let her words trail away because she could see Ma taking in her blush. Ma not buying her reason for being so disheveled. Ma pressing her lips together in disbelief.

Zoe folded her arms, irritated that Ma distrusted her after all her years of toeing the line with exact precision. She wasn't Belle, but it seemed her sister's penchant for rebellion had tainted all Ma's children in her eyes. "Wash has been a perfect gentleman, Ma."

Behind her, Wash's feet scraped against the boards and she heard him clear his throat.

What must he be thinking? He'd never even given any indication that he thought of Zoe in any way other than as a childhood friend. He was much more like a brother than anything, not that Zoe hadn't sometimes dreamed of there being more. Okay, maybe more than sometimes.

Heavens! Now look where her thoughts had taken her. If only she didn't blush so easily.

Ma continued to scrutinize her, one eyebrow winging upward suspiciously.

Zoe scrambled to produce the medicine from her skirt pocket. "Here. Pa's powders. How is he?"

That seemed to break through Ma's suspicions. She gave herself a little shake and took the vial from Zoe. "Thank you, Zoe. I'm sorry." Ma turned to Wash and repeated, "I'm sorry. Neither of you deserves my suspicion. Thank you for fetching Zoe home. Come in. I have dinner waiting for you both."

Wash dipped his chin a little and swept his hat off as he stepped through the door. "Thank you, Mrs. Kastain." He gave Zoe the briefest of glances and then turned to hang his hat on the peg by the door.

Zoe wished she could read that inscrutable look. Was he embarrassed? Horrified? Feeling sorry for her?

Ma started across the room. "Zoe, soup's on the back of the stove. Belle is"—she waved a hand—"gone again. Please get Wash some soup and then bring some of the broth to your pa's room. I'll mix his medicine with it and try to get him to eat something."

Zoe's heart sank. She'd really hoped that Pa would be up on his feet by the time she got home today. Ever since he'd been shot several years ago, he'd had bouts of illness with severe stomach pains. But sometimes he bounced back from them quicker than others. It looked like this bout was going to be one of the longer ones. Sometimes he was down for a week or more.

With Ma working at Dixie's Boardinghouse—which they were all thankful for—that left Zoe to do most of Pa's care at home, which meant she would miss school this week. And Mr. Haversham didn't like it when she missed classes. Zoe sighed as she led Wash to the table. She missed having Miss Brindle—now Mrs. Callahan—as her teacher and that was certain. Mrs. Callahan had often brought lessons to the house so that Zoe could keep up.

But Mr. Haversham only chastised her and deducted points

for every assignment she turned in late. And then made her do penance by doing his teaching when she *was* in attendance.

Zoe realized Wash stood by the table with his hands propped on his hips, scrutinizing her with those soft gray-green eyes of his.

She held a hand toward one of the chairs. "I'm real sorry about Ma. We don't talk about it much, but Belle has been... disappearing for hours at a time and we don't know where she's been going."

Wash pulled out a chair and sank into it. "I'm sorry to hear that."

Zoe shrugged. "She's always come back, but Ma worries about her something fierce. And I think she's worried that I might start becoming the hellion Belle has been. And Pa's been getting worse. Doc doesn't know how to help him except to keep giving him the powders for his pain."

She dished up a bowl of soup and set it in front of him as she talked. Then fetched the basket of bread rolls and the crock of butter too.

"Anyhow, I know you don't even feel anything—" Zoe felt the heat of her face turning crimson again. Blame this night! "What I'm trying to say is, Ma would normally never... Well, you get the idea." She scrambled back to the stove. "I'd better get this broth to Pa's room."

As she hurried from the room with the bowl of hot broth held carefully in her hands, she could feel Wash's gaze drilling into her back.

Pa lay against his pillows, the gray cast of his skin making him look even more sickly than the dots of moisture on his forehead already indicated. He smiled at her weakly. "There's my girl." His words were barely audible.

"Hi, Pa. I've got some soup for you." She set the bowl on the bedside table and tried not to notice how Ma's hands trembled as she sprinkled some of the powder into a spoonful of broth.

Zoe dropped one hand against Ma's shoulder. "I'll go check on the twins and Aidan."

"Thank you, dear."

Zoe heard Ma coaxing Pa to take the medicine, as she left the room and headed down the hall to check on her siblings. Aidan lay sound asleep with his blond hair tousled against his pillow. But when she poked her head into the girls' room, Sharon quickly thrust something under her covers.

Thankfully, Shiloh was breathing deeply on her side of the room.

Zoe tilted Sharon a look and held out her hand. "You have to leave for school first thing. You know Ma wants you to be asleep by this time. Besides, trying to read in the moonlight isn't good for your eyes."

Sharon gave a sigh of resignation and withdrew her book from beneath the covers. "I'll never sleep without knowing what happens to her!"

Zoe pressed her lips together as she took in the gilded letters of the book's title. *Tess of the D'Urbervilles.* "Where did you get this? Does Mother know you are reading this?" Mother surely wouldn't approve of such trash. But then... Zoe's lips quirked. She herself had read the book. She smoothed a hand over Sharon's hair. "What part are you at?"

"They are at Stonehenge. Tess is sleeping and the law just arrived."

Right at the end then. But still in the part where there was hope for something good to come to Tess.

Zoe tweaked Sharon's nose. "Sleep. You'll have something to look forward to tomorrow evening." She wouldn't tell the girl that she'd likely sleep a sight better without knowing the end of the terrible story. She would find that out soon enough on her own. She adjusted Sharon's blankets. "For now, I want you to think of something. How would things have been better for Tess and her family if only they had chosen to do things according to the Good Book, hmmm? Remember, dear Sharon, the devil wants only to steal, to kill, and to destroy. But Jesus has come that we might have life. Yes?"

Sharon scrunched her nose and grumbled. "It's just a story."

Zoe nodded. "Just a story that we can learn from. We can let it make us better or let it make us worse."

Sharon sighed. "I suppose."

Zoe bent down and pressed a kiss to her sister's cheek. "Thanks for getting Wash to look for me today. I know Ma appreciated your help. Night."

"Night," Sharon mumbled sleepily, and Zoe was gratified to see that her eyes had already slipped closed.

She set the book on the girls' dresser and then eased the door shut.

When she arrived back in the kitchen, Wash had just finished cleaning his bowl at the sink and was drying it with a towel.

"Oh, you didn't have to do that." Zoe hurried forward to take it from him.

But Wash held it out of her reach and kept drying. "Why not? This is the way we do it at home. Everyone cleans up after himself."

"But here you're a guest." She stepped closer to try to take the bowl.

He lifted it higher, with a grin. "A guest who can take care of himself."

"Wash give—"

Ma cleared her throat from the doorway, Pa's still mostly full bowl in her hand.

Zoe froze, suddenly realizing just how close she stood to Wash. He must have realized it too, because his jaw bulged and he stepped back, setting his clean bowl on the sideboard. He gave Ma a nod. "Soup was right delicious, Mrs. Kastain. Thank you."

Ma gave him a nod and strode to the sink, pumping in some water.

"I'll do that, Ma. You sit. You look done in. Did he eat anything?"

Ma sank into a chair at the table without protest. "More than he's eaten all day. But the powders make him tired. Then he only wants to sleep."

Zoe looked at the amount of broth left in the bowl and knew that whatever amount Pa had ingested, it wasn't enough to keep a grown man alive. She swallowed, willing away the concern that poured over her. How many days was this now that she'd been worrying over the fact that Pa was barely eating?

She took in Ma's sallow cheeks and the creases that puckered her brow.

"Did you eat, Ma?"

Ma straightened and tucked her lower lip between her teeth, as though she couldn't quite remember. She stared vacantly at the wall across from the table.

Zoe didn't bother waiting for an answer. She pulled two bowls from the sideboard. "I didn't get a chance to eat either. I'll join you, and Wash can tell us the news from town. It will be good to think of something else for a while." As she ladled soup into two bowls, she gave Wash a look that she hoped conveyed she wanted him to keep his story light—nothing sad or discouraging.

He gave her a nod, and eased into his chair. He launched

into a tale about Pricilla Hines getting cornered in the livery by Bill Giddens' big gelding, and Ma had even smiled once or twice by the time he got done with the story.

"Well now, that was some fix she got herself into, wasn't it?" Ma stood and Zoe was thankful to see that she had downed her soup to the last drop. "I can just see her in her fancy silks trying to circumvent that big galoot of a horse without getting her skirts mussed. But we shouldn't laugh, I suppose. She has come a long way since she arrived in town. I dare say Parson Clay's sermons have aided the Holy Spirit in doing some work on her."

Zoe met Wash's gaze. She wouldn't go that far with regards to the snooty wife of Wyldhaven's mercantile owner, but Ma was one of those people who never had an unkind word to say about anyone. And come to think of it, Mrs. Hines had smiled and greeted Zoe warmly last Sunday with no apparent ulterior motive.

Wash stood to his feet. "Thank you for dinner, Mrs. Kastain. It was delicious."

Ma nodded. "Thank you for tracking down my Zoe and fetching her home."

Wash's gaze landed on Zoe and for some reason Zoe couldn't quite comprehend, she felt a tingle zip down her back at his scrutiny. Everything inside her raised to awareness in the most pleasant of ways. He looked at her with a new light in his eyes that she'd never noticed before.

He cleared his throat and broke eye contact, bouncing a glance off Ma, who stood looking between them. "It was my pleasure, ma'am. I'd best get—"

"Susan..." Pa's call from the bedroom was weak but distinct. Ma plunked her bowl on the table and rushed from the room. Zoe stayed right on her heels.

Pa writhed on the bed, hands curled around his middle, face contorted in a grimace that bared his teeth.

Ma swiped a gesture at her. "The powders, Zoe. Fetch honey and water."

Zoe hoisted her skirts and dashed to the sideboard in the kitchen. She grabbed a spoon so hastily that it tumbled from her fingers and clattered beneath the table. With a huff of frustration, she snatched up another.

The jar of honey was thankfully still half full. And Wash was already filling a glass for her at the pump. "Thank you." She took it from him and hurried back to Pa's room.

Ma had helped Pa sit up a bit against his pillows, but Zoe had never seen his face so red, the tendons in his neck bulging as he clamped his teeth to withhold cries of pain.

Tears blurred her vision as she hurried to scoop a little of the honey onto the spoon and pull the cork from the tube Doc Griffin had given her. She tried to remember what he'd said about dosage. "How much, Ma?"

Busy laying a cool cloth against Pa's forehead, Ma flapped a hand. "Half honey half powder, till the teaspoon is full."

Zoe hesitated. "But isn't that more than—"

"Doc said toward the end we'd need to double up the doses as the pain dictated."

Toward the end. The words froze Zoe in place. Her focus honed in on Pa's twisted expression.

"Just do it, Zoe," Ma snapped.

"Yes'm." Zoe's hands trembled as she tapped out enough powder to fill the rest of the teaspoon and then slipped the dosage between Pa's lips.

"That's right, Pa. You'll be feeling the ease here in no time at all now. Here's some water. Can you drink? Here, I'll put it on the spoon for you."

Her words and her actions were mechanical. Stilted. But she forced herself to stay until she saw Pa physically relax.

One moment he was all tightness and tension and the next moment he eased out a breath and sank into his pillows, his eyes rolling back into his head a bit before falling closed.

Ma released a breath. "Thank you, Zoe. He'll rest for a bit now."

Ma's worried gaze landed on the tube of powders. And Zoe immediately knew her concern. If they were going to have to give Pa this much each time, they were going to run out in just a few more doses.

She forced herself to speak, keeping her focus on the steady rise and fall of Pa's chest. "He's not going to make it, is he?"

She heard Ma swallow. "I'm afraid not, Zoe. Doc feared the pains would only continue to grow worse until the end."

Zoe put the cork back into the tube and set it on the side table. "Is this going to be enough for the night? Wash and I can go to town and get Doc."

Ma brushed a hand over her face. "Send Wash. But stay with me? Please. In case..."

"Yes'm." Zoe gave a little dip of her knees. "I'll be right back."

She left the room, intending to stop by the settee to speak to Wash, but the moment she stepped from Pa's room, she knew she needed some fresh air. She rushed past Wash, flung open the front door, and charged onto the porch without even bothering to shut the door behind her. The rail felt cool beneath her palms and she leaned forward, drawing in long draughts of the crisp evening air, gulping her sobs into soft huffs instead of the wails that wanted to scream from inside her.

Behind her, the door clicked shut, and Wash's footsteps drew nearer. He stayed silent. Zoe forced herself to inhale slowly, and they stood near each other through the tympanic song of one bull frog and the simple serenade of a cricket. Finally, Wash leaned his forearms on the rail, looking up into her face. "What can I do, Zo?"

Zoe dashed at her cheeks with one palm, then rested her cheek against her shoulder and met his searching, concerned gaze. Through her tight throat she was barely able to eke out, "Ma wonders if you can fetch Doc for us?"

Wash's jaw jutted to one side and sorrow furrowed his brow, softened his eyes. "Of course. I'll go right away." He stood, brushing his hand across her back and squeezing her shoulder as he did so. "I'm right sorry, Zo. Right sorry."

Chapter Five

acinda's hands trembled as she hovered the boiled blade just above Zane's shoulder. She pierced Dixie with a look. "You're sure he's not going to feel anything?"

Dixie nodded. "I've helped Flynn with surgeries several times. This is how he does it." She swept a gesture to the small bowl-shaped mask that she'd placed over Zane's nose and mouth. "The chloroform makes the patients sleep deeply enough that they don't even feel the pain."

"Okay." She sent up a quick prayer and put the blade to use. And the good Lord must indeed have been watching out because she felt the metallic resistance of the bullet fragment in just moments.

The whole procedure, from first cut to final stitch, didn't take more than half an hour.

Even so, by the time Jacinda finished, she felt as though she'd been running for hours on no sleep. She sank into the chair by Zane's bed and swiped a strand of hair from her face.

Dixie stood across the room with Doc's spare doctor bag in her hands.

"I'll just run this home and then I'll be right back with some stew and biscuits for you. You look done in."

Jacinda glanced at Zane, taking in the rise and fall of his chest. "I feel done in."

"I'm sure you do. I'll be right back. Do you need anything else?"

Jacinda shook her head. "No."

Just for Zane to wake up and look at her with those silvery-blue eyes of his.

"I'll lock the door behind me and then knock when I return."

Jacinda nodded her thanks, never taking her focus off Zane.

What if he got an infection? What if she hadn't gotten all the fragments? She'd only found two, though one was quite large. Could there be more? Would they cause problems?

What if they'd given him too much chloroform? Had Dixie really known how much to administer?

Her stomach crimped into a tight knot.

Thankfully, Doc would be here in the morning and then maybe he could ease some of her concerns. If she hadn't done the job right, he would fix it. And if she had, he would let her know.

She sat right where she was, comforting herself with the steady rhythm of Zane's breathing, until she heard Dixie's soft knock at the kitchen door.

She pushed herself up and shuffled into the kitchen. She was too old for this kind of worry. After a quick glance through the curtain to make sure it was Dixie, she swung the door open.

Dixie frowned at her above the tray she held in her hands. She stepped inside, set the tray on the kitchen table, but then faced Jacinda and plunked her hands on her hips. "Jacinda Callahan, none of your worrying is going to change one iota of these circumstances, you know that right?"

Jacinda felt a little sheepish. "Yes."

"Promise me you are going to get some sleep tonight?"

Jacinda smiled wearily. "I promise. As tired as I am, I don't think there will be any way around it."

"All right then." Dixie pulled her into a quick embrace. "I'll send Flynn down to check on him first thing in the morning. He can fetch my tray and dishes home then."

"Thank you so much." Jacinda motioned toward the food.

"Of course. I'm happy to help."

Jacinda saw her out, locking the door behind her. Then she managed to down half the bowl of delicious stew and one of the biscuits. She set the rest aside. It would give her something quick to warm up for Zane if he woke up hungry in the middle of the night.

She yawned expansively. She had arisen before dawn and put in a full day of sewing before she and Zane had escorted Reagan and Charlotte to the train station. Weariness tugged at her. But she couldn't go up to her bed on the upper level. If Zane woke, she might not hear him. However, neither could she, a single woman, make up a pallet in his sick room. It wouldn't be seemly.

Instead, she dragged the settee from the parlor into the entry and pushed it to one side of her sewing room door—now Zane's sick room.

She fetched a pillow and a blanket from upstairs and then gave one last look at Zane before she laid down. She closed her eyes, but everything in her strained to hear Zane's steady breaths.

Every few minutes, she lifted her head from the muffling effects of the pillow to make sure he was still doing all right. Then she chastised herself to quit worrying and try to rest. And the cycle would repeat itself.

Finally, Jacinda punched her pillow into a conformed lump, and forced herself not to lift her head again. *Father, I'm in a bit of a pickle. I know that none of my worrying can help Zane, and yet, forgive me, but with the way we lost Wade, I fear that maybe you will take Zane from me too. I know in my head that your Word says you love us and only want good for us, yet my experience doesn't bear that out. So how do I get past that and let go of the worry?*

No answer came.

And if she were honest, she hadn't expected one.

❧

Lenny paced from the front of the cave to the rear and back again while Roddy rolled and moaned on his pallet. Bob had tried to extract the bullet from his gut, but hadn't been able to find it, and Lenny feared that Bob might have done even more damage to Roddy than the bullet had already done.

Now, curse it all, he had a decision to make. Did he go for the doc? Or didn't he?

Just the thought of seeing the doc again made his stomach ache. Was it really only six months ago that Doc had been treating Wanda at their little cabin out at Camp Sixty-Five? Of course he'd been going by a different name then. And praying every day that Doc wouldn't recognize him through his thick beard and long hair. Undeniably, the scar he'd sustained across his left eye and cheek from that fight in McNeil Island Federal Penitentiary had also helped to conceal his identity.

Lenny Smith, one of the infamous members of the Waddell Gang, had been a man with a rather forgettable face, but clean-cut and shaven.

Roger Polsky, the man whose wife Doc had been treating, was unshaven, unshorn, and wore a leather patch over one eye. Almost a different man entirely. But he couldn't begrudge that any. After all, it was the three months in solitary after that fight that had helped him escape. That and the fact that he'd grown up swimming in the ocean nearly every day.

When he'd been tossed in solitary, he hadn't let himself wallow. He'd made himself work. Exercise. Strengthen his muscles.

Even then, looking back, it had been a bit of providence that had helped him escape.

A thick fog had rolled in. And the single guard who'd come to pull him out of the stone-lined hole on the edge of the prison grounds hadn't expected his attack, much less the strength with which he'd launched it.

For three months, Lenny had sat alone and planned his escape. For three months he'd played through scenario after scenario of just how he could make it happen. He knew he had only a few feet between solitary and the confines of the jailhouse to make his escape. So he'd acted quickly.

Nonetheless, if the guard hadn't tripped over a rock when Lenny'd shoved him, he might not have made it. But the guard *had* tripped. And the rock had been right there near to hand. He'd bashed the man in the head, then used his keys to remove the cuffs.

And the thick fog had concealed it all from the guard-tower.

The wooden fence hadn't been hard to scale. And from there it had only been a short sprint to the south side of the island. He'd heard the alarm at the prison blare just as he dove into the water for the short, frigid swim to Anderson Island.

That was where he'd almost been caught because he'd paused to gulp down some raw mussels from the beach, but the search team hadn't expected him to be in such good shape, nor to be able to swim the couple miles to shore through the pounding surf.

And the fog had still been so thick that Lenny had hardly been able to see his hand in front of his face.

Lenny still relished in the victorious feeling that had rushed through him when he'd finally felt the sand of the Washington shore beneath his feet. He'd fallen to his knees and promised God that he was a changed man.

And he had been.

For nearly a year.

He'd married Wanda. And he'd loved her fiercely. But all that had come grinding to a halt six months ago.

Six bitter months that had made him realize God was a fickle tyrant who didn't care about anyone.

He scooped both hands back though his hair and then laced them behind his head and kept pacing. If he had called on Doc sooner, would it have made a difference for Wanda? A question that he would forever not know the answer to. A question that had plagued him ever since the day that Wanda took her last breath.

In all honesty, he knew Doc had done his best to help Wanda and the baby, despite that they'd had no money to pay for his services. But by the time Lenny had gone to fetch him, Wanda had already started having seizures. And Doc had told him after the first time he'd examined her that the chances for both her and the baby were very low.

Since he couldn't pay, Lenny had thought Doc wouldn't come again. But Doc had come. Every day until Wanda passed. And even afterwards, Doc had stopped to check on him a couple times.

But Lenny hadn't been able to remain there, working that low-paying job and living in that cabin with so many memories. He'd quit going to work, and then they'd terminated him only a couple days later. And at the same time, he'd determined that he would never want for money again, no matter what he had to do to obtain it.

That determination had brought him here. Because what

better place to exact his plan than on the town and the sheriff that had sent him away in the first place? And he'd wanted them to know just who they were dealing with! So he'd reverted to using his real name when he'd gathered up his men.

The men who were at this very moment scrutinizing him, waiting for his decision. Especially Jim, who made the skin on his neck crawl. Lightning Jim Roan, they called him. Lenny had asked him to join his team because of his reputed speed with a gun. What he hadn't counted on was the man challenging him at every turn. But hopefully when he'd drawn his gun on the man, Jim had realized Lenny wasn't someone to be trifled with.

His dilemma about Doc remained.

If he didn't go for the doc, he would lose the respect of his men, he could see that plain and simple. All of them kept looking at him, each of them with accusation in his eyes. Except Tommy. Lenny had known him since the days when they were both in the Waddell gang together. Tommy had been sent to live with a widow in Seattle after the law had caught on that he'd been working with the Waddell gang, but the woman had recently passed, and when Lenny went looking for men to work with, he'd found Tommy living off garbage scraps in a Seattle alley. He'd bought him a meal and ever since then Tommy practically worshipped the ground Lenny walked on. Poor dumb Tommy would love him till the day he died, but only because he was too stupid to do anything else.

On the other hand, if he did go for the doc, he risked revealing their location to the townsfolk. Because if a doctor went missing—especially one as kind and compassionate as Doc Griffin—the whole town would be out in force to find and deal with anyone who had dared to harm someone so valuable in the community. And if the truth were told, he didn't want to harm the man. If for no other reason than out of gratefulness for what he'd done for Wanda. Yet, could he risk bringing the man here and then letting him go?

He scrubbed one hand over his jaw and paced the other direction.

Another option came to mind... If they blindfolded the doc and brought him in to fix Roddy and then let him go again right away... Was that too risky? Would the doc be able to retrace the steps to their hideout?

He chewed his lip. Considered. Paced some more.

Not if they took a circuitous route.

Yes. That could work.

But getting to the doc without alerting the town that he'd been taken, now that could get tricky.

He paused in the entrance of the cave and studied the star-studded sky. Blast but he wanted a drink. They'd downed the dregs of their only remaining bottle last night. They needed to make a supply run too.

Beyond missing Wanda, he longed for the days when he'd simply been a lacky. Back when Patrick Waddell had been the leader. He gave himself a shake. What was he saying? No. He didn't want to go back to being a lacky. Playing the part of a lacky was what had gotten him sent to jail. He was smarter than that now.

He'd promised himself that he'd get rich. He'd worked hard to build up this gang. Been careful who he selected, other than Tommy who had mostly selected him because Lenny had never been able to stand seeing anyone so cast off by society.

He was the leader, so he was going to lead.

He could do this. He'd just keep Jim close so he could keep an eye on him.

He snapped his fingers at Jim Roan. "Jim. You and I are

going into town to fetch the doc. Saddle up three of the horses."
As Jim stepped past him, he turned his focus on Robert Shade.
"Bob, you keep watch over Roddy. Keep him cool if his fever
starts to rise, got it?"

Bob nodded.

"Good. Victor, you go check the snares. I know it's dark,
but we all need to eat. Take Tommy with you. If you catch
anything, make up a stew with plenty of broth. Roddy's going
to need that." He turned to the last member of the gang.
"Jango, fetch some wood to keep the cave warm tonight. Fill
the bucket from the creek and put a pot on to heat. If we
succeed in bringing the doc back, he's likely going to want
some hot water."

The men all looked relieved, and Lenny couldn't deny he felt
plenty of that emotion himself.

It felt good to have a plan.

Now he just had to figure out how they were going to capture
the doctor.

And decide what he was going to do if Jim challenged him
again.

⁂

Wash rode hard for Wyldhaven and slid from his horse in
front of the boardinghouse. Had Doc returned from the camp
yet?

He swept off his hat and pounded on the door.

Only a moment later Dixie answered, pulling a house coat
around her shoulders. She squinted past the lantern she held
up.

Washington gave her an apologetic wince. "Sorry to bother
you so late, ma'am. Is Doc home yet?"

"No. I'm afraid—"

"I'm here." Doctor Griffin called. Wash turned to see him coming up the street from the livery. "I just got in. What can I do for you? Someone sick at home?"

Wash shook his head. "Not at our place, sir. It's Mr. Kastain. He's taken powerful sick. They fear they are going to need more pain powders by morning."

Doc grimaced. "I'm sorry to hear that. I suspected his attacks might be getting worse. I hoped I was wrong."

"Looked pretty bad this time, sir. Zoe and her ma didn't seem to think he was going to make it through the night."

Doc sighed. "I fear they are likely correct. Well, I'll head right out there." He gave Dixie a weary look of apology and started to turn.

She reached out to stop him. "Before you go, I think you should go down and check on Zane. He's at Jacinda's. They ran into outlaws on their way back from the train station and Zane was shot."

"What?" Wash exclaimed, hearing Doc echo him. "Zoe and I were there. We had to hide in the brush, but I didn't see him get shot!"

Dixie's lips pinched together. "He drove the wagon all the way back to town before he told her he'd been hit. He'd lost a lot of blood and we didn't want him to lose more." She looked at her husband. "I took the extra bag you leave here, and Jacinda cut some fragments out of his shoulder. But I told her you'd come check on him."

Doc nodded. "Of course. Yes. I'll go check on him right now." He squeezed his wife's hand and kissed her cheek. "Go back inside and try to get some more sleep, hmmm?"

The two exchanged a look that made Wash feel a bit like squirming. He looked down at the crimped brim of his hat. He should walk away and give them some privacy, but he needed to warn Doc that he'd overheard the outlaws say they had need of a doctor.

He did step back though, as Doc leaned forward and pressed a kiss to Dixie's cheek and said a few low words.

Wash swallowed. Of all the crazy things...why did Zoe Kastain come to mind just now?

Chapter Six

*Lenny and Jim stood in the alley by Dixie's Boardinghouse, backs pressed against the building. Thankfully, Jim seemed to have moved past their disagreement. He'd done everything Lenny asked. And right snappy too.

So Washington and Zoe had been witnesses to that firefight? Lenny pooched out his lower lip. Good. Their gang's reputation would spread. There was nothing like fear to get people to cooperate in handing over their money. And if he could accomplish that without having to hurt too many of them, so much the better. As proven by the way he'd backed Jim down with his gun. A little fear went a long way. And would keep the population healthy enough to keep the money flowing. Hopefully make it flow a little faster too. He'd thought they'd be better off by now. Unfortunately, they'd only netted a sum total of nine dollars and seventy-three cents from the people they'd robbed, so far. Seemed people just didn't carry much money on them 'round these parts. What they needed was a big payoff.

The notoriety would do for now, but it also came with risks. He'd learned that from being in Patrick Waddell's gang. Patrick's downfall had come because he'd made too big a name for himself. Everyone had been hunting him there at his end.

Well, and maybe his pride had gotten in his way at the last

too. But that was part and parcel with the big name he'd made for himself.

Yes. There were definite risks, but for now it was good that they would be talked about. He'd just have to carefully navigate that in the future. Keep his finger on the pulse, so to speak.

A thought struck him. Word getting out with his name associated with it... Would there be people out looking to recapture him? He'd have to ponder on that.

Later. Right now, satisfaction curled through him. They'd winged the marshal! It would be better still if infection set in and took him—would be one less lawman 'round these parts. 'Course it wouldn't be better if any of the gang ever got caught, because then they'd have killing a lawman to account for in addition to their other crimes.

Still...they'd made it this long without getting caught—and much of that was thanks to his own smarts and intuition.

With that cognizance, he reminded himself to proceed with caution.

"We gonna grab the doc, or what?" Jim prodded.

Lenny rolled his eyes, irritation coming to the fore. It was certainly a good thing he was the one in charge and not Jim. He gave him a glower and laid one finger across his lips.

Jim's words had caused him to miss something the doc had said to the kid. And now they were walking away.

But he was likely headed to Jacinda's place to tend to the marshal.

Could it be that it was going to be this easy?

Lenny waited only a few seconds before he looked through the dark at Jim. He tipped his head toward the street that ran behind all these buildings, but in front of Jacinda Callahan's home and dress shop.

Jim nodded, and they both ran on silent feet.

Wash heard the door click shut and looked up.

Doc thumped him on the shoulder. "Walk with me for a minute. You said you and Zoe were there when Zane and Jacinda were attacked?"

Wash gathered the reins of his horse and hurried after Doc, who took First Street past the alehouse toward Mrs. Callahan's with distance-eating strides. "Yes, sir." He filled Doc in on the reason he'd been there and what he'd been able to see and hear in the dark. "Lenny Smith. You remember him? He used to run with the Waddell gang before Sheriff Callahan killed Patrick Waddell. He is the leader of this new gang. I'd lay money on it."

Doc sighed wearily. "That, unfortunately, makes sense. I heard he escaped, nigh on two years ago now. I feared he'd come back to take his revenge on the town, but when nothing happened... Well, it wouldn't surprise me to see him back here."

Doc suddenly stopped walking. He scrubbed a hand over his jaw in thought. "Did you get a look at him?"

"No, sir." Wash shook his head. "We were hidden behind some bushes and only overheard their conversation. Why?"

A swipe of his hand brushed away whatever thought had occurred to him and he started down the alley between the jailhouse and the alehouse. "No time to explain now. It's probably nothing."

Wash scrambled to catch up. "You should know I overheard them talking about a need for your services. One of them was shot."

Doc pondered on that a moment, then gave a nod. "Thanks for the warning. You say there were seven of them?"

Wash nodded. "From what I could tell. And I overheard several names, too."

"Good. Good. I need you to ride out to Deputy Joe's place and let him know everything you just told me right away."

Wash blew out a weary sigh. "Yes sir." Was this day ever going to end?

"Thank you. Obviously you need to tell him about Zane being shot, as well. He might need to cover some things at the office in the morning."

"Yes, sir."

"Thank you, Wash." Doc dropped a hand onto his shoulder. "You're a good man."

Wash couldn't deny that the compliment filled him with pride. He gave Doc a nod and swung up on his mount as they stepped from the alley onto Second Street.

Doc headed toward Jacinda's place with a wave.

Reining the horse around, Wash urged it into a canter, taking the road out of town toward the Rodantes'.

⌁⟿⧉⟿⌁

Lenny and Jim crouched in the shadows behind a large crate just outside the alehouse's back door and listened to Doc give instructions for the kid to go get Deputy Rodante.

The kid galloped by, turning left at the end of the street.

Lightning Jim's gold tooth flashed in the moonlight. He gave a nod. Taking the doc was going to be easier than anticipated.

"Let's go." Lenny jerked his head.

They crept out of the shadows and ran on cat feet down the street.

Lenny's heart pumped hard. Had he delayed too long? Ms. Callahan's place was only half a block ahead! But thankfully Jim was as fast on his feet as he was purported to be with a gun. He sprinted and was on the doc before the man even heard him coming.

Jim pressed his pistol to the back of the doctor's head. "Nice and quiet, Doc. Hands up."

Flynn jolted to a stop, then raised his hands, doctor bag still gripped in one. "Easy, fella. What can I do for you?"

"Do for me? Nothing. I wouldn't have bothered you none. But my boss here wants you to come doctor a friend of ours."

Lenny swallowed at the derision Jim put into the word "boss." He wished the man didn't give him such shivers.

"My oath compels me to help everyone. You don't have to kidnap me to get me to help."

"And my grandmother was Martha Washington," Jim snapped.

Flynn wagged his head. "I know that's harder to believe for some than for others. I'd just ask you to remember that I can't help a hurt man if I'm hurt myself."

Lenny had a moment of conscience. This was Doc. Doc who had come to his home so often in Wanda's last days. Doc who had been kind to him even when he couldn't pay for Wanda's care. Doc who had come to Wanda's service and brought him a pot of stew the next day.

He had to make sure the gang didn't do the man any harm. Not only because he was a good man, but because people needed to be healthy if they were going to work so they could fork over their money to the gang.

He smirked.

He caught up to Jim and the doctor.

Doc glanced up and there was a flicker of recognition before a frown of disappointment settled over his features.

Lenny pushed down the wave of guilt and allowed anger to build in its place. Doc had no idea what it was like to be a man for whom nothing had ever gone right. The man's wife was still alive and he'd never needed to escape so badly that he'd buried his sorrows at the bottom of a bottle. He'd never been fired from his job or sentenced to prison either. So who was he to stand in judgement?

Lips pinched, Lenny whipped his bandana from around his neck and gave it a few twists to roll it into a wide blindfold. This he wrapped around Doc's eyes and secured good and tight at the back of his head.

Next, he took the doctor bag from Doc's hands, and then prodded him in the back with his pistol. The man would have to be tied down once they got to the horses, but the least he could do would be to get there on his own two feet.

Jim met Lenny's gaze. "I should go after the kid."

"Get the horses."

Jim's jaw bunched. But he only hesitated a moment before he jogged toward where they'd left the three horses behind the livery.

With another judicious jab of the pistol, Lenny set Doc to walking forward.

Doc stretched his hands out before him. "I can't see, Roger. You'll have to lead me or tell me what to do at the very least."

Lenny pondered. Had Doc really not put two and two together the moment he laid eyes on him? He'd have to consider on that. The kid had mentioned his name just a bit ago.

As for his request, if he tried to lead the man, he'd be putting himself in the vulnerable position of not being able to keep his gun on him. "Just walk, Doc. I promise not to let you get hurt. I need you healthy. Got a man with a bullet in his belly. Soon as you fix him up, I'll return you to town."

Maybe.

If Doc recognized him as Lenny, would he still bring him

back? Another question to ponder. Up to this point he'd never killed anyone, so he'd just get sent back to prison if he was caught. But the moment he crossed that line, he'd be looking at a noose.

Flynn only inched forward. Doing his best to stall, undoubtedly.

"Don't try to do too much thinking, Doc. Just move." He prodded Flynn in the back again.

With a sigh, Flynn took a few ginger steps. "I have to confess...Lenny...that when I got word that you were the leader of this outlaw gang, I didn't believe it. Can hardly believe, even now, that I didn't recognize you for all those months. I never would have pegged Roger Polsky, a man whose wife adored him without reserve, for a former outlaw."

Lenny flinched, everything inside him tightened up. So his secret was out. "Wanda made a better man of me." She would be ashamed of him for returning to his old ways so soon after her passing. Of course, she hadn't even known he *had* old ways.

"Seems like she'd be mighty disappointed to find you going back to your former life. Or did she even know about your past?"

Was the man a mind reader?

Lenny's teeth clamped together so hard his jaw ached. "She's not here, now is she, Doc? So I guess it don't rightly matter what she would think. Just shut your trap."

It was a good thing for Doc that he'd been so kind and was the one man who would bring the wrath of the whole area down on them should something happen to him. Because right now Lenny could happily put a bullet in him and never think twice.

But something else registered. Doc had recognized him. So his earlier quandary, which had only been theoretical, was now a concrete problem. Could he afford to let Doc go after he fixed up Roddy?

He prodded Doc again. At this rate, they would still be right here when Jim returned with the horses.

"Why are you doing this, Lenny? Especially when you know how much Wanda would have wanted you to avoid going back to this life."

Lenny's hand trembled against the grip of the pistol. "Doc, your questions are grating on my nerves. And since I'm the one with the gun, you'd best avoid that. Just. Get. Moving." He gritted the command, his anger nearly to the point of exploding. But what was he angry about, really? The fact that he knew Doc was right? He shook his head and nudged Doc along a little faster. He gave the alley a quick double check, but thankfully they were still alone.

"Since I know it's you, we could probably take this blindfold off, don't you think?"

Doc was a sly one, he'd give him that. But he wasn't foolish enough to fall for his ploy.

Doc stumbled over a pothole and Lenny grabbed his arm just in time to keep him from going down. The man was quiet after that.

Only a couple minutes later, they met Jim coming their way with the horses. But in those couple minutes, Lenny had plenty to think about.

Perhaps his earlier thoughts about Patrick Waddell making too big of a name for himself had been a bit naïve. After all, he couldn't kill everyone who learned his name. Especially not if he wanted the reputation of the gang to spread fear. Maybe it was unavoidable to have his name known? Necessary even?

Imagine everyone in the area speaking his name with fear!

He grinned. Yes. Imagine.

And what about the bounty hunters?

They would only be a problem if he got caught.

The solution hit him with blinding clarity. It was such an audacious thought that he laughed aloud before he thought better of it.

All was not lost. They could deal with this.

They would simply take out all the lawmen before they could report that he'd been seen in this area! The citizens would then fall right into line and he would have an entire town under his thumb. It was brilliant and manageable, but he had to play his cards right.

The sheriff would be gone for the better part of a month, from what he'd overheard in the saloon. And he could be caught off guard on his way back to town and dealt with. The marshal was already wounded badly enough that he'd required the removal of bullets. Not many men recovered from such injuries. He was likely already a problem solved, especially since Doc never made it in to see him. That only left the deputy.

And the solution to that lay in Jim.

Lenny silently helped the doctor mount his ride, and then lashed his hands tightly to the pommel and double checked the blindfold to make sure the man wasn't going to be able to lead a posse right back to them. But he really wasn't too concerned about that at this point. After all, with no law in town, there wouldn't be anyone to come looking for them.

Despite that, it would probably be best to move camps after returning the doc to town. It was just too risky, staying in one place for too long, anyhow.

After he had mounted his own horse and gathered up the reins for the doctor's mount, Lenny pointed for Jim to go after the Nolan boy. "Wait for the kid and the deputy. Killing the deputy is the most important. But if you have to take out the kid, don't let that stop you."

"Lenny, what are you talking about?" Doc sounded aghast.

Jim didn't bat an eye, merely tipped his hat and mounted up.

As Jim rode away, Lenny eased in a calming breath. He'd made his decision and there was no going back now. Everything was going to be fine.

And if they escaped?

He shook his head. He would worry about that if the time came.

Thunder rolled in the distance, setting his every nerve on edge.

Pulling in a breath, he urged his mount into a trot.

If they were going to do this, they needed to do it completely and quickly. Could they pull it off? Because if they didn't, then the law would no longer passively hunt them down. It would be an all-out man-hunt. A tremor whipped through him. His horse snorted and side-stepped. Lenny eased his grip on the reins. He just needed to calm down and breathe a little.

There were only three. One was out of town. One was already down for the count. That left only one remaining. And if anyone would be able to take him out, it would be Jim. The man was meaner than a thirsty rattler on a desert rock. Another shiver swept down Lenny's spine.

As they rode out of town, they passed the skeletal framework of the town's new bank, and it struck Lenny how quickly things were changing in town. A bank must mean that there were some prosperous folks around.

They just needed to find them.

Chapter Seven

Wash would have loved to take a leisurely ride back to town and hopefully do some dozing in the saddle along the way, but Joe had kicked his mount into a trot the moment they left his yard and hadn't let up the pace since.

Above them, thunder rolled ominously, drawing Wash's attention to how dark it really was tonight. Storm clouds must be obscuring the sky.

They were just about to enter the draw that cut through the hills outside of town when Joe lifted a hand and pulled to a stop. "Whoa." He scanned the hills on both sides of the road.

"What is it?" Wash didn't see anything, but in this thick blackness with the moon behind the clouds, that didn't surprise him.

"Don't know." Joe shook his head. "Looked like my horse heard something."

Wash studied his own horse's ears. They were pointed toward a spot off to the right. If he weren't so tired, he might have noticed sooner. He bent down and stroked the animal's neck. "Yeah. Mine too."

"Get down. Now." Joe shucked his rifle from his scabbard as he swung down from his mount. "Stay on the right side of your horse. Whoever is out there has the high ground. But this pitch black is on our side."

Joe broke into a jog, and Wash moved out right behind him, keeping his head low behind his buckskin filly's neck.

The filly didn't like him being on the off side. She blew and bobbed her head, dancing sideways a little. "Easy, girl." Wash spoke softly and hung onto a handful of mane to keep her between him and the danger.

Something pinged off of the ground just behind Joe's horse, sending sparks through the blackness. The report of a rifle came only a moment later. Joe's paint reared with a screech. Wash's horse too. He barely managed to hold onto the reins. Both horses hit the ground itching to run. Joe was fighting to keep his paint close, but the horse had danced away from him, leaving him exposed.

Wash yanked his pistol and fired two blind shots into the trees. Pa would whup him but good if he knew he was shooting at something he couldn't see, but Wash figured in this case that was better than letting Joe take a bullet.

Another shot whined above Wash's head and he immediately realized his mistake. The outlaw had pinpointed his location by his muzzle flashes.

"This is no good," Joe grumbled. "Mount up and ride hard. I'll be right behind you."

"Yes, sir."

He swung into the saddle and kicked his heels firmly, and the buckskin was more than happy to give him the speed he asked for. When she wanted to stretch out, she could, and she devoured the road in ground-eating strides. Behind him, he heard Joe firing off a few shots.

Wash skidded to a halt at the back door of Dixie's Boardinghouse and whipped the buckskin's reins around the stair rail before he dove behind the water barrel.

He heaved for breath, trying to hear what was happening out on the road.

Silence. Too much of it.

Wash licked his lips. Had he left Deputy Rodante to be killed?

But in the next moment he heard the sound of galloping and Joe called, "You okay, kid?" He reined to a stop, rifle in one hand.

Wash nodded. "You?"

"Yeah."

"Did you get him?"

"I don't think so." Joe turned his mount in a circle, assessing the area. "We need to get inside. Let's talk to Doc and see if he learned anything from Zane. But let's go around front. I don't relish getting shot in the back while we're knocking on the door."

"Yes, sir." They hurried their mounts around to the front, and Wash felt terrible for banging on the boardinghouse door a second time in the middle of the same night. Especially when it was once again Mrs. Griffin who answered the door.

She was a bit wide-eyed when they asked to speak to Doc. "He never came back from Jacinda's place. Did you check there?"

"No, ma'am." Joe tipped her his hat. "Right sorry to have bothered you. We'll go talk to him there."

But when Jacinda opened her door, she frowned at them. "Doc never came by."

Wash looked at Joe.

This was not good. "Where could he have gone? I left him right behind the jailhouse and he was walking this way."

Jacinda clutched at her collar. "Something woke me about an hour ago. But there was no one in the street when I looked out."

Joe adjusted his hat, his boots scuffing on the porch. "You did say you overheard them discussing the need for a doctor."

Wash nodded. Swallowed as he realized the outlaws must have been very nearby when he was talking to Doc earlier. "Think they'll hurt him?"

Jacinda gasped. "Oh my! Flynn has been captured by outlaws?"

Joe ignored Jacinda and gave Wash a non-committal wag of his head. "Either way, we can't track them till morning. I just hope this storm holds off."

It suddenly hit Wash that if Doc had never made it to Jacinda's he'd also never made it to the Kastains'. He scrubbed the knuckle of his thumb over his jaw. "Doc was supposed to take more pain powders to Mr. Kastain. He was in a bad way. Mighty bad. I think I'd better ride out there. If Doc is there I'll come back and let you know."

Joe gave him a nod and Wash swung onto his mount and urged it back toward the boardinghouse. Mrs. Griffin was going to be none too happy to find him at her door yet again tonight, but he prayed she'd be able to give him the medicine the Kastains would need to keep Mr. Kastain as comfortable as possible.

He heard Joe riding right behind him and realized they were both headed to the same destination. Joe needed to let Dixie know her husband had gone missing.

⁓⁓⁂⁓⁓

Jacinda stirred the scrambled eggs and flipped over the fry bread. She'd slept so little the night before that she knew only a day of constant activity was going to keep her awake. Before he'd left in the middle of the night, Joe had said he'd be back first thing to talk to Zane and Jacinda wanted both men to get a good breakfast in them.

After Joe and Wash had left, she'd paced the house and prayed like she hadn't prayed in a long time. Prayed for Doc's safety. For Zane's recovery. For Joe to have wisdom to know what to do. For William's recovery and that if God didn't choose to heal him that he'd have peace in his last hours. For the rest of the Kastains to have comfort if he did indeed pass away. And then back to praying for Zane again.

Jacinda sighed. If there was one good thing in all of this it was that Reagan was gone and out of harm's way. Okay, two good things. Zane was injured too badly to be expected to go off hunting outlaws.

Her conscience struck her for the selfishness of her gratefulness.

Behind her, she heard a sound. She turned to find Zane, face contorted in pain as he tried to swing his gun belt about his hips.

"What are you doing?" Jacinda marched toward him and stilled his hand. "I fought hard to keep you alive and I'll not have you undoing all my hard work." She took the gun belt from him and plunked it on the table. "Back to that bed and I'll not hear a word of protest."

Zane swayed. He reached for the back of the nearest chair. "You know? I think maybe you're right. This time."

Jacinda hurried to the stove, tugged the pan to the coolest corner, and then returned to him. She tucked herself under his arm for support. "Come on. I'll walk you back."

Zane shuffled along beside her and nearly collapsed onto the bed when they reached it.

Lips pinched together, she lifted his legs one at a time and tugged off his boots, then helped him beneath the covers.

He captured her hand and when she tried to pull away, refused to release her. She snapped her gaze to his.

One corner of his mouth quirked up. "You worry too much, Jac."

She gave her hand a firm tug, forcing him to let go. "Did you hear Joe and Wash knock on the door in the middle of the night?"

His brow furrowed. "No."

"That's because you tried to play the hero and lost so much blood you were—are—as weak as a newborn mouse! So I'll tell you what you didn't hear. Doc was on his way here to see you, but he never made it. Disappeared somewhere between the boardinghouse and my front door. Joe thinks maybe the outlaws took him to tend to someone we wounded in that gunfight. On top of that, Wash says William Kastain took a turn for the worse. I should be cooking food to take out to that family. But you almost passed out in my kitchen and I can't leave because I can't trust that you'll stay in your sickbed. And I won't have you cracking your skull open in a fall!" She blinked hard, hating that her little lecture had nearly brought her to tears. Tossing her hands in the air, she spun toward the door. "And you're saying I worry too much!"

"Jac stop."

She complied, but didn't face him.

"Come here." His tone was cajoling.

She sniffed. Held her ground for a moment. Willed away the evidence of her heightened emotions with a few quick swipes of her fingers.

"Jac..."

The word was so soft and full of tenderness that she felt the impact of it in her knees.

She faced him.

He patted the quilt beside him, tilting his head against the headboard.

Finally, she strode over and sank onto the coverlet.

Averting her gaze from his searching silvery-blue one, she focused instead on the stubble of his firm jawline. She moistened her lips. Wished he'd get on with what he wanted to say before she gave into the temptation to press a kiss against that small scar where his beard refused to grow.

He lifted her hand and tugged it against his chest, curving his fingers around hers as if he simply needed to feel her close in this moment. "First, I didn't tell you about my wound, because I hoped you could avoid this very thing. This worrying. I honestly didn't know I was hurt as bad as I was till just before we reached town. I figured I could get Doc to tend it and you'd never need to be the wiser."

Jacinda frowned at that. Was her worrying so evident that Zane had felt the need to protect her from knowing he'd been hit?

"Second," Zane continued, "Joe's likely right. We probably hit one or more of the outlaws in that shoot-out. But those men know that if they kill a man like the Doc it will mean the end for them. He'll likely be fine."

She searched his face. Did he really believe that? Or was he just trying to spare her more worry? His skin was so gray it seemed it might only take half a moment to transform him into a corpse.

"Third... I've got no answers about Kastain. But you take them some food. I promise you I'll mind myself and stay in this bed." He tapped the quilt. "Right here. Without moving."

An assessment of his expression told her he meant what he said. Lurching to her feet, she said, "Fine. I'll—"

"Fourth." Zane held up a finger for her to wait.

Jacinda sank back down.

"There's a verse I want you to look up for me."

A frown tugged at her brow.

"Luke 12:27."

"Okay... What's it say?"

"You just look it up. Then we'll talk."

With a sigh, and a bit of reluctance, she stood. "Fine. I presume Dixie will want to come with me to the Kastains'. But I'll have Rose look in on you a few times. You might need help to get to the—well...you might need some help."

He nodded. "Jac?"

She met his gaze.

"I know you can shoot. But I'd feel better if you took someone with you to the Kastains'. Someone besides Dixie."

She gave him a nod. "I think Wash already rode out, but I'll see if Jackson Nolan can ride with us. He's a good lad."

Zane nodded and sank more fully against his pillows. "Thank you."

She took up a handful of her skirts. "I'll fetch your breakfast before I leave."

❧⁓❧⁓

If there was one thing Zane Holloway hated, it was feeling like a pup deprived of its milk. And that was just how he felt. He was so weak that if he encountered anyone on the wrong side of the law right now, he'd be out of the fight before one even began.

He hated to think of Joe having to face all this hullabaloo on his own.

Maybe he'd suggest that Joe deputize Washington Nolan. The kid was as level-headed as they came, and that would at least give Joe a partner in tracking down this gang, even if Wash wouldn't have a lot of experience. Zane hated that he couldn't be more of a help, but the truth was, though he'd never passed out, whatever he'd felt in the kitchen a few minutes ago had come mighty close to feeling like he might.

Imagine if he'd fainted with Jacinda looking on! He sniffed. No. He didn't want to have to live that story down. So it was best he listen to Jacinda's concerns and let his body recuperate a mite.

Could he have avoided this by telling Jacinda sooner that he'd been shot?

Perhaps, and yet, for the chance to keep her from worrying he might do the same again. However, as he'd been lying here on the bed in her spare room, he'd given that a good deal of thought. Was it in her best interest to help her avoid every worry she might come across? Yes, she'd faced great loss. Maybe more than most people. But it was still important for her to learn to rely on God and believe—truly believe—that He made no mistakes.

Maybe it was time he talked to her about Daniella. Because Lord knew that he'd suffered his own fair share of grief. And the bitterness that followed. Everyone handled such things differently, but the time had come for Jacinda to let go.

And if part of his reason for wanting her to do so came from the selfish desire to have her move on with him? Then so be it. Because if one thing had come from almost losing his life, it was the realization of what was important. And right now, Zane was very aware that the only thing he wanted was to spend the rest of his life with one beautiful, stubborn, prone-to-worry gentlewoman named Jacinda Callahan.

Weariness washed over him. All this thinking, along with the constant throbbing in his shoulder, had combined to tucker him right out.

He needed to come up with a plan. A woman like Jacinda wouldn't be easily won over. But perhaps with a little bit of charm and a lot of God's help, he'd be able to get the job done.

First—he sank further into the pillows—he needed to do a touch more study on the insides of his eyelids to make sure there were no holes.

Hopefully he'd have some of his strength back by the time he woke.

Chapter Eight

Zoe stared at Pa, heart aching like it had never ached before. At some point in the night, he'd asked for the kids, and Ma had woken the twins and Aiden and made them say their goodbyes. Now, they slept in a tangled pile of arms and legs against the far wall. Zoe knew it would likely be a boon for the kids to look back in the future and remember.

Several times, Pa had asked for Belle. And each time she'd had to tell him Belle still wasn't home, Zoe's anger had increased. Pa had finally given in to the tug of the other world, sometime just after the rains had started, though his breaths had still rattled.

"It won't be long now," Ma had said, wiping a cool cloth across his brow.

Zoe knew she should offer some words of comfort but hadn't been able to come up with any.

And now Pa's chest no longer moved. She watched closely. Willing him to take just one more lungful of air. His breaths had grown increasingly farther apart during the night. And several times she'd thought him gone, only to have him drag in one more. So now she waited, her own breath bated. She held it so long that a pain suddenly stabbed through her temple and she was forced to gasp.

Ma had curled against Pa's side at some point in the night.

Her hand rested gently on his chest, her head next to his shoulder. Now she raised up and looked over at Zoe. "It's done, Zoe." Tears shimmered on her lashes. "He's in no more pain."

Zoe nodded, then turned and pushed from the room. She rushed through the small sitting room and burst out the front door to heave great gulps of the chilly dawn air. The soothing sound of rain hammering against the roof grounded her.

Ma's pot of geraniums snagged her focus. Odd, the way they looked in the gray light of dawn. Without illumination, the geraniums seemed nearly as pallid as the sky. That was exactly how she felt. She'd just lost her light. Her world was now all grays and shadows.

A sob escaped. Followed by another. Yet she knew Ma was going to need her to be strong. She didn't dare fall apart just yet.

"Zoe?" There was a shuffle of sound behind her and she spun.

Wash was just coming up the porch steps. Water shed off his hat to stream down the back of his thick leather coat. In his hand was another vial of pain powder. The sight of them, stole her remaining resolve to remain strong.

"Wash!" She rushed over and threw her arms around him. Her legs lost all their strength as sobs overtook her and she buried her face against his damp collar.

"Aw, Zo. I'm so sorry." Wash sank onto the bench and gathered her onto his lap. He brushed wisps of hair back from her cheek, and cradled her close. "I've got you now."

She wasn't sure how long she cried. But it couldn't have been too long, because though the sky was lighter, the sun still hadn't crested the horizon when she sat up and pushed back from him. She swiped her fingers beneath her eyes, and looked at Wash. "Thank you. I'm sorry."

"Think nothing of it." He rubbed a hand up and down her back, then brushed his other hand down her arm.

His fingers left a warm trail on her skin.

"You're cold. We should get you inside." In the dawn-pallor of the porch with the rain still pattering all around them, she took in the sturdy angles of his face. The gray shadow of his jaw drew her fingers.

Wash swallowed hard enough that she heard it over the rain. His gaze drilled into hers.

She felt her heart pump against her ribs. Relished the prickly stubble of his jaw beneath the pads of her fingers. This was real. This was life.

This was color.

There was gravel in his voice when he said her name. "Zoe... Now's not—"

With a jolt, she realized the impropriety of her actions, where she sat, and how close his face was to her own. She scrambled to stand, but one leg tangled in her skirts and she lost her balance.

Wash's hands shot out to grip her arms. "Whoa, there. You good?"

"Wash, I'm—"

He released her. Raised his palms. "We're all exhausted. What can I do?"

Her gaze darted back toward the house. "I don't..." She felt her mouth go dry at just the thought of having to go back in there. Of having to help Ma...

Wash's fingers were warm at her elbow. "Come on, Zo. I'll walk you inside."

"Thank you." But, even then, her feet didn't seem capable of movement. What were they going to do now? They'd barely been making it before Pa passed. And that was only because

Mr. Hines, who owned the mercantile in town, had purchased their property and offered to let them rent it for a pittance until Pa got better. But now, the rent would go up.

And...

"Zoe?" Wash touched her chin, lifting her gaze to his. "One step at a time, hmmm? And I'll be by your side the whole way."

"I have to be strong."

He nodded.

And she took the first step.

⁘⁘⁘

Wash's heart felt like breaking as he helped Mrs. Kastain and Zoe carry the sleeping children back to their beds and then wrap Mr. Kastain into a clean sheet.

With that task done, Zoe's mother looked at him. "Thank you for being here." She squeezed his arm.

He swallowed. Nodded. Truth was, he wouldn't want to be anywhere else in Zoe's hour of need.

Mrs. Kastain looked down then. Her fingers laced together. "I've been buying one board a week, for several weeks now. I hope— I'm not—" She cleared her throat, her gaze darting to the sheet-clad body on the bed.

Wash understood. She wanted him to make a coffin but wasn't sure if she had enough wood. He tipped her a nod. "I'll get to work, ma'am."

Zoe stood quietly by the window, staring seemingly at nothing. He hesitated. Should he go to her?

Mrs. Kastain leaned close to speak low. "Give her time."

He nodded and reluctantly left her alone. If he could, he would take all her pain as his own.

He paused on the porch steps to study the yard.

Sometime in the past few minutes the rains had given way to

broken clouds. The sun poked above the horizon in golden glory, a reminder that light was stronger than the deepest darkness. Steam rose from every hill and fence the rays touched, creating a glorious golden haze along the horizon.

He found the pile of boards leaning against the back wall of the lean-to.

Seven of them. Not nearly enough for a coffin. But there was a crosscut saw hanging from a peg. And he remembered seeing a log on the east side of the cabin. Mr. Kastain must have hauled it home for firewood before he'd taken this last turn for the worse.

It would do, but was Zoe in a state of mind to help him? Pondering on that, he realized that even if she wasn't, Zoe would bring herself around to where she needed to be. She was the strongest girl he knew. A woman to ride the trail with, his pa would say.

He grunted. Where had that thought come from? He and Zoe were much too young to even be considering on something like that. Besides, he'd made up his mind that he was going to join the cavalry. And that was no life for a woman.

He took the Kastains' two horses from their stalls and harnessed them, then led them to the log. He would need to drag it up onto some blocks before he and Zoe would be able to saw any boards from it. The task took him an hour, and by the time he got done, he was famished. He tried to recall the last time he'd eaten anything. Not since that bowl of soup he'd had the evening before. And before that…breakfast yesterday before he'd gone looking for Zoe. But it wasn't like he could march into the kitchen and ask Zoe or her mother for food.

The sound of a wagon rolling into the yard came from behind him and he turned to find his brother escorting Mrs. Callahan and Mrs. Griffin. Mrs. Griffin's eyes were a bit red and puffy, which likely meant they'd had no news of Doc yet. And that rainstorm was going to make the job of tracking impossible. He kicked at the ground. At least Jackson was here. He could help with the sawing instead of Zoe.

"Good morning, Wash." Mrs. Callahan swung down from the seat and retrieved a basket from beneath the bench.

He tipped his hat to Doc's wife and then to her. "Ma'am."

"Any news?" She searched his face as she shrugged out of her rain poncho.

"I'm afraid Mr. Kastain passed just before dawn, ma'am."

The women exchanged a sad look.

Just then his stomach let loose a loud rumble. He gave a little cough that he hoped would cover it up, but Mrs. Callahan smiled at him.

"You've been on your feet or in the saddle every time I've seen you in the past day. You must be hungry." She opened the lid on the basket and flipped back a towel to reveal golden-topped blueberry muffins. "Take two."

He gave her a nod. "Thank you, ma'am."

She smiled at him. "As soon as Dixie and I get some bacon and eggs cooked up, I'll bring you and Jackson each a plate."

"Very kind of you, ma'am. I'm just"—he gestured to the log—"working on the casket."

She eyed the log a bit dubiously, before she hurried toward the cabin.

Jackson stopped by his side and took one of the muffins.

Wash glowered at him.

"Hey, I've been smelling these all the way from town. Liked to drive me mad." He took a big bite and then spoke around his mouthful. "You need help?"

"Yeah." Wash broke his remaining muffin in half and stuffed

one section in his mouth, then gestured from the crosscut saw to the log.

He and Jackson had always worked well together, and today was no different. The log was good and dry and while the boards they cut were rough, they would make adequate planking, especially for the floor and lid of the coffin.

They had just finished cutting the second board and Jackson was busy working over it with the plane when Wash heard a gasp.

He turned to find Belle at the edge of the yard near the tree line. Her blond hair curled out in frazzled waves all around her. Her blue eyes were red rimmed and bloodshot. And she was staring at the wood shavings and sawdust with an expression of horror.

Wash strode toward her. "Belle, I know your ma and Zoe were worried about you. Best you get inside and...let them know you're back." He noted a rolled-up piece of...was it fabric?...in one of her hands and a satchel over her shoulder. His curiosity piqued. Where had she been all night? He didn't suppose it was his place to ask.

"Wash?" Jackson called. "Do you want this last piece we cut for the side or the lid of the cof—"

Wash's eyes fell closed. His brother really could be an idiot sometimes.

"I'm really sorry about that, Belle. I didn't see you there," Jackson said.

At least he sounded contrite, though from the expression on Belle's face, his brother's words weren't offering any balm. Wash glowered at Jackson over his shoulder and gave a little bob of his head toward the shed.

Jackson scrubbed at the back of his neck, looking sheepish as he disappeared inside.

Belle's eyes were wide and one hand covered her mouth. "No. Tell me..." She shook her head. "No!" She backed a few steps like she might make a dash for the woods and never return. The rolled-up fabric in her hand tumbled to the ground.

Wash stepped forward and angled an arm behind her to stop her retreat. He stretched his other arm toward the house. "Belle, your ma needs you now. Zoe too."

That seemed to get through to her. She scooped a hand into her hair, finger-combing some of the tangles before she piled it all atop her head with a couple deft twists. She hesitated at the bottom of the porch steps, but then lifted her skirts and moved into the house.

Wash gave a sigh of relief. It was good for her to be here with her family, no matter how painful of a time this might be.

He bent and picked up what he could now see was a roll of canvas, lest the rain-soaked grass should ruin it. A splash of color caught his eye. Before he thought better of it, he unfurled it.

His breath caught.

He'd known that Belle was an artist, but not like this.

The painting was of the Kastain family, all dressed in their Sunday best. They sat in the wagon, and Mr. Kastain held the reins, the lines of his body strong and vibrant. His head was thrown back on a laugh as Mrs. Kastain leaned close with her hand on his arm to say something to him. Zoe, the twins, and Aiden were in the back of the wagon. And Belle sat on the seat by her mother. The details of the piece were so precise and accurate Wash could almost see the horses' manes blowing in the wind. It was as if Belle had somehow transferred a moment in time onto the canvas. And all with paint and brush.

Very carefully, he rolled the painting. He thought for a moment and then strolled over to where he'd slung his saddle over the top rail of the corral. He tucked the canvas into a saddle bag and then hurried back to the shed. Something like that should not be lost. If he gave it to Belle in her current state of mind, she might be tempted to destroy it. But later, it would be a precious memory for the Kastains.

⁓≫≫⁄≪≪⁓

Zoe sat at the table with Aiden on her lap, trying to convince him to eat some scrambled eggs. But her attention wasn't really on the task.

It was on Ma, who sobbed quietly as she talked to Mrs. Callahan and Mrs. Griffin in the kitchen.

Zoe's whole being ached. She felt hollow. Old before her time.

How could sturdy, steadfast Pa be gone? What would she do without his encouragement in her life? How many times had she been on the verge of giving up on something, only to have Pa give her a gentle nudge to keep going?

When she'd been trying to train Jinx to bark at the door if he needed outside, Pa had dried bits of beef and showed her how to use them to reward Jinx when he did what he was supposed to.

One time last year, when she'd been ready to throw down her pencil due to the complicated mathematics problems, Pa brought two pieces of pie and two cups of milk to the table. He'd closed her book and pushed it to one side, and slid the pie in front of her with a smile. After they'd spent thirty minutes savoring the tart berries and chatting about nothing in particular, he'd taken her plate and nudged the sums closer again with a quick wink.

Even though he'd never really recovered his health after Patrick Waddell shot him, Pa had maintained his kindness, patience, and gentleness.

Zoe blinked hard, forcing the painful thoughts to the recesses of her mind.

Aiden pushed the fork away and slumped against her. "I'm not hungry." He sniffed.

Zoe set the fork down and wrapped her arms around him, resting her chin on his curly mop. "I know."

Across the table, neither of the twins had touched their food either. The girls held hands, and they'd both slumped sideways in their chairs so that their shoulders and heads were propped together, as though neither had been able to carry on without the comforting touch of the other. Maybe it was a twin thing. Zoe had never felt that close to Belle.

The front door opened. Belle slunk in without meeting anyone's gaze.

The devil hath power to assume a pleasing shape.

Zoe's teeth clamped together. She tossed a glance toward Ma, but the three women in the kitchen were absorbed in their own world. Only a little bit of guilt pricked at her for the Shakespeare quote.

Pressing a kiss to Aiden's head, Zoe stood and settled him into the chair. She nudged the plate closer to him. "Try to eat, hmmm. We all need you to be strong now. You're the man of the house."

With one last glance in Ma's direction, she hurried after Belle. Her hands fisted so tight that her fingers ached, and by the time she caught up to Belle in the hall, she was nearly running.

She grabbed one of Belle's arms and jerked her around, then stepped right into her space. "Where were you? How could you be so selfish on a night like last night! We needed you here! Ma needed you here! And you didn't even get—" Zoe's voice broke, mostly because her throat had clamped off her ability to speak. She backed away from her sister giving her a look that she hoped conveyed her disgust.

Belle's eyes were bloodshot and red-rimmed. Her hair was tangled in a messy knot atop her head. And she wouldn't meet Zoe's gaze. In fact, she wasn't doing much of anything. Just standing there. Limp. Staring, unfocused, at a spot on the wall. Feeling guilty, most likely.

As she should.

The fact that Belle hadn't been here to say goodbye was a burden she'd have to bear for the rest of her life, but it wasn't something Zoe could forgive her for.

Zoe lifted her chin. Took another step back. "He asked for you, you know. Several times. He tried to hold out. Wait for you. But..." Sobs clawed up from inside her. She pushed them into compliance, determined to have her say. "He was...in so much...pain. And you...couldn't even be bothered...to be here."

She spun on her heel and left then, because she knew if she stayed, she might do something she'd later regret. Ma needed her help. And Pa wouldn't want her to fight with Belle, especially not today.

Feeling the necessity of solitude, she banged out the front door. Thankfully, there were chores that needed tending to. The rain had stopped, but the ground squished beneath her firm steps. She marched past Wash and Jackson, and grabbed up the pail of chicken feed from inside the tack room.

Feeding chickens. Milking the cow. Cleaning stalls. These were all things she could do.

Better yet, they kept her outside so she wouldn't end up in jail for clobbering her sister.

Chapter Nine

eart in her throat, Belle stood in the hallway, staring at the door to Pa's room. Despair weighed down every limb. She hadn't been fast enough. The painting that she'd hoped to show Pa had taken just one night too long.

Oh, Pa.

Something dripped onto the back of her hand and she realized she was crying. Giving her cheeks two quick swipes, she stepped forward and forced herself to press a palm to the door. Push inward.

Pa was already enshrouded in a sheet.

A sob escaped. She collapsed to her knees by the bed and pressed her forehead to the tick. "I'm...so...sorry, Pa." She rocked. "I painted us...before. You...strong. Ma...laughing." A groan emanated seemingly from her very heart. "It would have...made you smile."

But I was too slow.

Behind her, the door creaked. Aiden peeked his head around the frame.

Belle held out a hand to him and he hurried forward and scooted onto her lap. He leaned his head against her shoulder and hugged her arms close, as though he needed to feel wrapped in her comfort.

Belle rocked him, relishing the feel of him tucked close.

After a long moment, he whispered, "Is Pa coming back?"

Belle's eyes fell closed. "No, punkin'."

"Will we ever get to see him again?"

Belle hesitated. She knew the answer Ma would want her to give. The answer that came from the Good Book. That one day they would all be together in heaven again if they all gave their lives to the Lord and followed his commands. But she wasn't sure she believed it.

Pa had been a good man. So good that he'd been trying to help the man who shot him! He didn't deserve to die, much less to die after years of living in pain and agony with repeated bouts that took him to death's door.

Still, Ma would be sore disappointed if she told Aiden anything different, and Aiden didn't need more heartache, so she gave him a squeeze. "Of course we will. One day in heaven."

Aiden squirmed. "I don't want to wait till heaven."

"I know, punkin'. But we don't have a choice. Pa would want us to be strong."

Aiden sniffed but made no other reply.

After a long moment, Belle urged him to his feet. "Come on, let's go see if Ma needs our help."

Ma was seated at the table, and Mrs. Griffin was pouring her a cup of coffee. Ma looked up, her eyes hollow. She hesitated only a moment before she gave Belle a nod, but it was long enough that Bell felt the chill of her disappointment.

Ma would never understand the drive to paint that had sent Belle from the house for days in a row.

Pa had been the one to indulge her artistic bent. He'd been the one who saved up to buy her pencils and paints and canvas. The one who'd purchased her that book about the history of art. The one who'd always exclaimed over her pieces and told her how much better each one was than the last. When Ma had chided and said she needed to learn canning and sewing and cooking, Pa had winked and proclaimed that perhaps one day Belle's paintings would provide for them all. Pride had buoyed her in those moments. But now all she felt was a cavernous ache.

Just last week, right there at the table, Pa had leaned over her shoulder to examine the sketch she was making of Aiden refusing to eat his peas. Pa had laughed at Aiden's face and squeezed her shoulder.

She could see him in the sitting room peering at her above his newspaper and making silly faces as Ma read to them in the evenings.

Outside, there was the porch which she'd helped Pa construct when they'd first moved here. And the barn where Pa had led her two Christmases ago to reveal the easel that he'd built for her.

Memories. Everywhere, memories.

The strength left her legs and she sank down at the table.

Mrs. Griffin squeezed her shoulder. "Let me get you some food."

Belle wasn't hungry. In fact, she didn't think she'd manage to swallow even one bite, but she forced a quick smile and nodded her thanks.

She would stay for a few days until the family settled into a new routine, but then she would need to move on. Her desire to be an artist would only agitate Ma. Besides, the pain of seeing Pa in every nook and cranny might be too much to handle.

It would be better this way.

Ma would be happier. Zoe certainly would be. The twins likely wouldn't care one way or another. Aiden might miss her, but he would get over it.

Maybe she'd move to Seattle. There were probably more opportunities there for artists to make a living.

Yes.

She would try Seattle.

"Whoa!"

Flynn Griffin felt his first hint of relief since the rain had started. Maybe they were finally to the outlaw's hideout. Since Lenny had kept him blindfolded, he cocked his head and strained to listen, as he'd been doing for most of the ride from town.

At first, he'd figured Joe and Zane would be able to track him, but when the rain had started, he'd nearly given up hope. But then he'd consoled himself with the fact that if Lenny was keeping him blindfolded most likely he planned to let him live. And that was when he'd really started straining his remaining senses to take in every detail of the ride. Because if he could get back to town, maybe he'd have something useful to share.

Maybe the information he'd been able to gather would help Zane and Joe find this hideout.

After helping to tie him to the saddle, Lenny's partner had ridden away. Flynn had no doubts about where he was going. His only recourse had been to pray for Joe's safety. Wash's too. Had the man succeeded in his mission? Flynn's heart was heavy with the unanswered question.

Just out of town, they'd clopped across the bridge. That meant they were up in the mountains north of Wyldhaven. It had started raining somewhere along the way before they'd splashed across a river. Which had to be where Wyldhaven creek curved back to the east. That put them at least five miles outside of town and there were only a couple places that were shallow enough to cross. Then only about ten minutes ago, he'd smelled roses. Or maybe it was lilacs. Some sort of wild-flower. But the scent had been strong, so it was likely a large field of them. If they could find that, maybe they could find this place.

Providing they let me live.

He swallowed at that thought and willed himself to take a calming breath. If there was one thing he'd learned in all his years of doctoring, it was that worrying about the future never helped. He only hoped Dixie wouldn't stress herself too much with concern over him. That wouldn't be good for the baby. He suppressed a smile at that thought. She hadn't told him yet, but he knew. The signs were all there. He was going to be a father.

Please Lord, let me be around to raise that child.

"We're here, Doc." A horse stepped close to his and then light shafted into his eyes as the blindfold was snatched away. He squinted as a cold press of metal thunked against the back of his head. "Keep your eyes down and don't look at any of us if you want to live, got it?"

He fixed his gaze to where his hands were tied to the pommel. He definitely wanted to live. But he also wanted to figure out who these men were.

Who was this new voice? It certainly wasn't the same man who had helped Lenny capture him the evening before.

Footsteps crunched. "Oh good, you got 'im."

"Wh-wh-where's Jim?" a childlike voice that was too deep to belong to a child asked.

"Shut-up, Tommy," the first responded. This command was accompanied by a thump.

"Ow! Ju-just asking!"

Jim. And Tommy. Flynn tucked the names away in the back of his mind.

"I'm going to untie you. No funny business." A broad hand,

worn with age and sunspots, came into view and tugged at the bindings.

Flynn swiveled his wrists and massaged the places where the ropes had left indents in his skin. Slowly, he rotated his arms, restoring full circulation.

"Get down."

He followed instructions, but made the mistake of lifting his gaze. He only caught a glimpse of a game trail leading through the forest before the barrel of the gun smacked into the back of his head again.

"I said keep your eyes down."

He lifted his hands and kept his attention on the pine needles at his feet to show his compliance.

"Walk." The man gave him a little shove.

They walked for about five minutes before the man prodded him to stop. He thrust Flynn's bag into his hands.

"The man what's shot is in there."

Flynn lifted his gaze just enough to see the low opening of a cave before him. He bent down and had to stoop double to shuffle inside.

It was so dark in the cave that Flynn lost all sense of space. He paused to feel the ground before him with the toe of one boot, and his captor bumped into him from behind.

"Keep moving, Doc." A match flared, giving off enough light that Flynn could see to step forward.

The injured man lay on a bedroll against the far wall.

A moment later, the light in the cave increased and he heard the glass of a lantern being reset.

"Bring that light here, please." He was careful to keep his focus on the patient so his captor wouldn't be tempted to thump him again.

The lamplight grew brighter and Flynn set to rolling up his

sleeves as he assessed the man's injuries. He'd taken a bullet through this chest, high on the right side. No froth around the wound. The man was lucky it hadn't nicked a lung, but even so, his chances were slim. The wound was already shooting red streaks across the man's fever-dampened chest.

"What's his name?" Flynn knelt down and pulled his bar of soap from inside his bag. "And I need a basin of water."

"You don't need to know his name, Doc. Just fix him up. And alls we got is a canteen."

Flynn held out his hands. "That will have to do, then. Pour a little here, please." He'd only wanted to know the man's name so he could speak to him. Sometimes addressing a patient helped calm them, but he didn't suppose it would matter much, since this patient was currently unresponsive.

After he'd soaped up and cleaned both his own hands and the patient's wound, he dressed and bandaged it as best he could, then stood. The man had lost a lot of blood. He needed to be monitored. And he needed surgery.

"Your friend here will be lucky if he makes it. Bullet went clean through but shattered his clavicle and scapula. Maybe nicked a couple of ribs also. He needs to be brought into town where I can monitor him day and night and keep him in a cleaner environment than this cave. Do surgery."

Flynn's captor chuckled. "If you want to monitor him day and night, Doc, you can stay right here and do it. As for clean, this here's the best we got."

Flynn scrambled for a reason they should return him to town. "I have other patients that need tending. Several women with babies on the way." He swallowed. He wouldn't mention that one of those women was his own wife or that she wasn't due for several months yet.

He also wouldn't mention his concern for the marshal that one of them had shot the night before.

His captor only grunted. "Women been having babies on their own for decades before you came along, Doc. Don't suppose it will hurt them to continue in that way."

Flynn gritted his teeth. "Lots of babies died, and women too. I'm just trying to keep all my patients safe, including this one. He needs a dry bed. Clean clothes."

The man blew out the lantern and Flynn heard footsteps shuffle. "You just stay right here whilst I go and talk to the rest of the men. And there's no other way out of this cave except by the way you came in, so you might as well just rest a mite till I get back."

As soon as the man's footsteps faded, Flynn fumbled his way to the place where the lantern and matches were and lit the lamp. But his hopes immediately flagged. The man had been telling the truth. The back wall of this shallow cave was nothing but solid stone. And if he tried to go out the front, he'd likely be shot before he got two steps into the blinding light.

Flynn loosed a sigh of despair and sank down on one of the pallets. His eyes were gritty from lack of sleep, but he doubted he was going to get much rest.

He had just slipped into the zone of half-consciousness between wake and sleep when he heard a pistol cock next to his ear.

He came wide awake with a jolt.

Chapter Ten

acinda pulled the wagon to a stop in front of Dixie's Boardinghouse. They'd left Jackson at the Nolan homestead on the outskirts of town, but Dixie hadn't said a word from there to here. Jacinda leaned over to give her friend a side hug. "Try not to worry. Zane says the outlaws know how much trouble it will cause them if they harm Flynn. He thinks he'll be all right."

Dixie's shoulders slumped. "I suppose that is true, slim comfort though it is."

Jacinda squeezed her hand. "Maybe Joe has found their trail. He was going to head out at first light to search."

Dixie frowned. "The rain will make that more difficult."

More like impossible. But all she said was, "Yes. That's true," because she didn't want Dixie to think more on that. She wanted to encourage, but everything she'd tried all morning had only seemed to make Dixie more morose.

"What we have to remember is that we serve a big God who can bring the greatest good out of any tragedy." Which was so much harder to do than to say. She felt like a hypocrite.

Dixie nodded, then climbed down from the seat. She looked up and offered a forced smile. "I do believe that. It's just...we have no guarantees."

And didn't Jacinda know it. Her well of encouragement was now plumb dry. She didn't have even one more idea how to lighten Dixie's load. Some friend she was. "I'm sorry. I'll be praying." And doing her best not to think about all the ways things could go wrong if these outlaws decided killing a doctor was worth the risk.

"Yes. Me too. Thank you. Oh, with all my worrying, I forgot to ask… How was Zane this morning?"

Jacinda fiddled with the reins. "Weak as a kitten, but determined to try and help. He got out of bed and started swaying like a tree in a nor'easter. Thankfully, he laid back down and promised to stay there while we were out at the Kastains'."

Dixie waved a hand toward the boardinghouse. "Ma will have tonight's corned beef and hash just about ready. I'll bring a tray down to your place in just a bit."

"You don't have to do that."

"Nonsense. I'm happy to help. Besides, I need the distraction of activity."

Jacinda knew how that felt too. "When you put it like that, all that's left to say is thank you." She offered her friend a parting smile then snapped the reins and set the horses in the direction of the livery.

When she got back to the house, true to his word, Zane was still in bed—sound asleep in fact.

Since she didn't have the task of making dinner, she sat down with a cup of warmed-over coffee and set to making a list of all the things the Kastains would need help with. She would make the rounds of the town tomorrow and organize the women to make sure a meal was taken out to the house each day for at least a couple weeks.

Parson Clay already knew about William's passing. He'd been arriving at the Kastain place just as she and Dixie left. She put a check mark by that on her list.

Washington Nolan had volunteered that he would rally several boys in town to dig the grave. Check.

And Susan had requested that the service be held tomorrow afternoon, so there would be plenty of time to make a few cakes for the wake and get the church set up.

She would ask Aurora to play some music. That girl could coax the church's old out-of-tune piano to play the most melodious notes.

And if they had to repeat all of this for Dixie in the next day or two? Jacinda's stomach rebelled at the thought. She jotted Dixie's name down. The town might need to step in to help her too.

She glanced toward the window. If she hadn't fallen asleep, might she have seen something the night before that would have helped capture these outlaws.

Jacinda's hand trembled as she set down her pen and gripped the back of her neck.

At least Dixie would be able to provide for herself with the boardinghouse if something happened to Flynn.

What were the Kastains going to do for money now that William was gone? She penned a few dollar signs next to their name. Things had been tight for them for the past several years, but William had been able to do some hunting and planting. Susan was going to have a time of it with all those kids to feed and clothe. And hadn't she heard that Jerry Hines had purchased their land? They would have rent to pay too. She wrote down "rent" and "food."

Her thoughts flitted back to Doc. His loss wouldn't only affect Dixie. What was the town going to do if the outlaws killed him?

And oh—Jacinda's breath hitched—what if Dixie couldn't handle the painful memories here? What if she decided not to stay in town? Would she decide that she needed to take Rose and move back east? Then Wyldhaven would lose its doctor and its only respectable hotel.

And what about Zane? What was she going to do if he developed an infection? Without Doc here to treat him, what if he died? Her stomach crimped into a tight knot and she clamped her lower lip between her teeth. She scribbled a few more lines before she stood and paced to the window, hands over her queasy mid-section.

Something shuffled behind her and she turned to find Zane slipping into a chair at the table. He lifted his palms. "Don't worry. I'm not going far. I just needed a few minutes out of that bed or I was going to go crazy." His gaze settled on her. "If I'm any judge, you've been whiling away the time worrying over all that's happened."

With his boot, he nudged out the chair she'd just abandoned and patted the table in front of it.

Jacinda smoothed her hands over the table and sank into the seat with a sigh. "I suppose if I'm honest, I'd have to say that's true."

He cocked his head. "You didn't read that verse I gave you, did you?"

Jacinda glanced toward her Bible, sitting unopened at the end of the sideboard. "No."

Zane swung a finger toward the book. "Help an invalid out and fetch it, would you?" He winked at her.

She hesitated. "Do you need anything? Dixie will be here with corned beef in just a bit, but I can get you something to tide you over."

He shook his head. "I'm fine. Rose came by not long ago and I ate a good-sized slice of ham, biscuits, and two potatoes."

"Coffee?"

His lips quirked. "Just the Bible, Jac."

"Right." She stood and fetched it for him.

He opened to the book of Luke and flipped to the twelfth chapter. He spun the Bible to face her and stabbed his finger down at the twenty-second verse. "Start here."

Jacinda couldn't quite pin down why she felt a bit peeved with his insistence that she read these verses. Perhaps it was the way he'd said it? Like she was failing in her duty to God in some way. She was a grown woman, after all. One who'd been walking with the Lord for many years. She didn't need someone pointing out scriptures to her. She knew the Bible backwards and forwards and was plenty aware that she had a good deal of shortcomings.

"Need me to read it for you?"

She wrinkled her nose at him. "No. It says, 'Then He said to His disciples, "Therefore I say to you, do not worry about your life, what you will eat; nor about the body, what you will put on. Life is more than food, and the body is more than clothing. Consider the ravens, for they neither sow nor reap, which have neither storehouse nor barn; and God feeds them. Of how much more value are you than the birds?'" She lifted her gaze to Zane. "I have always trusted in the good Lord's provis—"

"Keep going."

She pressed her lips together and found the place where she'd left off. "'And which of you by worrying can add one cubit to his stature? If you then are not able to do the least, why are you anxious for the rest? Consider the lilies, how they grow: they neither toil nor spin; and yet I say to you, even Solomon in all his glory was not arrayed like one of these. If then God so clothes the grass, which today is in the field and tomorrow is thrown into the oven, how much more will He clothe you, O you of little faith?'" Once more she lifted her gaze to his. "Zane, I'm not sure what you are trying to say to me, but I honestly have trusted God for more in my life than most people. Especially after Wade passed."

"Have you? Or have you worried your way through them until you somehow were brought out the other side?"

The words jabbed like a barb.

"Read to the end of the section, please."

Jacinda sighed and kept going. "'And do not seek what you should eat or what you should drink, nor have an anxious mind. For all these things the nations of the world seek after, and your Father knows that you need these things. But seek the kingdom of God, and all these things shall be added to you.'"

When she lifted her focus, Zane's silvery-blue gaze was on her, soft and probing.

She swallowed and closed the Bible. "Zane, I—"

His hand shot out to cover hers.

She froze. Stared at the back of his broad strong hand. Willed down the tympany of her heart.

"Jacinda, do you consider me a friend?" His throat worked as his focus roved over her features.

"Of course I do. You know that." She ought to withdraw her hand. Keep the boundaries they'd established firmly in place. Yet somehow, she lacked the will to do it.

His thumb swept a trail of warmth over her knuckles. "I have come to think of you as more than a friend. To hope that you will one day see me as...more."

Jacinda snatched her hand to the safety of her lap. What was he saying? She shook her head, feeling a pinch of a headache coming on. "Zane—"

He held up a hand for her to let him finish. "I know, Jac.

You've kept me carefully at arm's length, hoping to avoid the risk of loving again."

Her face flamed and she pushed away from the table and paced to the window. "I'm not following how this relates to the Bible passage we just read." Maybe that would help get him back on track. *Heaven's mercy, please get him back on track.*

"It's related because you keep people at a distance to avoid your propensity for worry. If you don't let them close, you can pretend they don't matter as much to you."

"That's not true!" Was it? She did plenty of worrying. Her lips pinched together. And only a moment ago she'd been irritated with him for pointing that passage out to her because she felt she was doing pretty well in her relationship with God. How was it this man seemed to be able to cut to her very heart and still make her want to throw herself into his arms for comfort?

"And yet, here you are"—she heard him lift her list— "worrying about the Kastains, and Dixie, and the town, and me. Worry is a sin, Jac. Has all that worrying solved anything? Made you any happier?"

Zane tapped a finger against the table and waited for a long silent minute.

Jacinda didn't have a response. Undeniably the answer was no, it hadn't, yet she couldn't get the words past her tight throat. Her feet shuffled and she fiddled with the cameo at her collar.

Finally, she heard his chair scrape against the floor. "I want you to be happy, Jac. Peaceful. Joyous even. And you can't have any of that when you are striving to come up with all the answers on your own. Not only that, but it robs you of the joy of contentment. God's will cannot be avoided, battled, or negotiated—only accepted. It's also robbing you of companionship." He cleared his throat. "Love."

Her eyes fell closed. Why had he done this? They'd had such a wonderful friendship. And now he was going to force her to cut things off, all because he'd let feelings get the better of him. She couldn't send him packing just yet, not in his condition, but as soon as he was on the mend, she'd have to figure out a way to keep from spending so much time with him.

She forced herself to take a breath. "I'll think on what you've said. For now, you'd best get back to your bed, I don't want you overtaxing yourself." She bit her lip. There it was again. Her propensity to worry, as he'd put it. Was it really such a sin? How could caring about another person enough to worry about them be a sin?

And he was wrong about her keeping people at arm's length! She cared about everyone in this town. Would even go so far as to say she loved many of them.

As she heard Zane shuffle back to his room, she gritted her teeth.

Zane Holloway simply didn't know what he was talking about.

Zane sank against the pillows and propped his good arm behind his head, resting his other arm carefully to avoid jostling his shoulder. Right about now he might wish he was a drinking man if he hadn't seen all the destruction drink created—not only to deplete the pain in his shoulder but also his irritation with himself. She'd accepted his input just about as well as she might have accepted a pig in her dress shop.

He puffed out his cheeks. He honestly hadn't been trying to rile her. Maybe this courtship he'd been pondering would be buried six feet under before it even started.

A knock sounded on the door out front and he heard Jacinda

move to answer it. A moment later, Joe stepped into his room with her on his heels. Joe's expression was dour, and Jac wrung her hands.

Zane clenched his teeth. Not only was she irritated with him for bringing her attention to her worrying, but it looked like she was ignoring everything he'd said to boot.

Zane sat up and met Joe's gaze. "What is it?"

Joe slid the brim of his hat through his fingers. "Rained good and hard this morning. I've got no trail."

Zane sighed and scrubbed his fingers across his jaw. He'd give half a day's wage for a shave about now. "And nothing else to go on?"

Joe shook his head. "One of them laid in wait and took shots at Wash and I as we rode for town this morning. After I couldn't follow Doc's trail, I tried finding something out there, but again, no luck. Just wondered if you had any other ideas?"

Zane scratched three fingers along the underside of his chin, pondering. He let his gaze drift to the window. "Mighty big country out there. We could search for a month of Sundays and still not find them."

Joe's only response was a shuffle of his feet and a dip of his chin.

Zane didn't like their options any more than Joe did. "I don't suppose we have much choice but to wait and pray. Doc's a smart man. If they don't let him go, he'll figure something out."

When he looked back across the room, Joe was studying the ground near his boots, but Jacinda glowered like he might have just lit her house on fire. Obviously, she didn't like his reasoning. She wanted a practical solution. But there really was nothing they could do and her peeve irritated him.

Zane met her glower for glower.

Silence hung heavy in the room until Joe glanced between the two of them. His brows lifted a little.

Zane blurted the first thing on his mind. "What I'm more concerned about is the fact that one of them laid in wait for you and Wash. This is escalating and—" He paused. Were the outlaws escalating because they'd heard that Reagan was out of town? Perhaps they'd been of the opinion that they could easily move in and take over while the sheriff was gone. If so, maybe he and Joe could take advantage of that?

He focused on Joe. "You think they maybe figured to cash in on Reagan's absence?"

Joe tilted his head in thought. "Could be. But even if not…"

"Maybe we could bait the trap? They already know I'm wounded. What if we use that to our benefit? There's the new bank. Money's not due to arrive for weeks, but…"

Jacinda gasped. She hoisted her skirts and barreled from the room. And suddenly Zane's earlier misery dissipated. Because if she was that riled, it must mean she cared for him, at least a little.

Joe's puzzled expression made Zane realize he was grinning. He scrubbed a hand over his mouth. "Right, let's come up with a plan. How would we get the outlaws the information? I think we're going to need to deputize someone."

Chapter Eleven

ashington swung down from his mare the next morning and stood outside the cemetery gate for a long moment. Heart heavy with the task before him, he took his time untying the shovel from the back of his saddle.

The lone maple tree on the knoll at the back of the cemetery cast dappled shade across the green grass that Parson Clay watered and trimmed each week.

And there, just at the foot of the knoll, Parson Clay had staked out the plot that needed to be dug.

Wash swallowed and stepped through the gate. Might as well get started.

As he walked past the few graves—the girl, Tess, who had died when the church burnt down last year, Old Man Jonas, and a couple others—hoofbeats drew his attention over his shoulder. Kin Davis gave him a nod and swung down from his mount, shovel in hand. And beyond him, Wash could see Jackson, and Nathaniel Burberry making their way up from the church.

Not feeling like talking, he stopped by the marked plot and sunk his shovel into the sod. He stared at that first shovelful for a moment before he tossed it. He looked at the gouge in the earth. Green grass chopped away in its prime, crumbling brown clods left instead. Fitting. He sunk the shovel in again, using his boot to thrust it home.

The other fellas set to digging too, each from a separate corner and, thankfully, in silence. Wash didn't think he could handle idle talk. Not today.

Soon the hole was deep enough that they took turns getting down in it and before an hour had passed, they had Mr. Kastain's grave ready.

Wash shook Kin and Nathaniel's hands and gave them a nod of thanks, then clapped Jackson on the shoulder. "We'd better get home to do chores before we need to clean up and get back here." The last thing Jax needed to be doing today was running wild with Nathaniel.

Jackson shrugged away from his touch, but he did get on his horse and rein it toward home.

They'd just reached the edge of town by the Wyldhaven Creek bridge when Wash heard someone call his name. He pulled to a stop.

Deputy Joe stood in the middle of the street in front of the sheriff's office. "Can I talk to you for a minute?" He waved an arm for him to join him and then stepped back into the office.

Wash glanced at Jackson, who rolled his eyes. "I'll get started on the chores." He nudged his horse across the bridge.

Reining around, Wash trotted his mare to the hitching rail. He tied off, glancing up and down the street as he did so. Things seemed oddly quiet today even if it was a day that called for more somberness than usual. Because of yesterday's rain, not even the normal dust devils danced on the breeze.

Deputy Joe sat behind the desk filling out a piece of paper.

He glanced up, then motioned to the armchair across from the desk. "Have a seat, Wash, and I'll get right to it. Wyldhaven needs your help. I was talking with Zane and we've decided that if you'll take the job, we'd like to make you a deputy for a few days."

Wash froze, only halfway into the chair. He blinked at Joe, and processed all he'd just said to make sure he'd heard right.

Joe grinned and tossed a brass star onto the desk. "You heard me right. The pay's not very good—only a dollar a day—but it beats doing chores for free, I bet." He spread his hands. "So what do you say?"

Wash sank the rest of the way into his seat, eyes glued to the star. He swallowed. A dollar a day! Even if he was only deputized for two weeks, that would be fourteen dollars he could give to the Kastains. And if he did a good job, maybe Joe and Zane would give him a recommendation that he could show to the Cavalry when the time came. But...

"I'd need to talk it over with Pa. Can I let you know this afternoon at the funeral?"

"Of course. That will be fine." Joe stood and reached across the desk.

Wash surged to his feet and took his hand, gritting his teeth so he wouldn't grin like a kid on Christmas. He gave Joe a nod. "I'll let you know."

⁕⁕⁕

The steel of the gun barrel pressed cold against Flynn's temple. A tremble swept through him. Was this to be his end? Shot in an unknown cave where Dixie would likely never find his body?

"On your feet, Doc. Seems we don't need you here anymore." This voice was different from the last.

Flynn carefully kept his hands in sight and moved slowly. He stood, keeping his gaze fixed to the cave floor, even though it was still so dark he couldn't see more than shadows. "What about your injured friend? I told the other fella that he needs to be in town where I can take care of him better. Give him a clean environment. Otherwise he's likely to take a worse infection. Maybe die."

The gun jabbed him in the ribs. "Old Roddy is made of rawhide and grit. Isn't likely thet a little ol' bullet hole is going to do him in, but one just might be your demise. Now move."

Roddy.

Flynn tucked that name away with the others. He shuffled forward toward the dim glow of the entrance.

The moment they reached the pine-needle-strewn area outside of the cave, the man behind him kicked him in the back of the legs. "On your knees, Doc."

"Oh no. Oh no. Gonna sh-shoot the d-doctor." The childlike voice that belonged to the man named Tommy called out.

A pistol cocked.

Jesus. Flynn had no time for more of a prayer than that.

"Don't shoot him!" That voice was Lenny's.

"D-don't shoot him," Tommy echoed.

Flynn swallowed and closed his eyes.

Lenny cussed the man clean through to his bones.

"Why not? He done what we needed him to, didn't he?"

"Jango, you have to be the stupidest outlaw this side of the Mississippi." Feet scuffled and then came the relieving sound of a cylinder being opened and emptied of bullets.

Pain bloomed across the back of Flynn's skull.

And then all went black.

Lenny's heart pounded like a runaway stallion. Mostly because he now had to prove to the gang that he was indeed the leader here.

He cussed Jango liked he'd never cussed anyone before. Why had the man put him in this position?

His authority had just been challenged. Jango knew without a doubt that the doctor was to be kept safe. He'd given the decree to everyone as soon as Victor had come out of the cave after taking Doc in to tend Roddy. The aggravation of it was, he hadn't quite decided whether to let Doc live or not. But he'd given the order for his protection because if anyone was going to kill him, he wanted to be the one to do it so's it would be quick and painless. Wanda had always said she appreciated his merciful side.

But now he couldn't let any harm come to Doc simply because the men needed to know he meant what he said. He narrowed his gaze on Jango. Certainly, now was not the time for mercy.

Everyone seemed to be frozen. All of them watched him.

Well, Tommy was looking everywhere *but* at him. His feet shuffled. His head wagged from side to side. His hands fidgeted in a nervous washing motion.

Lenny's lips thinned. Sometimes he thought that maybe Tommy was the smartest of them all.

Yes, Jango needed to be taken care of, but he couldn't have Doc being witness to that.

He snatched the pistol from Jango's hand and emptied the cartridges into his palm. Then he flipped the barrel into his grip and knocked Doc out with the handle.

Jango smirked. "Not as final as what I'd planned, but..."

Lenny silenced Jango with a glower before he turned to Victor and handed him Jango's pistol and the bullets.

And then before he could lose his nerve, he drew and fired.

One moment Jango was standing there smirking. The next, he was falling to his knees, eyes wide as he clutched at the hole over his heart.

There would be no need for Doc to tend him.

Jango toppled and lay still.

Lenny willed his hands not to tremble as he reholstered his Colt. He clasped his hands behind his back and made eye contact with every other man standing there. "When I give an order, I expect it to be followed to the letter. Do I make myself clear?"

They all nodded.

"F-followed to the l-letter, Mr. L-Lenny," Tommy stuttered, nodding rapidly and still not meeting his gaze.

Behind them, hoofbeats sounded and they all turned to see Jim riding into camp.

Lenny gestured from Victor to the body. "See that he's buried good and deep. Tommy and Bobby can help you dig."

He strode to where Jim was stripping the saddle from his mount.

"You get him?"

Lenny felt his aggravation rise when Jim's lips pinched into a disappointed line. "'Fraid not. Thought I had them dead to rights, but in the pitch black and with the wind blowing…" He shook his head. "Actually, I'm not sure how I missed. They somehow took wind of me 'fore they rode into the gully where I'd laid my trap." Jim took stock of Victor and Bobby hefting Jango's body out of camp, but he made no comment.

He did have a little more respect in his eyes when he turned back to Lenny, however.

Lenny threw back his shoulders and lifted his chin. Maybe he wouldn't need to feel so inadequate around Jim anymore.

He was debating how to explain when Tommy took care of it for him. "H-howdy, Jim. J-J-Jango done t-tried to sh-shoot the doc after M-Mr. L-Lenny done said he w-was not to be hurt. I-I'm g-gettin' sh-shovels."

A queasiness swept over Lenny. But his men didn't need to know he'd never shot anyone before.

He clapped Jim on the shoulder. "We'll figure it out. For now, we get Doc back to town before they send out a search party. Then we change camps."

"You sure that's the wisest move? Why don't we just shoot the man and be done with the bother?"

Lenny's teeth banged together. Why did everyone have to question him? Every decision be challenged?

He narrowed his eyes. "He goes back to town."

Jim lifted his hands and stalked away.

⁂

Zoe stood in her petticoats staring down at the black bombazine dress she'd just tossed on her bed. It was a hand-me-down. One that used to be Belle's. Zoe had worn it a couple years ago to Tess's funeral, but hadn't needed it since then. She'd just tried it on and realized with horror that she couldn't go out in public in it. It was already several inches too short and much too tight through the shoulders and...she folded her arms...other areas. She really ought to put it away for one of the twins, but she didn't have anything else to wear to Pa's funeral. All of her other dresses were much too bright and inappropriate.

She couldn't mention anything to Ma because she had been crying for most of the morning and Zoe didn't want to burden her with yet one more thing.

If only this was the kind of thing she could go to Belle about. But Belle hadn't spoken to her since she'd offered that piece of her mind yesterday.

Zoe's stomach crimped. She probably deserved that, however this was not the time to ponder on her personal failures.

She reached for her blue day dress and slipped it on. There was only one other person she could think to ask for some help.

She was just stepping from her room with the black dress draped over one arm, when Belle stepped into the hallway from the children's room. Belle simply looked at her, lower lip tucked between her teeth.

Zoe ought to apologize. She knew it. Her words had been harsh and unkind. Yet, hadn't Belle deserved at least some of what she'd said? Didn't Belle herself need to offer an apology for being absent when the family had needed her so badly?

Zoe lifted her chin and her arm to draw Belle's attention to the dress. "Please tell Ma I'll meet you all at the church. I'm going to Mrs. Callahan's for some help with this dress."

Belle gave her a nod. "I was just checking on the twins. They are dressing now. And Aiden's Sunday suit is only a little tight. He can manage."

As though they'd both been drawn to thoughts of Ma at the same time, they turned to look at the still-closed door down the hall.

Zoe lowered her voice. "Has she come out at all today?"

Belle shook her head. "I haven't seen her."

"Do you think we need to go in and check on her?"

Belle pondered for a moment. "You go on and get your dress taken care of. I'll check on her if she doesn't come out soon."

With a nod, Zoe lifted her hand and headed for the door. "See you in town."

The walk into town only took thirty minutes, but it was refreshing to get out into the silence and simply be alone for a few minutes. She breathed deep of the solitude, knowing that the rest of the day was going to be a whirlwind of activity as everyone, with the best of intentions, offered their condolences and regrets.

No matter how much she craved solitude during times like this, Pa—and Ma, for that matter—would want her to be polite and accommodating. She laid a hand over her stomach as she crossed the bridge into town.

She was just passing the jailhouse when Wash stepped out onto the porch. She hesitated. Frowned. What was he doing in the jailhouse?

He shoved his fists into his pockets and studied her, his gaze soft and comforting. "How are you?"

Just that one little question made a reservoir well up inside her. Before she knew it, tears were on the verge of spilling over. She couldn't have this. She swallowed hard, pushing down the emotion. With Belle acting unpredictable, and Ma falling apart at the drop of a hat, she had to be the strong one.

She brushed a hand through the air and turned her focus to the alley. "Oh...you know... busy. Speaking of which, I'd better get going. Have a lot to do before..." Her throat closed off.

She waved a goodbye and dashed down the alley, willing herself to think on anything but the expanse of loss and burden that stretched before her.

"Zo, wait." She heard the slap of his boots on the gravel behind her. His hand wrapped around her arm.

"No!" She tugged her arm from his grasp and held up a palm. Kept walking. "I really don't have time to talk right now, Wash."

"All right." There was an edge of hurt in his tone.

But she didn't have the energy to soothe it. She left him standing there and when she got to the end of the alley and glanced back, he was still in the same place, hands on his hips with two fingers tucked into his pockets.

His expression held understanding and he gave her a nod. "Praying for you, Zo," he called.

"Thanks." She turned the corner, thankful to leave behind the temptation to let it all go and throw herself into his arms and sob her cares away like she'd done in the wee hours just after Pa passed.

She set her jaw in firm resolve. Took the steps up to Mrs. Callahan's porch with purpose. And knocked on her door.

She would take care of the dress.

Get through this afternoon's service.

And then maybe she'd give herself the freedom to fall apart.

Chapter Twelve

fter Zane and Joe had decided on the beginnings
of a plan to trap the outlaws, and Joe had headed
off to find Washington Nolan, Zane settled against
the pillows and let his mind ponder what to do about Jacinda.

Was he just deceiving himself into thinking she might have
feelings for him?

Before he was shot the other day, he would have scoffed at
anyone who told him she carried a torch for him. But after...
she'd been mighty prickly and irritable, but had given him
some looks that lifted a man's hopes right through the roof.
Then when they'd talked over those Bible verses, she'd acted
prickly again, yet revealed her concern once more when he and
Joe had been discussing how to use his injury and the bank to
lay their trap.

Of course, she *had* lost her husband to an outlaw's bullet.
Maybe she just didn't want to lose a friend in the same manner.

But...if there was one thing this situation had driven home,
it was that he was tired of pussyfooting around his feelings. It
was time he laid his cards on the table and let the chips fall
where they may.

He swallowed.

It could potentially mean a loss of her friendship. Was he
willing to deal with that?

She bustled in just then with a tray which she set on the

foot of the bed. It held a steaming wet cloth, a bowl of hot water, a razor, and a shaving cup full of frothy soap.

She shook open a dry towel and stepped closer. "Saw you scratching at your chin, earlier. Figured you might want a shave before the funeral?" She looked everywhere but into his eyes.

Was she upset with him over the verses he'd made her read? Or over his and Joe's plan? Most likely the latter. Maybe a little bit of both.

"I know you are worried about Joe and me trying to capture these outlaws, but I promise you I'll be careful."

Her gaze did snap to his then. "Like you were careful the other day when we were surrounded?" Her voice broke a little. She dropped her focus, fiddled with the towel, and blinked hard. She waved a hand. "Sorry. It's just this whole situation with William's passing has me a bit emotional." Her gaze flicked to his for the briefest of moments before returning to the towel.

Interesting.

Zane scooted a little closer to the center of the bed, giving the mattress beside him a pat. "A shave would be really nice." But mostly because of who would be doing the shaving. There was no time like the present to put his own personal plan into action.

And if he ended up being tossed out on his ear?

Well, at least he would have tried.

Jacinda leaned forward and draped the towel over his chest, then sank down as close to the edge of the bed as she could without falling off.

The man was entirely too handsome.

And grinning at her like he knew it.

"So the only reason you're upset is because of William?" His tone indicated he knew she'd been lying.

Her conscience pricked her for it. Because while she was sorry about William Kastain's passing, her tears had been due to the fact that she'd almost lost Zane.

Zane tilted her a look. "Kind of hurts a man's feelings to be lying at death's door but have the prettiest eligible woman around indifferent to it."

She rolled her eyes at his teasing. "Would be a shame if I accidentally poked that shoulder of yours."

He covered his wound with one hand and faked a crushed expression. Then he smiled. "You're too kind to do something like that. And that's what makes you so captivating."

Her heart forgot to beat and then fluttered to catch up. She was doing a terrible job of resisting his charm. How could she even consider the risk of loving such a man ever again? And yet...she feared her sentiments had run away without consulting her on the matter. "You and I both know we have too much in our pasts to ever be good for one another, Zane."

His expression turned immediately serious. "Do you *truly* believe that? Or is it worry holding you back?"

She gritted her teeth. So he was back to that. And? Did he have a point? Reluctantly, she had to admit that he might be right. But today was not the day to solve matters of the heart.

"You're not the only one to suffer a previous loss, you know. I lost my wife and our babe on the same day."

Her conscience pricked her. She searched his face. "Did you love her?"

He swallowed. "Very much."

"How did you get to a place where you were willing to risk again?"

He frowned. Considered. "I guess I've come to realize

that while what I went through was hard, God *did* bring me through it. I learned. Grew. Became more compassionate to others who've faced loss. I hope I won't have to go through that again, but if God has more he wants from me, I'm willing to accept that. Especially if it means I get a few years to know you better."

With a sigh, she reached for the damp towel. "Drape this over your face for a few minutes." Would he accept her change of subject?

He only hesitated for a moment before he drawled, "Yes, ma'am." Though his fingers lingered too long against hers as he took the towel from her and his humor-filled gaze dared her to protest.

She snatched her hand back and busied herself with whisking the froth in the shaving bowl, even though it was plenty whipped already.

He slowly settled the towel over the lower half of his face, but kept his scrutiny on her the entire time.

After a long moment, she tossed the shaving brush into the bowl and glowered at him. "What are you looking at?"

He was grinning, she could tell by his eyes, even if his mouth was covered with the still steaming towel.

"Just looking at you, Jac. Prettiest woman in all of Washington state."

Despite the fact that she felt her face heat, she rolled her eyes at him. "Only a moment ago I was only the prettiest *eligible* woman."

"The two are not mutually exclusive. If you're the prettiest in all the state *and* you're eligible, then it stands to reason that you are the prettiest eligible woman." He winked.

"Do go on with you." She whipped at the froth some more, but couldn't seem to prevent a little smile. Maybe she was wrong to refuse to consider his attentions. Maybe she was wrong to worry that God's plan for her future might involve the death of another loved one. After all, if that was what God had planned, didn't she believe that His plans were perfect? Carried out for the good of all those who love Him? As Zane pointed out, He'd helped her through Wade's death. And His Word promised to never leave nor forsake her, so who was she to doubt that He couldn't see her through again?

She met Zane's silvery-blue gaze and pondered what life might be like if she were to marry again—not that he'd mentioned any such thing. So here she was worrying endlessly over something that likely wasn't even going to happen.

In exasperation, she flapped a hand at him and forced her focus to the bowl of shave cream. "Zane Holloway, stop looking at me so. You've got my thoughts swirling every which way!"

From the corner of her eye she saw him settle more comfortably against the pillows. Heard his soft chuckle. But at least, by heaven's mercy, he did close his eyes.

She breathed a little sigh of relief. "All right, hand me the towel. I need to get this done so I can go bake a couple cakes for the ceremony."

Keeping his eyes closed, he tugged off the towel and stretched it toward her. "Make one of them chocolate. You haven't made chocolate in a long time." At least he seemed to be following her instructions, though she did find herself missing that particular shade of silver-blue.

She leaned over him and set to daubing the cream on his cheeks. Drat. Did he have to smell so good? Cedar and leather and...she leaned a little closer. Some sort of spice she couldn't quite identify.

He reached up and touched her chin with his thumb.

She gasped and pulled back a fraction, but then the

magnetism of his gaze had her in its grip. "You're a cheat," she whispered.

His eyes twinkled in acknowledgement. His words were whisper soft when he spoke. "I do believe I need to amend my earlier statement."

Jacinda fought through a haze of warm confusion. Her focus dipped to the pink of his lips just visible through the white froth of the shaving soap. "What...statement?" She felt her brow furrow.

His thumb stroked across her chin. "I said Washington state. I should have said this side of Washington D. C." The warmth of his hand settled against the side of her face.

Jacinda swallowed and licked her lips. The man wasn't fighting fair. "Zane, I—"

A knock sounded loudly against the front door.

Jacinda leapt to her feet as though someone might barge in and catch her staring at Zane's lips with one of those newfangled Eastman Kodak hand-held cameras. She smoothed trembling hands over her hips and down the front of her skirts.

He tucked his good arm behind his head and grinned at her. "Get the door. I'll shave myself."

"Left-handed?"

He nodded and as she moved to see who was at the door, she fleetingly wondered how many other times he'd been injured and had to take care of himself one-handed.

The realization that it was probably more times than she wanted to know didn't do anything to reassure her concerns over her relationship with Zane.

⁓≈≫•≪≈⁓

Zoe was still fighting her emotions and determined not to let them carry her away when Mrs. Callahan opened her door.

But she wasn't in such a gone state that she didn't notice Mrs. Callahan's high color.

Her concern immediately rose. She touched Mrs. Callahan's arm. "Are you okay? Is it Doc? Did you get news of him?"

Mrs. Callahan blinked and a little furrow settled between her brows. "No. No. We haven't had word. Why do you ask?" She stepped back and gestured for Zoe to enter.

Zoe stepped through to the dining table and set her black dress down, then gave Mrs. Callahan another scan. "You looked a little flushed is all."

From the bedroom just behind her, Zoe heard the marshal give a soft chortle.

Mrs. Callahan's color deepened further.

Zoe's brows arched as she considered. The marshal and Mrs. Callahan? Why had she not thought of them as a pair? It made perfect sense.

She stared down at the dreaded black dress.

Normally at this point, she would pry for details, even though Ma would chastise her for the impropriety of it. But today she couldn't muster up the desire to do so.

She brushed a hand through the air. "Must have been my imagination."

That blasted dress was still there on the table. The thing of nightmares. Only this was one she would never have the freedom to awake from.

Mrs. Callahan stepped close and wrapped an arm around her shoulders. "Need help with this dress?"

Zoe knew if she tried to speak in that moment, she would lose her precarious control, so she only nodded. Blinked hard. Gritted her teeth.

Mrs. Callahan lifted the dress and held it up to give it a once-over. Then she draped it over one arm and wrapped her other around Zoe's shoulders. "Come on. We'll go up to my room and you can try it on so I can see what needs to be done."

Just as Wash rode into the yard, Pa rode in from his shift. Pa swung down and laid his crosscut on the two saw horses where he would spend the next hour sharpening each tooth.

Jackson stepped out of the barn, pushing a wheelbarrow. "Howdy, Pa. I hope you notice that I'm here doing chores while Wash there has been lazing away in town." He grinned.

"That so?" Pa gave Wash a wink. He looped his horse's reins over the corral rail and tipped a nod for Wash to take care of it.

"So?" Jackson prodded. "What did Deputy Joe want?"

Wash darted a glance toward Pa as he dismounted. He'd hoped to bring up the subject at just the right moment, but of course Jackson would flap his jaw.

Pa stilled and turned to face him full on. "What's this about the deputy?"

Wash busied himself with unbuckling his saddle. "Jackson and I were on our way home after digging Mr. Kastain's grave and Deputy Joe asked to speak to me."

"You been causing a ruckus that I ain't heard about?" Pa's long red mustache twitched irritably.

"No, sir." He tugged the saddle into his arms. "He wants to deputize me." Wash held his breath and didn't look at Pa as he hoisted the saddle onto its peg. He didn't look at Jackson either, because he knew what his brother was going to think of the whole matter.

"Aw, Pa!"

Wash unbuckled Pa's saddle and kept his gaze averted. Just as he suspected. Jax was none too happy.

"If he's off lawing that's going to leave me the bulk of the chores!"

Pa remained silent.

"Pays a dollar a day." Wash dropped that little nugget into the silence that followed Jackson's caterwauling. "And Lincoln and Grant are both old enough to take on a few more chores." That was the truth, too. Ma had passed when Wash was only twelve and he'd been doing a man's chores ever since. And Grant, his youngest brother, was already fifteen. He couldn't help but sneak a quick glance at Pa's expression.

And just that quick glance eased all his tension.

Pa was grinning. From ear to ear. "My boy! A deputy! Well, ain't that something!"

Jackson cussed.

Pa cuffed him upside the back of his head. "Watch how you talk, boy."

Wash hoisted Pa's saddle onto its peg. "Deputy Joe figured it would just be for a few days. And I thought the money could go to help Mrs.—Widow Kastain." He swallowed the lump in his throat. Somehow saying the title out loud drove the reality home. Zoe had no pa.

Jackson rolled his eyes at him while Pa was busy settling onto this stool and taking up his rasp.

Wash gritted his teeth and held his silence. Jackson obviously thought he was just shining up to Pa with the comment about the money. He took up the curry comb and gave first his own horse and then Pa's a quick rubdown. He turned them into the corral. Forked them each a measure of hay. Hung the reins on their pegs in the tack room and still Pa hadn't said anything.

Jackson loitered nearby doing a little of nothing while he too waited to see what Pa's decision would be.

Finally, Pa looked up and pegged Jackson with a look.

"Don't suppose those leavings are gonna empty themselves out of that wheelbarrow."

"No, sir." With a quick glance in Wash's direction, he hefted it and trundled away.

Pa set down his rasp and propped his hands on his knees. He fixed a serious gaze on Wash. "Being a lawman ain't nothing to doddle with. It's an honor that you've been asked, and I won't stop you. But I want you to think on one thing 'fore you give them your answer."

"Yes, sir?" Wash's heart pounded in excitement. He was going to be a deputy!

"Comes down to it, you might be faced with shooting a man. Can you live with that on your conscience for the rest of your life? More than that, can you take necessary action to save lives without hesitating?"

Wash swallowed and held his silence, knowing better than to give a quick response. Truth was, when he'd fired off those shots at whoever was shooting at him and Deputy Joe, it was the first time he'd ever fired a gun toward someone. How would he have felt if he'd actually hit someone? He hadn't really thought of it till now.

Pa took up his rasp and set to work again. "Just something to think on."

Wash resettled his hat on his head. Much of his excitement had dissipated. "Yes, sir."

❧⸱⸱⸱⸱❧

Two hours later, Zoe stepped off Mrs. Callahan's porch wearing the black mourning gown. Her heart wasn't any lighter, but she was ever-so-thankful for Mrs. Callahan's kindness. And for the amazing hand-crank Singer sewing machine she had purchased last year.

They'd been able to enlarge the bodice of the dress, and thanks to Mrs. Callahan's skill, no one would be the wiser except for the two of them. Well, and Ma and Belle, but they didn't count.

Zoe had feared the tight bodice was unfixable, but Mrs. Callahan had taken part of the skirt and made some V-shaped panels under the dress's arms. Then she'd used an extra piece of black silk she'd had in her sewing room to create a tiered skirt that was now the proper length.

Zoe promised to come by and do some work to pay for the materials and time, but Mrs. Callahan waved away the offer. "That piece of silk has been in that drawer since before Mrs. Heath passed away more than ten years ago. Honestly, you were doing me a favor to use it up."

Once again, Zoe's emotions had threatened to pull her under. But she'd pressed her lips together and given Mrs. Callahan a hug, even if she couldn't get words past her tight throat.

Now she stood in the street staring at the alleyway that would lead her out to Main Street and on to the church. Somehow, she had to find the courage to put one foot in front of the other and walk to the church. Walk *into* the church. Somehow, she had to find the strength to keep her chin held high and be strong for Ma. And for the twins and Aidan. But she still had at least two hours before the ceremony.

She turned instead toward the livery. She'd always loved to climb high into the haymow and look out of the window toward the mountains in the distance. Pa had been the first one to show her that view when she was only seven, and it seemed fitting that she go there now.

After today, she would be too much of a lady to do such things, for she'd vowed to herself to make Ma proud and not burden her with any more mischief from this day forward.

One last goodbye to the view from up there.

One last goodbye to the memory of Pa squatting and settling her on his knee as they'd taken in the misty mountains together.

One last goodbye to life as she'd known it.

Chapter Thirteen

When Flynn came to, he was once again blindfolded. But this time he was draped over the horse like a sack of grain.

His horse jostled down an incline and a shard of fire shot through his skull. He winced and tried to adjust his position, but his hands were tied at the wrists and his ankles were bound also.

"Lenny, we really gonna just ride into town and dump him off behind the livery? That's asking for trouble."

"Hard as I conked him, he'll be out for at least another hour. By the time anyone finds him and he comes to, we'll be long gone."

Flynn gritted his teeth. So it had been Lenny who knocked him out. He strained to hear the conversation over the forest sounds, clopping hooves, and creaking saddles. He recognized the first voice as that of the man who'd initially taken him captive with Lenny.

"You certain this is the best thing to do? Seems like it might be prudent to...make him disappear since he's seen all of us."

"I'm getting mighty tired of everyone questioning my orders, Jim!" Lenny's words were harsh.

Jim hesitated, then finally responded. "You're the boss. But what if he tells them where we are?"

Lenny gave a disgusted huff. "I got a plan. You want to hear it? Or would you rather keep bellyaching?"

"Fine. What's yer plan?"

"First off, we'll move camp soon as we get back. Second, when we get to town, you're gonna ride on ahead and check to make sure no one is at the livery. Then you're gonna send ol' Giddens on an errand. And signal to me when it's clear. We'll unload the doc, and be gone 'fore anyone even knows Doc is there."

"Can I also stop by the alehouse to buy a few drinks? I've had a powerful thirst on me." Jim's sarcasm practically dripped from every word.

"Don't think we better risk it."

Flynn pondered. Was Lenny really that oblivious to the fact that Jim realized he was the one being put in danger? Or was he purposely being obtuse?

Jim grumbled a little, but then there was a long stretch of silence. Finally, Jim spoke again. "What sort of errand?"

"What?"

"What errand do I send Giddens on?"

"Do I have to do *all* the thinking? I don't know! Tell him you saw some suspicious activity on the north end of town and that someone ought to inform the deputy. That ought to send him scuttling. You know how ol' Giddens likes to poke his nose into every curiosity that comes up."

"And what will you be doing?"

"I'll be standing guard over the doctor until you signal me! What else do you think I'd be doing?"

Silence settled after that.

Flynn did his best to be still so they wouldn't know he'd come to. Thankfully, it sounded like Lenny planned to let him live, but if he pretended to still be unconscious until they offloaded him, then maybe he could get someone's attention and they could catch the men before they rode out of town.

Maybe his capture would be a good thing in the long run.

Old Mr. Giddens, the liveryman, smiled sadly at Zoe when she stepped into the barn, making a lump rise up in her throat. He reached out a gnarled hand and patted her on the shoulder. "I 'as right sorry to hear about yer pappy, Miss."

She swallowed. "Thank you."

"What can I do fer ya?"

Zoe suddenly felt a bit foolish. She folded her arms and poked at a bit of straw with her toe. "I was just..." She lifted her gaze to his. "Going to go up to the loft for a bit."

Bill tilted her a kind look. "Course. Go right on up."

"Thank you."

He moseyed back into the tack room.

Zoe gripped the ladder and stood at the base, simply staring up at the roof for a long moment. Before she climbed, she could stand here and pretend that Pa was waiting for her. When she reached the haymow, he would tweak her nose and give her a wink.

Tears misted her vision. She pressed her cheek to her shoulder. Maybe this wasn't such a good idea?

No. She gave herself a little shake and set to climbing.

She would take this one moment of solitude today to reminisce about Pa on her own terms.

In the loft, hay rustled a warm welcome beneath her boots. She hoisted her skirts and worked her way over the slippery mound until she could see out the window at the back.

She sank down before it, rested her arms on the sill, and settled her chin on her wrists.

The mountains in the distance were cut crisply against the sky today, as though they'd only recently been chiseled.

Yesterday's rain had cleared the air and the blue canopy contrasted vividly with the snowcapped peaks. Two fluffs of cloud floated off to the right. The mountains gave way to the nearer green forested foothills that in turn gave way to the browns of meadows. And the road leading into Wyldhaven from the south cut a sepia river through the middle of it all.

In the distance, a lone rider on a black horse clipped along the center of the road, coming toward town.

A man riding like Pa never would again.

The tears came then, and she let them fall this time. Here, where no one could see her misery, it seemed safe to do so.

But she was careful to make no sound. She didn't want Mr. Giddens getting worried and coming up to check on her.

✿⚜❀⚜✿

After they finished altering the dress, Jacinda had followed Zoe down the stairs. Her heart broke by increments at the heaviness that seemed to weigh down Zoe's countenance and posture. The girl's eyes held the weight of the world.

Zoe paused by the front door and opened her mouth like she wanted to say something, but then changed her mind and simply offered a hug instead. Without another word she stepped onto the porch, tugging the door shut behind her.

Jacinda pushed the lace curtain that hung over the door's cut-glass window to one side.

Zoe stepped into the street, shoulders sloped. She glanced toward the alley, but then turned in the opposite direction.

Jacinda frowned. Where could she be going in that direction? The only thing on that end of town was the livery. But then, with as down as Zoe was, and with the service not for a couple hours, perhaps Zoe was just giving herself some space to think. Maybe taking a walk.

The thought of the service reminded Jacinda that she hadn't yet started on the cakes. As she hurried toward the kitchen, she tugged her necklace watch forward to check the time. Too late to make cakes. Looked like she'd have to come up with something else to bring to the service.

But when she bustled into the kitchen, she froze.

Zane stood across the way, his arm in the sling she'd fashioned for him, but with an apron draped around his neck. Instead of tying the strings—a feat which he'd obviously failed to accomplish one handed—he'd simply stuffed them into the pockets of his denims. He leaned over a piece of paper on the counter and when she stepped nearer, she recognized it as the recipe she'd copied down from Rose Pottinger for her lemon pound cake.

Zane must have heard her come in, because even though he didn't turn to look at her, he said, "What in tarnation is lemon zest?"

Jacinda grinned and stepped to his side. "What are you doing?"

He brushed his good hand at a smudge of flour on the back of the one in the sling, only succeeding in adding more flour to it. "Figured you were busy helping Zoe get that dress fixed, and I was doing nothing but lollygagging, so I thought to help out." He gestured to the mixing bowl half filled with ingredients. "Couldn't find the recipe for chocolate cake, but this here lemon one sounded promising."

Jacinda grinned and gestured him toward a chair at the kitchen table. "Sit. I'll pour you coffee. But first, tell me what you have already put in the bowl."

"Everything in order right up to whatever zest is." He sauntered to the chair and sank into it with a huff. "And don't think it was easy cracking them eggs, one-handed. Some pieces of shell fell in there, but I got them all out. I think."

Jacinda's brows rose as she peered into the bowl.

Sure enough, all the ingredients from eggs to butter to sugar and flour were all heaped together in the bowl. Nothing had been creamed or folded as the recipe called for. She could already see portions of the flour gumming together with parts of the eggs.

She released a breath and pushed the bowl back from her. Jim Dandy, this was going to take some whisking to get the batter smooth. She would get Zane's coffee first and then get started on it.

But she was just setting a steaming cup before him when a knock came on the front door.

Zane stood. "This must be your day for visitors. Get the door and I'll finish the cakes."

"No!" Jacinda held up her hands. "Just sit. Sit. I'll see who's at the door and then come finish. You shouldn't be up yet, anyhow."

She hustled from the room without giving him opportunity to argue.

When she opened the door, Bill Giddens stood on her porch, hat in hand. "Beggin' your pardon, Mrs. Callahan. Beggin' your pardon. But...uh...well...you see the fact is..."

Jacinda tossed a glance toward the kitchen, trying not to imagine what mischief those blobs of butter might be making with the baking soda at this precise moment. "What can I do for you, Bill?"

"Well, it's Zoe, you see."

Cakes forgotten, Jacinda stepped out onto the porch. "Zoe? Is she hurt? What happened?"

"No. No. She ain't hurt. Well, least wise not in body ma'am.

It's just...she's up in the loft down to the livery right this moment and well, I thought...maybe a woman's touch might be in order. You was the closest one I could think of."

"Of course. She actually just left here and I was worried about her. Give me just a moment and I'll be right there."

Bill tipped her a nod and tugged on the brim of his hat as he replaced it and stepped off the porch.

Jacinda hurried back to the kitchen. She flapped a hand at Zane as she reached for her shawl from the peg near the back door. "Sorry, I know I'm changing my mind, but I think I'm going to need you to finish those cakes after all. But that lumpy mess is going to take a good deal of time to whip into a smooth batter. Didn't you read that you are supposed to cream together the butter and sugar before adding the other ingredients?"

Zane frowned at her over the rim of his coffee cup, then set it down with a thunk. "I started reading right at the top. There wasn't anything about adding cream. Did I miss something?"

"Not *adding* cream. *Creaming.* You know..." She made a stirring motion. "It says so right in the directions."

"Where?" Zane stood and crossed to the recipe card.

Jacinda stabbed a finger at the instructions toward the bottom of the card. "Right there. See?"

"Oh. Well, I haven't gotten to that part yet."

Jacinda rolled her eyes. "Thank you for trying to help, Zane, especially when you aren't feeling well. But you are supposed to read the whole recipe first, then follow it."

"Why wouldn't the creaming instructions be right after the mention of adding the sugar and the butter?"

"I don't know. That's just how they've always been written." She reached past him to grab an apple from the bowl on the counter. Maybe she could coax Zoe into eating a little bit.

Zane was grumbling something about lack of logic as she left.

If she wasn't so concerned about Zoe, Jacinda might have chuckled, because she had to admit that maybe Zane was right on this count.

꒰ঌৎ৵/ৡৄ꒱

Zoe only let herself indulge in tears for a few minutes. Ma had always said that tears were the key to the doorway that let in healing. And she certainly could use a little healing right about now. But if she let herself cry for too long, she wouldn't be able to bring herself back into control. And she must be in control by the time Pa's ceremony rolled around.

She lifted her skirt and found a section of petticoat and dried her face.

The rider was closer now. And he kept checking over his shoulder and all around. Something about the uneasy way he rode made prickles snake down Zoe's neck.

She frowned and pulled back into the shadows as the man rode onto the hard-packed area behind the livery and swung down from his horse. She couldn't quite make out his face shaded as it was by the brim of his hat, but something about him struck a familiar chord. Something she ought to recognize, but...couldn't quite place.

Behind her, she heard a rustling of hay. She spun toward the sound.

Mrs. Callahan stood at the top of the ladder. She tilted Zoe a mournful look. "I'm so sorry to intrude. Mr. Giddens thought you might need...a woman's comfort."

Zoe ran her fingers under her eyes. She turned and looked out the window. She could no longer see the rider. He must have led his horse past the side of the livery and on into town.

She shoved aside the thoughts of the stranger. It was probably nothing. Maybe just her heightened emotions spilling over into her imagination.

She took one last look at the view she and Pa used to enjoy so much. Then she stood and brushed the hay from her skirts. "I'll be fine. Pa, he and I used to..." She gave a lame gesture toward the window. "I just...came to say goodbye, I suppose."

Mrs. Callahan stretched her arms wide. "Oh darling, if I could take your pain, know that I would."

Zoe let herself be enfolded in the firm embrace. It felt good to have her pain acknowledged. Sure, at home everyone understood. But they were all going through their own dark valleys. And she knew Mrs. Callahan had traveled through grief of her own several years ago and seemed to have made it out the other side. She supposed that meant they would too, even if it didn't feel like they would right now.

Mrs. Callahan simply held her. Zoe didn't allow any more tears, but it felt good to know that there was someone else who cared.

Below them, a horse clopped into the barn.

The door of Mr. Giddens' tack room squeaked. "Howdy there. What can I do fer ya?"

A voice Zoe didn't recognize responded. But her curiosity was once more piqued. Was this the man who had just ridden into town?

She pushed back from Mrs. Callahan's embrace so she could hear better. They couldn't see the men below because of the hay mound and loft floor, but that was probably best. Something told her they shouldn't let the man notice them up here in the loft. She put a finger to her lips to caution Mrs. Callahan to silence.

She frowned and mouthed, "What is it?"

Zoe shook her head. She still wasn't sure what it was about the man that had her hackles up like Jinx with a skunk.

"Just wanting to stable my horse. But I thought I should let someone know... I just saw some monkeyshiners on the north end of town."

The north end of town? Well then it couldn't be the man who had just ridden in from the south. She tiptoed toward the rail. But the man stood behind a support pole and she couldn't see his face. He wore denim breeches, a dusty white shirt, and a brown leather vest that had seen better days. Had that been what the rider was wearing? She hadn't been paying that much attention.

"Monkeyshiners, ya say? What makes ye say such?" Mr. Giddens' voice held a definite note of curiosity and Zoe knew he would totter right down to the jailhouse to let the law know as soon as he had more details.

She suppressed a smile as she inched her way to the right, trying to get a better glimpse of the newcomer.

"Can't rightly put my finger on it," the man replied. "Just saw a group of boys, looked like they were up to no good, is all."

"Hmmm, mayhap I ought to go let the deputy know he should check it out. Been some outlaw activity 'round these parts." Mr. Giddens shuffled toward the door. "Ye can have thet last stall there on the left. Care and feeding be two bits a day. Leave yer coins on the table, and I'll fetch 'em when I get back."

"I'll do that." The man stepped forward, and slapped his horse's reins against a gloved palm as he watched Mr. Giddens hustle away.

Zoe's heart pinched. It *was* the man who had just ridden in from the south. So what was he doing telling Mr. Giddens that he had seen troublemakers on the north end of town?

This close, she could see a puckered scar on the side of his face. Her heart threatened to seize. That was it! Her gaze darted to Mrs. Callahan's to see if she noticed it too.

It was clear from her wide eyes and parted lips that she had seen it also.

Mrs. Callahan raised a finger and jabbed a motion for Zoe to get out of sight.

She didn't have to worry. Zoe didn't want to draw the attention of one of the area's meanest outlaws. A man whose picture hung on the wall down at the jailhouse! She crouched behind a large wooden barrel which held a couple of pitchforks and a shovel, but couldn't resist peering around it.

Had Mr. Giddens recognized him? He certainly hadn't acted like he had.

As soon as Mr. Giddens was out of sight, the man whipped his horse's reins around a tie and hustled toward the door. He glanced both up and down the street, then slipped outside.

Zoe frowned at Mrs. Callahan. "What do we do?"

Mrs. Callahan motioned for Zoe to hurry. "We get out of here, now!"

Zoe pinched her lips together and turned to look toward the window once more. "I just saw him ride into town from the south. But he told Mr. Giddens that he had witnessed troublemakers on the north end of town."

"I think he was trying to get rid of Mr. Giddens for some reason. We must hurry."

Feeling the urgency of Mrs. Callahan's words ignite inside her, Zoe grabbed the top of the ladder and stepped down as quickly as her skirts would allow. As soon as she reached the ground, Mrs. Callahan followed. Zoe hurried toward the exit.

But Mrs. Callahan took her arm. "Not that way. He might be waiting for someone just outside."

Zoe stilled. "I didn't think about that. Did you see the scar?"

Jacinda frowned. "Yes. In the shape of a lightning bolt, just like on the wanted poster."

Zoe shivered.

"Out the back." Jacinda nudged her in the direction of the large sliding door on the other end of the livery. "We'll hurry to my place and then I'll go down to the jail and let Joe know what we've seen."

Zoe hesitated before the door. "What if he's out there?"

Mrs. Callahan's lips pinched. She glanced back toward the main door, but then motioned that they should continue with their current plan. "Cautiously," she whispered.

Zoe's heart gave a thump in her chest. The back slider was already open by a couple feet to allow a cross breeze. Zoe peered out. She felt Mrs. Callahan leaning with her. They froze. Two men were propping Doc, limp and unconscious, against the back wall of the barn. He'd obviously just been dragged from the empty saddle of a nearby bay Morgan.

Mrs. Callahan jerked her head back inside, but Zoe felt tears prick her eyes. Was Doc dead? She searched the faces of the two outlaws for the answer. Surely if he was dead, their expressions would reflect that in some way?

Mrs. Callahan snatched at Zoe's arm, urging her to back into the barn, but Zoe's gaze had frozen on one of the men. She'd heard his name the other day. But seeing him was another matter. By rights she oughtn't to recognize him, what with his eye patch and long beard. But his was a face she wasn't ever likely to forget. Not after he'd captured her and tied her to a chair so he could kidnap her teacher.

Lenny Smith was partly responsible for Pa being laid to rest today. How had he escaped jail? And what was he doing here? Free and clear when her pa was about to be put six feet under!

She felt her pulse pounding through her head. Heard the rush of it in her ears. Vaguely felt Mrs. Callahan tug a little harder on her arm, and then...

Smith looked up. He froze. "Jim."

The scar-faced man spun to face her. His lips curled into a snarl and his hand dropped toward his pistol.

"Zoe!" Mrs. Callahan's whisper was near to a panic now as she yanked on her arm.

Zoe jerked back. She thrust the door shut, but there was no lock on it.

She and Mrs. Callahan lifted their skirts and dashed for the exit at the other end of the barn. They had to get to the sheriff's office was all. Just past the new bank down the street!

"Go, Zoe! Run!"

Behind them the door swished open.

Their exit to the veritable safety of the public street lay only a few paces ahead. A patch of sunlight streaming through the door stretched like a flag of freedom.

"Freeze! I will shoot!"

Zoe burst into the sunlight and kept sprinting. They'd made it!

She'd always been fast, and she thanked the good Lord for that now as she leapt up the steps in front of the sheriff's office and yanked open the door.

Zoe bent double and propped her hands against her knees. She gulped for breath. "We just barely...escaped...from a couple of...outlaws." She wheezed and pointed back toward the livery, still unable to stand straight.

Silence greeted her and a prickle of awareness swept down her spine. She lifted her gaze. No one sat behind the desk. The sheriff's office lay empty. What were they to do now?

"Mrs. Callahan?" Zoe straightened and turned to face her companion.

And that was when she realized that Mrs. Callahan wasn't there either!

Chapter Fourteen

acinda froze with her hands in the air. She made her stance as wide as possible to block the man's aim from Zoe, and cringed, expecting at any moment to feel a bullet tear through her torso. At the same time, she mentally urged Zoe to speed and safety.

Behind her, the outlaws' boots slapped against the barn floor.

Jacinda closed her eyes in thankfulness when she saw the girl yank open the jailhouse door and disappear inside.

The outlaws were too late.

The man with the jagged scar cursed. And in the next moment he had her by the arm. He hauled her toward him and glowered into her face. "Who was that with you?"

"I-I—" How many times had she looked at the eyes on this man's wanted poster and shuddered? She'd always thought he looked like a snake about to strike. Now, staring him face-to-face, she could only think that maybe if she delayed long enough Zoe would be able to get Joe here to save her.

The other outlaw had already turned for the back doorway. "We don't have time. Bring her. We ride now!" Who was that second man? He looked somehow familiar, but she'd never known a man with an eyepatch before. Had she known him before that injury maybe? If so, would he know who she was? Whoever he was, he was obviously the man in charge.

Would he want to ransom her? Her mouth went dry. Or simply kill her and be done with it?

Scar man—she racked her mind, trying to remember the name on the poster—was already dragging her toward the exit.

If they took her with them, she would never return alive! That was one thing Wade and Reagan, had always emphasized. *Never let them take you.* It was better to fight and be injured near help, than to be dragged into the wilderness by men with ill intent.

She shoved her captor as hard as she could. Yanked to loose her arm.

But she might as well have pushed a rock wall and tried to free herself from a bear trap.

He slapped her.

Pain seared through her and her vision blurred.

She tried to shake away the pain, but he had already hauled her through the back door and was handing her up to Lenny.

Only a moment later, they were galloping out of town.

Help was rapidly disappearing behind her!

She assessed the distance to the ground. The speed with which it streamed by. She must jump! She took a breath. Prepared herself for the landing.

But in the next moment, something slammed into the back of her head.

Pain seared through her.

And everything went dark.

Zoe clutched her head and tried to think what she ought to do! Of course Deputy Joe had probably gone to check on the supposed trouble that Mr. Giddens would have reported to the north of town!

And she'd left Mrs. Callahan behind! How could she have done such a thing?

Terror pulsed so violently that she could feel the pounding of it in her chest.

Had she left the sheriff's mother to be murdered? Mrs. Callahan could even now be dying because of a gunshot wound! She couldn't just leave her there! She yanked open the jailhouse door and lurched onto the porch before she realized that she hadn't heard a single gunshot.

That didn't mean Mrs. Callahan was all right, however. The outlaws wouldn't have wanted to draw attention. They'd likely used a knife! Or maybe simply bashed her over the head!

She had to go help! But if she charged into the barn and got herself killed, who knew how long it would be before anyone found their bodies. And then the outlaws would make a clean escape.

What would Pa tell her to do?

She squinted, trying to see into the livery. There was no movement, but she couldn't tell if anyone stood inside the edge of darkness. What if they were even now aiming a gun at her?

She lurched back into the office. "Oh Lord, what do I do?"

At the window, she gingerly peeked above the sill. She glanced up and down the street. Not a soul was in sight. Metallic fear prickled over her tongue.

The closest help was Marshal Zane. He would know what to do.

She just had to make it down the porch steps and around the corner, then she'd be out of sight from the livery. From the back end of the alley, she only had to run one block to reach Mrs. Callahan's front door.

Taking a fortifying breath, Zoe yanked open the jailhouse door. She scampered off the porch, halfway expecting to feel the pain of a bullet in her back at any moment. But it was only a few steps to the relative safety of the alley. She sprinted, skirts hoisted. At the other end, she paused only long enough to see that the street was empty before she dashed down Second. She took Mrs. Callahan's porch steps in one leap and pounded on the door. "Marshal Zane! Open up! I need your help!"

Her loud banging and yelling sent a sweep of fear through her. She spun to check the street in the direction of the livery. Had the outlaws seen or heard her? All remained quiet. Maybe even now they were making their escape from town.

Forget waiting on the porch! She burst inside.

Marshal Zane stepped into the entry. His brows arched quizzically. "Zoe!" He was wiping a hand on an apron of all things.

"Marshal"—Zoe slammed the door and swept a gesture toward the livery—"Mrs. Callahan—the livery—there were outlaws and—" Her tongue felt thick and her mind a'muddle.

The marshal grabbed her arm and tugged her away from the door. He stepped close to it and peered through one of the cut-glass flanking windows. He gave the street a quick assessment, then set to yanking the apron off over his head. His other arm lay in a sling beneath.

"Are you sure you should be up?"

"Spit it out, Zoe. What happened." Though she saw him wince, his voice was remarkably calm.

Right. Mrs. Callahan was the only thing of importance, at present. "We were in the livery. In the loft. It was Pa's and my place and I went up there to—"

"Skip to the important details, and fetch my boots from the bedroom, while you talk." He sank onto one of the dining room chairs and set to tugging up his stockings with one hand.

Was the marshal going to go after them with his arm in a sling?

He pointed at the bedroom. "Zoe, the boots. What happened?"

She jolted into action. "Yes, sir. A man came in. He told Mr. Giddens that he'd seen troublemakers on the north end of town." She scurried into the bedroom and saw the boots by the bureau. She snatched them up. "But I'd just seen him ride in from the south. We recognized him from one of the wanted posters." She plunked the boots down before him. "He has a jagged lightning bolt scar. We tried to go out the back but they were there— Doc!"

The marshal lifted his gaze to hers.

"They were propping Doc against the back side of the livery when they saw us. He was all limp and..." She bit back a sob. "Maybe dead. We tried to make a run for the sheriff's office. I thought she was right with me." Zoe wrung her hands. "But when I got there, Deputy Joe wasn't there and Mrs. Callahan wasn't with me. I didn't know what to do, so I came here!"

Zane clenched his teeth as he fumbled one-handed to get the first boot on. It didn't help that he trembled from head to foot. Jacinda in danger. Queasiness rumbled in the pit of his stomach.

Focus. Get details.

"You did the right thing. Did you see where they went?"

Zoe shook her head. "No, sir."

"So you don't know if they are still in the livery?"

Her fingers twisted together. "I'm really sorry. I thought she was with me and I feel—"

"It's not your fault, Zoe."

His frustration ratcheted up a notch. Not knowing if the outlaws had fled would slow things down. They couldn't just go rushing up to the livery if men were inside waiting under cover to pick them off.

Zane gave up on tugging the boot and stood, stomping his heel into place instead. His focus snapped back to Zoe as he repeated the process. "Sit down. Take a breath." He strode over before her and squatted to the balls of his feet, looking into her face to ensure that he had her attention. "I need you to listen carefully, Zoe. Doc's not dead or they wouldn't have brought him back to town. And Deputy Joe likely went to the north end of town to see what the report was about."

She nodded.

"I need you to go find him. Tell him everything you just told me. And that I'm approaching the livery from the west, got it? From the west. He'll know what to do."

She stood. "Yes, sir."

He patted her shoulder. "Quick as you can now. Mrs. Callahan's life may depend on it."

"Yes, sir."

He was thankful to see that she was already scurrying out the door.

He hurried for the kitchen and snatched his gun belt from where Jacinda had left it on the table earlier. He braced himself for the pain. He just had to get the blamed thing on. In all his years of practicing shots with his left hand, why had he never thought to practice putting the gun belt on with a bum arm, too?

He extracted his arm from the sling and gritted his teeth as he forced himself to hold one end of the belt in place while his left arm slung the rest of it around. He used the wall to trap it and then winced his way through threading the end into the buckle and getting the pin into the hole. It only took him half a minute, but fresh blood marred the bandage on his shoulder.

It didn't matter.

His gun belt was on. He settled it into place and bent to tie it down.

Jacinda could kill him later for opening the wound again. And he would happily let her.

He returned his arm to the sling. Grabbed his hat from the peg where he'd hung it by the back door—was it only the evening before?—and then dashed across the street and hurried toward the livery.

Lord, I'm asking You to keep Jacinda safe.

⁂

Lenny leaned over Jacinda where he'd propped her against a pine trunk, heart in his throat. She ought to have awakened by now, shouldn't she? Had he hit her too hard? Killed her?

He reached out and patted her cheek. "Mrs. Callahan. Wake up. Come on now."

Behind him, Jim paced. "We should just kill her and go back for the girl."

Lenny spun on him. "Is that really the only solution you can think of for everything? The girl has already talked! You know she has. So exactly what good would it do us to go back for her?"

Jim continued pacing without reply.

"It would only put us in more danger." He sank into a crouch and patted Jacinda's cheek once more.

"You're too soft. She's slowing us down. I still say we kill this one and move on."

Lenny loosed a huff. If only he'd had the time to consider the smarts of his crew when he'd put them together. "Jim, you have no idea who this is, do you?"

Jim leaned over his shoulder. "She someone special?"

"She sure is. This here is the mother of Wyldhaven's sheriff. And I happen to remember just how close they were." He smacked her other cheek, this time with a smile. "I do believe that providence might finally be smiling on us."

Jim glanced at him. "Why's that?"

"Because now we have leverage! We trade her. For something good."

Jim considered. "Have you noticed that new bank going up in town?"

Lenny felt this excitement begin to rise. When he and Jim worked together, they were good. "We'll need to formulate a plan. But first, we need to chain her up."

"Chain her up? You're not taking her back to camp?"

Lenny did his best not to roll his eyes. "No. We're not taking her to camp. That's why I stopped here." He swept a motion to the thick patch of mountain huckleberries backed by what from this angle simply appeared to be a large rocky precipice jutting up in the middle of the forest. Shady as it was here the bushes had grown as high as a tall man's head. "Look behind those. No, a little further to your right."

Jim stepped forward and parted the branches. He made a little noise of surprise and squinted. "What is this place?"

"Take the trail just around the corner after it climbs up the rock face a ways. You'll find a cave. Waddell used it from time to time. Take a branch for a torch. Make sure the manacles are still securely in the wall, would you?"

From the forest floor, Jim hefted a short stout pine branch with a good end of dry needles.

"And be careful you don't break any of those huckleberry branches. We don't want to leave any trace that we were here."

Jim grunted his irritation at the obvious instructions.

Lenny bit back a grin. For some reason it gave him joy to make the man feel stupid.

Jim paused and turned back to face him. "Did you say 'manacles'?"

Lenny forced a dramatic sigh. "You didn't think I was going to leave her here of her own recognizance, did you?"

Jim's brows slumped only a little this time before he stepped through the huckleberries and scooted out of sight.

Lenny grabbed his canteen and flicked some water into Jacinda's face. "Come on, woman. You have to wake up if you're going to be the butter for my bread."

She didn't move. The lump on the back of her head, where he'd whacked her with the butt of his gun, was mounded up and bleeding.

He frowned. Maybe he'd hit her too hard? He'd been so panicked to get away from town.

He pressed his fingers to her throat. Relief coursed through him. Her heart still beat strong and steady.

He angled a look at the sky. The sun was much lower than he would like. Men from the town would be crawling all over these woods before nightfall.

They needed to get back to the camp and get everyone out of there. And they would need time to cover their trail before the lawmen and a posse arrived. He and Jim had traveled fast after they left town. But ten minutes back, after they'd turned the big corner south of town, he'd slowed and made sure their trail was covered. Still, situated as their camp was, right on the banks of the creek not far from here, he wouldn't be surprised if the law stumbled on it. And they needed to be clean gone by then. They couldn't travel fast with an unconscious woman to deal with. Beside which, he didn't want any of his men getting any ideas and harming the goods before they could be traded.

A few minutes later, Jim stepped from behind the huckleberries. "The bolts are still good and tight in the rock wall."

"Fine. Put that torch out, toss it, and help me with her."

Jim looked from Lenny to the torch. "Thought we were trying not to leave sign that we've been here?"

Lenny ground his teeth. That was true enough, but he couldn't admit it now without looking foolish. He brushed a hand through the air. "Good a job as we did covering our trail between the road and here, no one's going to stumble onto this exact spot."

Jim shook his head and looked at Lenny. "Those are the kinds of careless mistakes that get men killed!"

Lenny very seriously contemplated pulling his gun and doing away with the attitude of Jim Roan. But that would only leave more evidence. Besides, he needed Jim's help to move the Callahan woman, and he *was* right. They'd done a good job of covering their trail.

"Forget it. Just help me with her. We don't have time to stick around until she wakes up. We'll just have to chain her and come back for her later."

And hope she was still alive to be traded.

Jim blew out his torch and thrust the non-burnt end into the ground. "I'll take this with us when we leave. We can toss it when we're away from here."

Lenny had to confess, if only to himself, that it was a good plan.

Together, they carried Jacinda behind the bushes and into the darkness of the cave, where they cinched the manacles tightly around her wrists. Lenny tugged off his bandana, tied a knot in its center, and then shoved that into her mouth before tying it securely at the back of her head.

Though everything in him pressed to get back to camp and get the men moving, Jim didn't let them leave until he was certain that no trace of their footprints remained and all the bushes looked natural and undisturbed. He filtered leaves carefully over the entire area until even Lenny couldn't tell that anyone had been here.

Lenny rolled his eyes. "Can we go now?"

Finally, Jim gave a nod of satisfaction.

As they rode away, Lenny thought of Jim's comment about the bank.

A thrill of excitement zipped through him.

Finally! His luck had turned.

Chapter Fifteen

Zane was nearly crawling out of his skin with impatience as he forced himself to cautiously approach the livery. He pressed his shoulder to the back of the bank—the newest building in town, actually not even completed yet—and peered toward the barn.

No one in sight.

He eased forward, staying low, Colt palmed in his left hand and ready.

How long until Joe could get here? Providing Zoe found him right away, it shouldn't be long.

Movement at the front corner of the barn had him lifting his gun, but then he froze. "Doc!"

Holding the back of his head, Doc staggered forward. He waved a frantic hand. "Marshal."

Zane motioned for him to hurry forward. "Did you see anyone in there?"

Doc shook his head. "Livery is empty. But the outlaws have Jacinda! I saw them ride away just a bit ago. But I didn't have a weapon..."

Zane's heart fell. "I know. There was nothing you could have done. Which way did they ride?"

Doc motioned south.

Joe rushed up just then, with Zoe and Giddens fast on his

heels. "Doc. Glad to see you're all right." He glanced at Zane. "I'm sorry I fell for their ruse."

Zane shook his head. "You couldn't have known. We always check out any reports of troublemaking. They knew that."

Bill Giddens rubbed his hands. "I ought to've recognized that snake. Zoe tells me he's on a poster." He pulled a face. "These ol' eyes ain't what they used ta be."

Zoe wrapped an arm around the old man's shoulders. "It's not your fault, Mr. Giddens. If you hadn't gone off to tell Joe, who knows what that man might have done to you! I'm glad you didn't get hurt."

Joe propped his hands on his hips. "So what now?"

Zane motioned toward the south. "Doc says they rode that way."

Joe started toward the barn. "I'll saddle our horses." He paused to give Zane an assessing skim. "You sure you're up for this?"

"Just saddle the horses." Zane motioned Zoe toward Doc. "Help Doc home, would you?"

Doc waved a hand to brush away the idea, but at the same moment seemed to lose his balance. He propped one foot to the side in a wide stance.

Zoe slipped beneath Doc's arm and supported his weight, giving Zane a nod. "Yes, sir."

"After you get him home, I need you to go for Wash, hear? Tell him Joe and I are on the road south out of town and we need him to keep an eye on things in town."

Zoe's eyes widened. That was a big honor for them to trust Wash with such a thing. "Yes, sir."

Zane was already headed for the back of the livery. The sooner they found the trail, the sooner they could be on their way.

But another thought registered. He leaned in the back door of the livery. "Joe?"

"Yeah? Almost ready."

"Saddle up whatever horse Jacinda rides most often, would you?"

"Yeah. Good idea."

Zane set to studying the collage of prints in the dust behind the livery. His heart sank when he saw how many prints there were in the roadway.

Tracking them was going to take longer than he'd hoped.

Pain pulsed through the haze between wakefulness and sleep.

She moaned. Turned her head. Groaned.

Why was her arm in so much pain? She needed to turn over.

Something clanked loudly.

She stilled.

Agony begged for her attention.

Her eyes didn't want to open. Why wouldn't they open? She blinked. Then realized she sat in total darkness.

Slowly she became cognizant. She was sitting. On a hard surface. Head hanging. Arms bound above her. Something cold brushed one arm.

She lifted her head. Searing heat knifed through her shoulders so swiftly that she couldn't stop a cry.

Something skittered in the darkness.

She stilled. A frown furrowed her brow.

Where was she?

How had she come to be here?

Another thought brought her up short.

Who was she?

A wave of dizziness made her feel like everything around her swayed. Nausea roiled.

She couldn't give in to it. Mustn't give in to it. The gag would make her choke on it.

Despite the darkness, she squinted her eyes shut and pulled in a slow breath. She tipped her head against the wall.

Pain pounced so swiftly that she hardly had time to feel it before she slumped into the oblivion of unconsciousness.

⁂

Irritation swept through Zane as he and Joe led their horses down the road, scouting for sign. He wanted to be galloping after Jacinda. Instead, he was stuck moseying along so they didn't miss the place where the outlaws would likely turn off the road.

His pulse jumped. His forehead dripped sweat. His shoulder throbbed.

The sun shone mercilessly. The top layer of dust on the road was dry as powder. But after yesterday's rain, the road beneath was damp enough that they had been able to pick out what they hoped was the right trail. Two horses. One with deeper prints that could indicate it was carrying double the weight.

He only hoped they were right. And that they wouldn't be too late.

His mouth went dry at the thought.

The trail fizzled out. Zane gripped the back of his neck. *God, please…*

"Zane, here." Joe leaned over the lip of the embankment. He lifted his gaze to the forest beyond. "I think they went in here." The grass at the edge of the road was bent at a slightly different angle than the grass around it. Half of one hoof print was visible in a bare spot. Small evidence to go on.

Zane glanced ahead. Something... What was bothering him? The trail had disappeared. That meant that either the outlaws had paused to brush out their trail, or they'd left the road. His focus honed in on the road.

Zane clapped Joe on the shoulder. "We keep going."

Joe frowned. "You sure?"

"Look at the road. What do you notice different between there"—he pointed ahead—"and there." He pointed back in the direction they'd just come.

Joe glanced both directions and then his eyes widened. "*All* the prints are gone up ahead."

Zane nodded. "They brushed their trail. Mount up."

As Zane swung into the saddle, he hoped he was right. *Please, let me be right.*

He and Joe urged their mounts into a trot now, leading Jacinda's.

When the prints started up again, that would likely be the place where the outlaws had left the road. Unless of course these outlaws had thought far enough ahead to realize they could throw them off their trail by doing this.

Zane ground his teeth.

He pulled his horse to a stop and glanced back the way they had just come.

Joe reined in and looked at him.

"Do you think I'm right, Joe?"

He nodded. "I think you're right. Why would they brush the trail if not to keep us from following it?"

"Maybe one of them rode ahead brushing the trail while the other took Jacinda off back there?"

Joe considered. "These outlaws took Doc right from the middle of town. So, I'll acknowledge that they have some brass. But..." He glanced back toward town. "They also returned him in the middle of the day and got caught doing so." He shook his head. "I don't think they have the smarts to think very far ahead."

True enough.

Zane kicked his heels in, urging his mount ahead. "I pray we're right. Let's ride."

❧✿❧

As Zoe helped Doc up the steps to the boardinghouse, Parson Clay was just stepping out. He moved out of the way and held the door for them. "Flynn! You're all right. So glad to see it. I've been praying up a storm. Here Zoe, let me take him."

Zoe nodded, unable to deny that she was thankful to be free of Doc's weight. The man was barely keeping to his feet.

Miss Dixie—Mrs. Griffin, Zoe silently corrected herself— hurried down the stairs just then. "Oh, Flynn! I was just heading over to the church for William's service!" Zoe felt the words like a punch, even as Mrs. Griffin flung herself forward to wrap Doc in an embrace.

Doc canted backward like a tree out at the logging camps about to fall.

"Whoa there!" Parson Clay, curved a strong arm behind Doc, even as Zoe surged to prop both hands against his shoulder blades.

Zoe bit back the bitter taste in her mouth and looked away from the warm reunion. She ought to be thankful that Doc was home. Instead all she could think about was the fact that Pa would never be home again.

Mrs. Griffin withdrew, concern etched in the scan she gave her husband. "I'm sorry. You're hurt. I was just so glad to see you. Let's get you upstairs where you can rest."

"Parson?" Zoe followed along behind as Mrs. Griffin led the way. "Will you be all right if I leave? Marshal Zane said I should give Washington Nolan a message."

He grunted beneath Doc's weight as he helped him up the first step. "He'll likely be at the church in just a few minutes."

Right. Pa's ceremony again. Zoe smoothed her hands over her black skirts. No matter all the uproar, there was no escaping reality for long.

She paused in the doorway and looked past the empty lot across the street toward the church on the hill. Already wagons and horses filled the shaded area under the big oak. Several women bustled into the church with pots and platters in their hands.

Ma stood on the top step in solid black. Belle at her side. Zoe could tell it was them only because she knew them so well. Ma would be smiling at everyone and thanking them for coming. Belle would be more sedate in her greetings, polite, if a bit distant. The twins and Aiden were already likely seated on the front pew at the church.

Was Pa already there? In the pine box Wash had fashioned?

Her stomach threatened and Zoe laid a hand over it, thankful that she hadn't eaten anything today.

She cast another look toward the oak and paused. Wash stood just outside of the shade, and he was looking her way. After a brief hesitation, he started down the hill toward her.

Zoe expelled a breath.

At least it hadn't been hard to find him.

Carefully lifting her skirts, she stepped onto the road and started forward.

This time it was the cold that woke her. That, and the fact that she couldn't feel her arms.

She rolled her shoulders and blood surged into her numb limbs.

Agony flamed.

She whimpered.

Again, something skittered in the dark—this time dashing over her extended legs.

She gasped and drew her knees up to herself.

Her head throbbed. She tried to see where the creature had gone, but it was still so dark. How long had she been unconscious this time? Without the aid of the sun it was hard to tell.

Thirst thickened her tongue.

She worked her mouth. Then realized it was the gag making her mouth dry.

Another roll of her shoulders made her clamp her teeth on the gag. Could she use her shoulder to push the gag from her mouth?

She pressed her cheek firmly against one arm and tried, but to no avail. It was tied too tightly.

She gave up in defeat, and dropped her head against one of her bound arms.

A memory surfaced. She was a young mother and her son, Reagan, had begged her to play "sheriff." No wonder since his father made a living as a lawman. Reagan had "tied" her to one of the straight back chairs from the dining table—really nothing more than a few loops of rope around her. He left the room then to "hunt down the outlaws who had dared to capture his mother," and Wade came home just then. A spark glinted in his clear blue eyes as he took in her predicament.

He leaned close, propping his hands on the arms of the chair. "I see you've been captured by outlaws again."

She smiled. "Some lasses are forever charging into trouble,

don't you know? But God will protect me and the ones I love. He always does."

"Mmhmm. That's the Jacinda Callahan I know and love." He gave her a lingering kiss before straightening with a wink. "I'd better go find our illustrious sheriff so he can rescue you before dinner burns. Again."

She laughed. "Couldn't his partner free me just this once? After all, the good Lord sent you at just the opportune moment."

He shook his head. "Oh no! Never take away the thrill of a man's job. The rescue is the only reason for all the risks we take in this line of work." He leaned close and whispered warmly, "I promise to hurry him along. And then later you and I can celebrate your rescue good and proper." He gave her a double-pump of his brows.

She'd laughed. "If I have to scrub burnt pans again, I'll be too tired to celebrate."

He had rushed from the room on the run, causing another round of chuckles.

Jacinda sighed and relaxed. *Thank You, Lord, that I can always rest in Your will, knowing that You take care of me.* Verses she'd memorized as a young mother filled her mind. *Because you have made the Lord your refuge, Even the Most High, your dwelling place, No evil shall befall you, Nor shall any plague come near your dwelling; For He shall give His angels charge over you, To keep you in all your ways.* A warm feeling of contentment washed over her, despite her circumstances. God had promised that nothing evil would befall her. Somewhere out there was a man who loved her. He would come for her. God would see to it.

And at least she'd remembered who she was.

She gave in, once more, to the tug of oblivion.

Chapter Sixteen

꩜

The footprints in the roadway reappeared again as suddenly as they had disappeared. And up on one embankment lay a broken pine bough, dusty from its work of brooming away the prints.

"Just stay mounted." Joe was already off his horse and leaping up onto the bank. "I'll check it out."

Irritated that his bum arm had Joe pampering him, Zane scouted ahead a few feet. He leaned out of his saddle to get a better view of the ground.

He didn't want to miss anything. They couldn't afford to miss anything.

A careful search of the road didn't reveal any of the prints they'd followed from the livery. He looked hopefully to Joe who was still scouting back and forth through the grass between the roadbed and the edge of the forest. Joe suddenly stopped and studied something more carefully.

"Here," he called, already starting back for his mount. "There's a crushed fern."

Zane's stomach rolled. He hated that they were basing Jacinda's rescue on things as slight as erased footprints and crushed foliage, but what else was there to go on?

He swung down and led his mount and the spare up the embankment as Joe returned for his. He found the crushed fern and stepped into the cool shade of the woods, hearing Joe right behind him.

They proceeded quietly. Cautiously. Well aware that this could be an ambush and shots could ring out at any moment.

The going was slow. Painstakingly so. And there was no further evidence that the outlaws had actually come this way. He and Joe scouted wider, sweeping the area searching for even the slightest sign that the forest had been disturbed.

Zane's skin crawled with the urge to rush ahead, calling out Jacinda's name, but his years of experience held him in check. He wouldn't do her any good if he rode right into an ambush.

After an hour with no luck, they came to a sheer mossy cliff that stretched as far as they could see in both directions. If the outlaws had come this way, they would have either turned back, or ridden along the face.

Zane tied off his mount and the extra. He pointed Joe in one direction. "Meet me back here in ten minutes."

Joe nodded and started off.

Zane took the other direction. But he found nothing. No tree was scuffed. No rock was scraped. No brush lay crushed. No prints, partial or otherwise, indented the ground. Despairing, he turned back and met Joe in the middle.

Joe shook his head. "Maybe you were right. Maybe this whole thing was a setup . Maybe they did go off the trail back where we first thought."

Zane scrubbed his good hand over his face and glanced around. Terror pulsed through him. He'd made the wrong decision. There was nothing here but tall pines, huckleberries, and stone.

"We go back." He reached for the horses' reins.

And stilled.

"Joe?"

"Yeah?"

Zane nodded toward the horse Jacinda often rode.

The animal's ears were perked toward the huckleberry bushes, all attention focused there.

Zane studied the bushes. Had the horse simply heard a forest critter? The bushes grew right up next to the cliff's face, so that had to be it, didn't it? Nothing lay beyond.

Joe shook a couple of the huckleberry branches, then stepped back.

Something scurried through the underbrush and dry leaves.

Jacinda's horse stepped forward, ears still perked in the direction of the brush.

Zane leaned forward and pushed aside a couple branches, peering into the depths of the bushes. This time of year, the bushes were covered with small pink and white blossoms that carried a sweet, tart fragrance. There was nothing at the base of the bushes, and the rock wall rose straight up behind them, but he knew when a horse was curious, and this was too important to simply sweep aside. He was probably wasting time. They should go back to the first place they'd seen the outlaws leave the main road and search from there, but something wouldn't allow him to let this go just yet. He moved down the row of huckleberries parting the branches and peering between them.

Nothing. Nothing. Nothing.

"Hang it!" He kicked at the ground, sending leaves, twigs, and debris flying.

There was simply nothing here to indicate Jacinda had been here.

Except the horse was still singularly focused on the huckleberries. The huckleberries that had revealed nothing after a thorough search.

In disgust, Zane bent, snatched up a branch, and chucked it into the bushes.

A rat the size of a barn cat dashed out, leapt off his boot, and scuttled through the legs of Joe's horse, to disappear beneath a fallen tree.

Joe's horse whinnied and sidestepped. Jacinda's mount laid its ears back and bent to rub its nose against its knee.

Joe and Zane met each other's gaze.

Disappointment marched through Zane's chest. Small as the chance had been of finding something, his hope had been riding just beneath the surface.

He reached for his horse's reins. "Let's go back to the first spot."

Joe nodded.

⁂

Wash's gaze was so soft as he met her in the road that it was almost her undoing. He tilted his head. "Your ma worried where you were." He left the question unasked, but she could tell by his searching look that he had wondered too.

Zoe tucked a loose curl behind her ear. "Something bad has happened."

Wash reached out and squeezed her shoulder. "I know, Zoe. I'm right sorr—"

"No. Not Pa." She stepped back from his touch. She'd never be able to keep herself together if she gave in to Wash's comfort right now. "Marshal Zane sent me to give you a message. He said for you to keep an eye on things here in town. He and Deputy Joe are on the road south out of town."

Wash tossed a frown in that direction. "Right now?"

"Mrs. Callahan has been captured by the outlaws."

"What?!"

Zoe felt tears sting. "It was my fault."

Wash stepped closer but he didn't touch her this time. His voice was low and husky when he said, "I'm sure that's not true."

Zoe folded her arms, refusing to meet his gaze. If she looked into those empathetic gray-green eyes of his, she would be overcome by the threatening emotions right here on the street. And she must stay strong. "I need to go to Ma." She couldn't talk about anything more right now or she was going to fall to pieces.

Wash stepped out of her way. "I'll keep an eye on things. Go on and let your ma know you're fine." He motioned her toward the church steps.

She nodded. Then left him before she did something silly like throw herself into his arms right here in front of the whole community and beg him to make everything better.

***

Discouragement weighing heavy on his shoulders, Zane gathered up the reins of the extra mount and turned toward the road. But he couldn't seem to take that first step. He had failed her. Failed to keep her safe.

Just like he'd failed Daniella.

He gritted his teeth. His rational side said there was nothing he could have done about Daniella dying in childbirth. His heart said, as small as she was, he never should have gotten her with child in the first place.

And now...even knowing that there were outlaws roaming the area, he'd let Jacinda leave the house alone.

Lord, I don't know what You are trying to teach me here, but I sure wish You'd quit taking it out on the women I love.

The memory of the verses he'd been prodding Jac with only

this morning swept over him. He clamped his jaw. What a hypocrite he was. Because here he stood, just as worried about Jac as she'd ever been about anyone else. It was one thing to spout phrases about leaving things in God's hands, when they were mere acquaintances and friends. But trusting God with the people you loved was a horse of a different color. Zane knew from experience that God's plans for a loved one weren't always in lock step with his own wishes.

So how did one go about reckoning with that? How did one trust that God was good, even when He let bad things happen to those you loved?

Zane shook his head. He didn't have the answers to that. What he needed to do right now was keep using the skills the good Lord had given him to find the woman he loved. He would keep searching until he found her, no matter what came. And he'd deal with his feelings toward God after he knew what to feel.

"Ready?" Joe prodded.

He tipped a nod.

What was he going to do if they never found her? He'd gone through this torment once. Had never wanted to go through it again. Didn't know if he could survive going through it again.

Behind him, he could hear Joe catching up his horse. His tongue clicked as he urged it to step out. Chains clanked.

Zane froze. *Chains?*

He looked back.

Joe had stilled too.

Both of them studied the huckleberry bushes again.

Zane was the first to move. He slapped both the horses' reins around a tree branch and strode to the bushes. "We're missing something."

"Agreed."

Zoe sat on the front pew of the church, trying not to look too often at the casket that sat before the pulpit.

It was fitting that Pa's memorial had been turned into a prayer vigil for Mrs. Callahan. Pa would have liked that. The parson had asked Ma what she wanted him to do and she'd insisted that Pa's service could wait. And so the townspeople who'd come to say goodbye to Pa sat in the pews and prayed instead that they wouldn't soon be saying goodbye to yet another fine member of the community.

Zoe had done her duty and prayed for Mrs. Callahan's safe return, but guilt over her part in the capture kept pulling her focus from prayer. If only she'd done something different at the livery, there would be no need for this vigil.

Zoe's feet swung forward and back beneath the pew. Sitting still could really be torture, sometimes.

She closed her eyes. Thought back. What ought she to have done differently? She could have withdrawn when Mrs. Callahan first urged her to, before the outlaws even saw them. She could have run straight for Marshal Zane, instead of going to the sheriff's office. Should have realized that Deputy Joe wouldn't be in the office! That had been a stupid blunder. But even then, when she'd seen he wasn't there, if she had run for Marshal Zane immediately, maybe that would have saved Mrs. Callahan from being taken from town.

Instead, she had frozen. Panicked. And if something terrible happened to Mrs. Callahan, it would be all her fault.

Zoe stilled.

What was she thinking? Something terrible had *already* happened to Mrs. Callahan. Imagine! Being captured by outlaws and carried off to who knew where!

She leaned past Belle and touched Ma's arm. "I'm going out to the necessary," she whispered.

Ma nodded and Zoe fled. It was an excuse to get out of the building. To put some of her pent-up energy into pacing beneath the large oak outside the church.

She heard footsteps and spun to face them.

Belle stood a few feet away, arms folded, a soft look in her gaze. "This wasn't your fault."

Zoe resumed her pacing. "I should have done so many things different."

Belle looked down and scuffed one toe against the grass. "You'll do yourself no good rehashing what you ought to have done differently. Nor her either, for that matter."

For the first time in a long time Zoe felt the comradery she and Belle used to share. She paused and wrapped Belle in a hug. "It's just been a terrible day. And I don't know if I'll be able to forgive myself if they don't find her."

Belle rubbed her back. "I'm sorry I wasn't there for Pa." Her voice broke. "You've no idea—"

Zoe pulled back and gripped her shoulders. "No. I'm the one who's sorry. I never should have said all that."

Belle looked toward the church, swiping her cheeks with the cuff of her sleeve. "No. You were right. I should have been there. I just thought I could... I was making a painting."

"A painting?"

"Of us. Before. I wanted to show it to Pa."

Zoe felt even worse for her earlier outburst. "Belle, I'm so sorry. Ma was so worried about where you were running off to. Why didn't you tell us?"

Belle shrugged. "You know how Ma is about my painting. And...I wasn't sure it would be any good."

Zoe huffed. "Your paintings are always amazing!"

Belle gave her a self-deprecating smile. "You have to say that. You're my sister."

"That's not true. I want to see it. Did you get it done?"

Belle's face contorted. "Not in time."

Zoe tugged her close once more and curled her arms tight. "He can see it. Pa can see it. And better yet, he's not in any pain anymore. He's probably rushing through the halls of heaven hollering for the attention of anyone who will listen and pointing out your painting."

Belle chuckled through her tears. "Parson Clay would likely have some theological rebuttal for that."

Zoe gripped Belle's shoulders once more and winked. "I'm sure the good Lord won't begrudge us our fantasy. But I want to see the painting. Do you have it?"

Belle's expression fell. "I lost it. I was coming home to show it to Pa and when I got to the yard and saw Wash and Jax building the coffin, well... I'm not sure what happened to it. I can't find it."

Zoe put an arm around Belle's shoulders and turned them toward the church. "We'd best get back inside, but I'll help you search for it when we get home. I wish you would have told us what you were doing."

"Ma is just always so...insistent that my painting is a waste of time. Pa was the one who encouraged me to keep at it."

Zoe touched her head to Belle's as they walked. She wished she had an answer for that. But she knew Belle was right. Ma wanted all her girls to be proper ladies, domestic and docile. Pa had encouraged each of them to be themselves. To pursue their passions.

She sighed and released Belle as they reached the bottom of the stairs.

They were all going to have a lot of adjusting to do after this day was through, Ma included.

As they resumed their seats on the front bench, Zoe renewed her prayers for Mrs. Callahan's safety with greater purpose.

She didn't want any other family in town to have to suffer what they were suffering right now. It would be terrible for Sheriff Reagan to come home from his wedding tour only to learn his mother had died.

Chapter Seventeen

Zane parted branches more forcefully this time. "Jac? You here?" he called, figuring it was safe to call out now since they knew the outlaws weren't in the area.

Joe moved off a few steps and started doing the same. "Jacinda?"

Zane thrust his arms into the thick brush and separated the branches as much as he could. He ignored the pain throbbing through his shoulder and put a damper on his despair when all he saw was that blasted rock wall. He stepped to the right, repeated the process.

Nothing.

"Zane!" Joe called. "Here!"

His heart leapt and he rushed forward.

He and Joe clambered through the bushes onto a thin hard-packed path where nothing grew. The trail curved with the precipice wall, so narrow it was well-hidden behind the wild huckleberries.

"Hurry." Zane prodded Joe from behind.

As it curved around the corner, the path rose on an incline, a thin ribbon of granite shelf with a sheer drop-off on one side and the rock wall on the other. Only a few moments later, the wall opened up and dank air swept over them. A cave! The opening was not much taller than a man, and barely wider than a wagon. Ivy cascading down the wall had helped to disguise it from below.

Zane's first instinct was to surge ahead, but Joe stopped him with a hand to his arm. Of course he was right. Zane pressed his back to one wall, while Joe did the same to the other. Both of them drew their weapons. It wouldn't do Jacinda any good for them to get themselves killed just as they'd found her. Backlit as they would be by the daylight, they would be easy targets.

Together, they stepped forward into the darkness.

Jacinda woke to the sound of footsteps and for a moment terror clawed through her. But then she remembered her faith that God would send her husband to her rescue. She strained to see through the darkness, but the blackness refused to give up any shapes.

Her wrists throbbed. Her arms trembled, half-numb from their forced position, and half-tingling with shards sharp enough to feel like broken glass slivers.

How did she reconcile her current circumstances with the verse that said no harm would overtake her? Her faith faltered.

Did she try to cry out? Were the footsteps help?

Or did she remain absolutely silent? If her captors were back, it might be better to appear unconscious.

Despite the fact that she'd remembered her name, she fought through a foggy haze trying to recall how she'd come to be here. Why she'd come to be here. Who had brought her here. But her head only ached and refused to give up its secrets.

Was it Wade coming for her? If so, how had he found her? Confusion swirled and made her want to cry out with frustration.

With the footsteps coming stealthily nearer, she chose her second option. If she didn't know them and they took her outside, she would try to make a run for it. But for now, it was better that whoever approached find her limp and unresponsive. If God had allowed this much pain and suffering into her life, who was to say there might not be more to come?

Her reality felt like a betrayal. Had God abandoned her?

She hung her head, biting back a cry of agony as her weight transferred to her wrists once more.

Her breaths came in frantic puffs and that was no good. Anyone who saw her would know in an instant that she was not unconscious. She willed herself to calm. Breathe slowly. Relax.

She would do herself no favors by panicking.

❦

It only took a few steps into the darkness of the cave before Zane heard Joe pause.

"Zane?" he whispered. "This is no good. We need light."

Zane glanced back the way they'd come. A light would make them sitting ducks to anyone guarding the cave further in, but it couldn't be helped. And it wouldn't be any more dangerous than walking blind into a situation where they were silhouetted from behind.

"You got matches?" He always carried some but bum-handed as he was, he wouldn't be able to get them out of his pocket.

Joe's answer was the flair of a match.

In the brief surge of light, Zane noted that the cave curved sharply just ahead.

Chains clanked again, but more softly this time, as though someone had heard them coming and was trying to be quiet.

"I'll be right back." Joe stepped outside and jogged down the trail.

Tempted as he was to press ahead without him, Zane forced himself to wait, and thankfully it was only moments before Joe was back with a candle for each of them. "Keep these in my saddlebags for situations just like this," he offered.

Zane was thankful for his foresight, but he couldn't hold a candle and his gun. "I'll follow you."

Joe's gaze flicked to his sling, before he nodded, snuffed one of the candles, and stepped out.

The light flickered eerily in a breeze, as they approached the corner. They paused to listen and let the flame right itself. There was no sound.

Zane's heart pumped. Was someone lying in wait for them just around this bend? What was he going to do if they found nothing? Or even worse, found Jacinda dead?

He couldn't hold back any longer. "Go!" he whispered, then surged around the corner, gun at the ready.

His heart caught in his throat. Jacinda was there, head hanging limply between arms that were chained above her head. Her hair had come loose of its pins and cascaded in a curtain over her face.

"Jac!" Zane wanted to forget caution, but his years of training forced him to assess the rest of the cave. It dead-ended here, the back wall a sheer rise of gray granite. There was an empty stone shelf. A firepit. The iron ring pounded into the wall. The chains. And Jacinda.

He gritted his teeth. The outlaws had just left her here? Chained up like some animal? What if a wolf had found her?

Zane took a breath to momentarily temper his anger. He holstered his gun and fell to his knees beside her, brushing her hair back from her face. "Jac, I'm here. I'm here to bring you home." He tugged the gag from her mouth, slipped it free and tossed it to one side.

She made no sound. Just hung there limply.

His heart threatened to stop. She was still warm, but... He touched her throat. A sigh of relief puffed out. Just unconscious. His hand swept over her skull as he pushed her hair back and he felt the swollen sticky lump behind one of her ears. His jaw clamped. They had to get her out of here quickly because the outlaws could decide to come back at any moment. But also because light would allow them to better see how to help her.

He leapt up. "Help me with these. Here, I'll hold the candle." Thankfulness that Joe was here to aid in freeing her from the manacles filled him.

Joe examined the clasps. "We'll not get these undone without the key, but this chain is pretty rusty. If I had a hammer..."

"A rock will have to do." Zane tipped a nod to the stones that rimmed the firepit.

Joe nodded. He hurried over and picked up one that fit in his hand.

Zane dribbled some wax on the shelf and stuck the candle into it so it would remain upright. Then he pulled the chains taut until they stretched tight against the rock wall.

Joe aimed for the rustiest part of the links and set to smashing the chain between the rock in his hand and the wall.

Zane pulled with all his strength. They just had to get one link to break. That would free the manacles from the wall and they could take her back to town and cut the cuffs free at the livery.

"Almost there, Jac. We're going to get you free."

They didn't have keys to the manacles, and they were doing their best to get her free. Did that mean she could trust them?

The one who kept talking to her had a nice voice. Comforting. Like the low rumble of a creek tumbling over rocks.

He called her Jac. She fought for recollection. Did that name mean anything to her? Wade called her Jac. She stilled. Wade. Just the thought of his name gave her a sense of well-being and belonging. But...she couldn't recall the last time she'd seen him. Was it really him? What did he look like?

She couldn't help herself. She lifted her head. "Wade?" The word emerged as nothing more than a croak past her dry lips.

"Hey! You're with us. Are you all right? We've almost got you free."

A curl of hair blocked one of her eyes. She shook it away, gasping at the fissure of pain that split through her skull.

"Sorry. Just be still a minute. I'm sure all this banging makes your head feel like it's on an anvil."

She squinted through the darkness. But with the candle up high on the shelf, and his hat shading his face, she couldn't make out his features.

The second man gave the chains another whack and she felt the tension on her arms give.

"There! Got it."

The chain rattled loudly as it clattered to the floor at her feet. She brought her arms in front of her and couldn't suppress a groan as every muscle cried out with the change of position.

The man with the kind voice reached out and brushed her hair back. "Sorry, Jac. I'm so sorry. I should have done a better job of protecting you. Do you think you can move? We need to hurry."

She nodded. He felt it was his job to protect her? That must mean she trusted him, right? Or was he misleading her? If she could see his face, maybe she would recognize him. If only her head would quit pounding so she could think!

They'd freed her from the wall, that was a point in their favor.

But her wrists remained cuffed and chained to each other. Did they really not have a key? Or were they leaving her hands bound for another more sinister reason?

She would let them help her from this dark place and then she'd decide what to do.

"That's my girl. Let me help you up." He clasped her forearm.

That was when she noticed that his other arm was in a sling. "You're hurt," she said. Or tried to say. Her voice completely failed her and only rasped.

"We'll get you some water as soon as we get to the horses. Can you walk?"

"Yes." At least she thought she could walk. She tried a tentative step. Her legs wobbled, but she would be fine.

One of the men moved out ahead, but the injured one stayed right by her side, one hand at the small of her back.

He seemed honest, didn't he? Dare she trust her instincts?

"Careful here. Don't step too far." He guided her onto a ledge outside the cave. The sunlight shafted into her eyes, momentarily blinding her. She stilled, scrunching her eyes shut tight.

"It's all right. Just give yourself a moment to adjust. We'll get those cuffs off the minute we get you back to town." Wade murmured the words in a soothing tone.

Wade? She frowned. Was it truly him? Would she even know? He certainly seemed to know her, but was it all just a charade?

"Think you can walk? Or should I have Joe carry you?" he asked. The urgency in his voice prodded her to hurry, even though he said nothing about it.

She opened her eyes. They seemed to have adjusted, because she could see fine now. She searched his face. He had nice eyes. Silvery-blue with a dark rim.

The man in her memory had blue eyes too, but... She tried to recall the features of the man from her earlier memory, but they were indistinct. A haze cloaked them, keeping them just out of reach.

The man before her blinked at her scrutiny. Were his eyes familiar? His dark hair and angular jaw made him a striking man. And nothing in her sounded alarm bells, even with him this close. She gave her head a little shake. She didn't have the capacity to puzzle this out, at the moment. For now, she would think of him as Wade.

His brow furrowed a little. "You all right? Want me to get Joe?"

"No. I'll walk." She stepped out, following the descent the first man—Joe—had taken. But she was thankful for the sturdy presence of the man beside her because the drop-off made her head spin. The man called Joe waited for them at the bottom of the trail, holding some huckleberry shrubs back so she could pass by. He gave her a nod and an assessing look as she passed through the branches.

The leaves were glossy. Smooth as silk when she reached out to stroke one. Why did she know what huckleberries looked like, but couldn't remember what her own family looked like?

Wade nudged her from behind. "Just a few more steps." His watchful gaze searched the brush and trees all around them.

Ahead, three horses stood tied.

Her heart pounded. If they got her up on a horse, she might be able to make a run for it.

She glanced over at the two men. They stood close to one another just this side of the huckleberries, speaking in tones too low for her to make out. Every once in a while, they glanced her way.

Uncomfortable, she looked down. The manacles pinched her

wrists, making every movement painful. Did they really plan to remove them? Or was that just something they told her to keep her compliant?

Her quandary mounted. She should run. Get as far away as possible and give herself time to...what? She wasn't sure. And who would she run to? Where would she run to?

She frowned. Tucked her lip between her teeth.

If only she had an inkling of what to do next.

***

Zane's heart weighed heavy as he stepped closer to Jacinda. It was clear that something was wrong. She had a lump the size of a man's fist on the side of her head and she had a blank look in her gaze when she met his perusal.

He offered her a smile. "Let me get you that drink and then we need to get you back home. We'll have Doc come take a look at your head. So long as you are in agreement?"

She nodded, but there was a veil of mistrust in her expression. It was almost like—he stilled, hand on the canteen. He searched her face.

A touch of fear widened her eyes. "Do I know you?"

Zane's heart sank. He'd heard of cases where people had memory loss after a hard blow to their heads, but he'd never encountered it...until now.

He faced her full on and made sure he had her attention. How terrifying it must be for her to find herself in this situation, not knowing if she could trust him or not. But he didn't have time for long explanations. They needed to get away from this place and take her to safety. He would come back later and settle this score with the outlaws. He searched for something quick to ease her mind and settled for, "Yes, you know me. And I'm here to help."

He wanted to ply her to see what she *did* remember, but he highly doubted that pestering her with questions was the best way to make her feel comfortable. Maybe something familiar would ground her. He grabbed the canteen, uncorked it, and held it out to her with a smile. "I'm glad you are all right. Reagan would have my hide if he came back from his wedding tour and something had happened to you."

He watched her closely.

Her face lit up for just a moment. "Reagan...yes." The furrow returned between her brows. "Wedding tour?"

Zane proceeded cautiously. "He and Charlotte will return in a few weeks."

"Charlotte." She said the name as though she was tucking it away in her memory for future use.

His heart thudded with an urgency to rush her along. But he took a breath and forced himself to be gentle and easy. To proceed with caution until Doc could take a look at her and tell him what he thought. He didn't want to give her more stress than she had already been through.

She guzzled thirstily from the canteen and then handed it back to him with a swipe at her chin.

He motioned toward her horse. "Let's get you up on the black. Remember him?"

She cocked her head at the animal, but no light of recognition lit her eyes. Thankfully, the horse seemed to sense that they spoke of him. He stepped forward with a soft whicker and nuzzled her shoulder.

She smiled and lifted her hands to gently stroke the black cheek. Something about the interaction seemed to put her at ease. "He seems to know me." There was a little awe in the words.

Zane nodded. "He does." He wanted to add that they needed

to go but refrained, reminding himself not to push. He didn't want to cause her fear or confusion. "Let's get you up." He motioned that he would help her into the saddle.

She shook her head. "I'll do it. I wouldn't want to hurt your arm more."

He stepped back, giving her space, but he couldn't help a smile as he watched her mount up. Even though she couldn't remember who he was, she was still the same caring woman.

It somehow did his heart good to realize that.

It was the horse that made her decision for her. The horse definitely knew her. And if these men were her captors, what was the likelihood they would be so gentle and kind?

She settled into her saddle and only felt a little dizzy for a moment until she acclimated to her perch. She watched the man with the injured arm mount his horse. He was sure footed, agile, and familiar with long days in a saddle, that she could tell, though she wasn't quite certain how she knew it. But his easy grace put her at ease, and...she glanced down at her pommel with a slight smile...maybe her decision not to run had a little bit to do with his kind eyes. She only hoped she wasn't going to come to regret it.

They rode three abreast into town, a man on either side of her. Both of them were attentive to her every move and she had the feeling they were poised to catch her should she grow dizzy and start to fall.

One or the other kept a constant eye on their back-trail and that too gave her a measure of comfort because somehow she sensed that they searched to make sure her captors weren't after them.

Ahead, a town abutted against a river, a large barn on the near end of the street.

"Here we are, almost home." The man she'd dubbed Wade smiled at her.

When they reined to a stop behind the livery, an elderly man tottered out and threw his hands into the air. "Lord Almighty be praised. They found you!" He hustled to her side and took her hand, then helped her from the saddle.

The two men who'd found her dismounted too.

"Whoo-eee!" The elderly gentleman made no bones about the fact that he was checking her head. "That's quite a bump you took there, pardon me for saying so, ma'am. And look at you, still trussed up like a turkey ready for a Thanksgiving oven. Come inside. Inside. I have a hacksaw that will have you free of those in no time."

Wade gave her a nod and settled a hand to her back. "Right in here, for just a minute or two, then I'll get you home." He leaned closer and lowered his voice. "That's Bill Giddens. He runs the livery here in town."

She studied his face, wishing he would think to confirm to her his own name. When she'd asked if she knew him, he'd only said yes, but hadn't told her who he was.

Joe cleared his throat. "I'll fetch Doc and let the townsfolk know that we found her."

Her escort nodded.

Mr. Giddens waved a hand at Joe. "Doc's down to the church, much to his wife's chagrin. They's all having a vigil, praying for your safe return, you understand, ma'am. They's all gonna be so happy to hear of it. Yessir. Mighty happy."

While he talked, he motioned for her to lay her hands out on a table in the tack room. "Rightchere. Yes'm. Just like that. We'll have these off in no time." He picked up the saw and set it carefully against the hasp of one of the manacles. "I'm right sorry that I was the one who got you into this mess."

She frowned. What did he mean by that?

Taking note of her frown, he paused his sawing. "If I hadn't have come to get you to comfort Miss Zoe, you would have been home, safe in your kitchen, when those outlaws rode in."

Her guardian settled a hand against Bill's shoulder. "This wasn't your fault Bill. Not your fault at all."

She looked up and studied his face. His tone had held a note of self-crimination, like maybe he felt it had been his fault.

Bill shrugged. "Well, I 'preciate that, but I can't help but feel I played some part."

She frowned, racking her memory for any inkling of what had happened to put her in that cave, but it was like her mind was a large dark canvas. Very unsettling. Her hands trembled.

Bill must have noticed because he hurriedly resumed his sawing. "Almost done now, Mrs. Callahan, and then the marshal there can escort you home and I'll take care of unsaddling yer horses. Mighty glad to have you home safe and sound. Yes'm, mighty glad."

With one more thrust of the saw blade, the hasp gave way and her first wrist was free.

She rubbed at it, wincing when she realized her skin was raw and bloody in places.

Mr. Giddens made quick work of the hasp on her other hand, and it was only a moment before the manacles fell free.

He gave a little bow and then shooed them toward the door as he hustled to their horses.

"Thanks, Bill." Wade once more settled a hand at her back, hovering near as though he feared she might disappear if he didn't keep a hand on her. "Let's get you home."

She was thankful when he led her to a clapboard house only

a couple blocks from the livery, because her head pounded by the time they reached the top step of the stoop.

He unlatched the door and pushed it open, motioning for her to precede him. An apron lay haphazardly over the back of one of the dining room chairs.

He snatched it up and scooted the chair out for her. "Here, sorry about that. I was in a bit of a rush when Zoe came and told me you'd been taken. Sit, sit. I want to wash your wrists and then I'll help you upstairs. I'll be right back. Don't move." He hustled off to the kitchen.

She frowned. How did she know that was the kitchen? She just somehow knew. Like she knew that her room was up the stairs and the first door on the left. Like she knew that there was a wedding picture of her and Wade on the bedside table. Why could she remember all that, but she couldn't remember a thing about her captivity or the kind men who'd come to rescue her, or the liveryman who'd seemed so overjoyed at her return.

Wait... A wedding photo on her bedside table? She blinked and her gaze traveled to the last place she'd seen him a moment ago. A wedding picture of Wade. And he'd talked of the apron like he'd been wearing it when—had he said Zoe?—came to get him. All of that must mean he was her husband, didn't it?

She closed her eyes. And she'd almost run from him. Thank the Lord above that she hadn't.

Something clunked softly on the table beside her and she looked down to find him kneeling before her with a soft cloth in his hands. He dipped it into the water and carefully dabbed it across the cuts on one of her wrists.

Her head ached, but she couldn't seem to bring herself to shut out the sight of him. She wanted to know everything she had forgotten about this man she had married. "How did you hurt your arm?"

His gaze flicked to hers, then back to her wrist. "What can you remember?"

She glanced around the house. Most of it was familiar. "I remember this house. I remember Reagan, and that he has a wife named Charlotte—though maybe I only remember that because you mentioned it, since I can't recall her face."

He set to work on her second wrist. "Thinking back, what's the last thing you remember?"

She tried to think, but frowned. Every flit of an image that she tried to extract from her mind seemed permanently embedded in a concealing black tar. She shook her head. "I'm sorry, I can't—"

"No. It's fine. Don't worry about it. I'm sure with rest things will start to come back. He lifted a clean strip of bandaging. "Let me just wrap your wrists and then we'll get you upstairs."

She did let her eyes fall closed then. Yes. Upstairs sounded good. She wanted to simply fall into her bed—their bed—and sleep for a month of Sundays.

"There, that should do you. Ready?"

She swayed for a moment when she stood and he stepped close and wrapped an arm around her waist.

"Only a minute more and then you can rest."

"I'll be fine." Despite her reassurances, she didn't know if she would have made it up the stairs without his help.

In her room, he helped her sit on the edge of the bed and then snatched his hat from his head, crimping the brim in his good hand. He glanced around the room, and his gaze settled on the wedding picture. He seemed a bit ill at ease.

Her heart went out to him. Of course he was ill at ease. How must it feel for your own wife not to remember you?

His feet shuffled. "Right, well, I'll let you rest and bring Doc up the moment he gets here. Do you need anything?"

She shot a hand out and clasped his arm. "Stay with me? I just want to lie here with you and feel...safe."

Chapter Eighteen

A commotion started at the back of the church and Zoe turned to see Deputy Joe walking up the aisle. He reached out to touch his wife's shoulder where she sat on the end of a pew closest to the aisle, but he didn't hesitate for but a moment before resuming his trek toward the front.

Zoe grabbed Belle's arm. Did he have good news? Or bad? She couldn't tell from the enigmatic expression he wore.

Parson Clay stood from where he'd been praying in his chair on the platform, and Aurora McClure stopped her playing at the piano.

Deputy Joe spoke some low words to the parson and then they both smiled.

The congregation let out a collective breath and murmurs of excitement filled the room.

Parson Clay lifted one hand. "Ladies and gentlemen, there's good news and bad news."

Immediate silence descended.

"The good news is that they have found Mrs. Callahan alive."

Zoe felt a surge of sheer joy rise up inside her.

"However, she has suffered an injury to her head and seems to have lost much of her memory. So now we turn our prayers to those of thanksgiving and healing."

Zoe slumped against the seat, elation and horror vying for preeminence in her mind. Deputy Joe was already at the back of the sanctuary, leaning past Rose Pottinger to speak low to Doc. Doc stood, squeezed Mrs. Griffin's shoulder, and then scooted by his mother-in-law to follow out the door.

Zoe leaned over Belle. "Ma, can I go see her? Please? I just need to see for myself how she is."

Ma pinched her lips for just a moment before giving a nod.

Zoe leaped up and Ma snagged her wrist before she could dash down the aisle at a full sprint.

"Like a *lady*. And stay out of the way and be helpful."

"Yes'm." Zoe gave a little curtsy, then forced herself to walk sedately.

Standing at the back of the room with his arms folded and one boot propped against the wall, Wash gave her a curious look. His brothers and Kin Davis sat on the pew next to him. His gaze swept the room attentively before returning to hers. Still taking the job he'd been given seriously, she supposed. She felt the full impact of the question in his eyes. Did she need his help?

She shook her head at him, still not in a frame of mind to accept any of his kindnesses lest they drag her down into a pit of sorrow she'd never be able to escape. But seeing him there made her thankful that she'd taken the aisle like a young woman and not a wild guttersnipe.

Still, the moment she reached the church steps, she raced at full speed to catch up to Doc and Deputy Joe.

Pa was probably chuckling at her from the windows of heaven.

Jacinda felt disappointment as Wade practically leapt back

from her touch. His brows shot up and his face turned a red to match the shade of the lamp on her bedside table. "Uh..."

Downstairs, a knock sounded on the front door.

"That's probably Doc." He scrambled out of the room so quickly he might have been running from a fire. Through the doorway, she saw him pause at the top of the stairs and look back at her. He swallowed, then disappeared below the rail, calling, "I'll just get the door."

She frowned. Why had asking him to stay put him ill at ease? She reached for the photograph on the bedside table. It was a bit faded, and my they looked so young. She studied Wade's face. Frowned. Why could she remember him so clearly from the day they'd married, but not remember anything of the recent years they'd shared together?

She squinted at the grainy face in the image. Tilted her head. He looked quite a bit different now. Age had graced him with many favors. Why was it that men aged so well?

She returned the photo to the table and looked at herself in the mirror above the dressing table across the room. She pulled a face and scooped a hand through her wild array of blond hair. Maybe there was more than one reason that had sent her husband running from the room.

She heard the stairs creak, and a moment later a nice-looking man paused in her doorway, a doctor bag in his hands. Behind him, a beautiful young girl with red hair and a smattering of freckles across her nose peered over his shoulder.

"Come." Jacinda motioned for them to enter.

The doctor set his bag on the end of the bed and smiled at her. "I'm Doctor Griffin. And this here is Zoe. She was worried about you and just wanted to see that you are indeed all right."

The girl sank onto the bed beside her and wrapped an arm around her shoulders. "I'm so glad you are okay. I just didn't know what to do when you weren't behind me at the sheriff's office and then I panicked and took too long to get the marshal and I'm so sorry I left you behind. I was so worried about you."

Jacinda had no idea what the girl was blathering about, but appreciated her kindness, nonetheless. She offered a smile. "I'll be right as rain in just a few days."

She swallowed and flicked a glance to the doctor, wishing she actually believed it. What if she had to go through the rest of her life in this black fog of forgetfulness? She pressed away tears of despair at the thought.

The doctor touched Zoe's shoulder. "How about you go downstairs now and let me talk to Mrs. Callahan alone, hmmm? I'm sure Zane and Joe would like to ask you a few more questions about what you saw this morning. And Parson Clay will want to start your father's service as soon as you can get back."

A cloak of sorrow swept over the girl's features.

Her father's service? Jacinda felt like there was something she should know, but again her mind withheld it.

Zoe stood. "Yes. Of course. I'm sorry to intrude. I'm just so happy to have you back home so soon, Mrs. Callahan." The girl gave a sketch of a curtsy and then left her alone with the doctor.

Jacinda forced a smile. "Nice girl."

"She is that. Deputy Joe tells me that you took a pretty good knock. Mind if I take a look?"

She shook her head and swept her hair away from the painful lump.

His fingers were gentle as he assessed the contusion. "A good knock indeed. Do you remember what happened?" His gaze probed hers.

Irritation snapped through Jacinda. How many times was

she going to have to explain that she couldn't remember anything? "No. It took me a bit to even recall my own name."

"I see. Do you have a headache?"

If only he knew. "Yes."

"Well, some memory loss can be normal after a hit like this. I'll get you some pain powders that will also help you sleep." He turned to his bag and she caught sight of a white bandage at the back of his head.

She studied him, realizing that he seemed pale and shaky. "You look a little worse for wear, if you don't mind my saying so."

He smiled softly. "I'm afraid you and I have been victims of the same outlaws."

"I'm sorry. Do you have memory loss?"

"No." He tapped a few powders into a glass tube. "Head injuries are still somewhat of a mystery. Most times there are small ill-effects. A headache. A bit of dizziness that dissipates within a few days. But in more severe cases like yours, there is memory loss."

Jacinda swallowed. "Do you think I will get my memory back? I don't even remember the last few years with my husband."

The doctor stilled and looked at her. He frowned and glanced toward her door and then back to her. "Uh... I'm sorry to have to be the one to tell you, but your husband passed away several years ago."

Jacinda propped a hand against the bedside table as a memory suddenly came rushing in. Wade, chest bloody, lying in her arms, face pale as the life drained out of him. Reagan as a young man, hovering nearby, pacing, biting his thumb. God had indeed abandoned her, but it had happened long before she'd found herself chained in a dark cave. "Wade's dead. Yes,

I remember now." She whisked a look to the door. "Then who is that man downstairs?"

Dr. Griffin settled a hand to her shoulder. "You must be referring to Marshal Zane Holloway. He was injured recently and you took him into your spare room downstairs while he recovered."

Jacinda pressed a hand to her forehead. She'd asked the man to lie with her! What must he think? Heavens! "If you don't mind, doctor, I would like to rest a while."

He nodded. "Let me just get the gash on your head cleaned and bandaged. I don't want you taking an infection. But first..." He stepped out the door, leaned over the rail and called down. "Someone bring up tea and honey, please?"

"Right away."

That comforting tumbling-water voice. Which probably meant he'd be the one to bring the tea and she'd have to face him again. She felt her face heat at the mere thought.

Dr. Griffin paused with a roll of white bandages in one hand and a bottle of ointment in the other. "You look a little flushed. Any other symptoms you need to tell me about?"

Would this day never end? "No. Just a little warm is all." She snatched up the fan from her bedside table and put it to good use while Dr. Griffin cleaned and bandaged her head. He was just tying the bandage into place when Marshal Holloway stepped through the door with a tray balanced on one hand.

"Thank you, Marshal." Dr. Griffin took the tray from him and set it on her vanity. He shook out enough powder to fill the teaspoon and then stirred it into the cup of tea along with a dollop of honey.

The marshal propped his good hand against his hip, pushing back his long duster to reveal a tied-down holster. "How is she, Doc?"

Jacinda absentmindedly returned the fan to its place. Why did the sight of that tied-down holster give her both comfort and a measure of unease? Since coming to, she felt like her emotions were a whirlwind that couldn't quite decide where to land.

The doctor handed her the teacup. "Drink it all, if you can." He spoke to the marshal as he set to gathering his medicines back into his bag. "Time will tell if she regains her memory. But other than that, I think she will be fine after a few days of rest. Which"—he reached an arm to prod the marshal's withdrawal—"she will commence as soon as she finishes her tea. And I dare say you could use something to ease your own pain about now?"

The marshal ignored the doctor's question and peered over his shoulder at her. "I'll be right downstairs. Just call me if you need anything."

Jacinda nodded, but felt her face heat all over again. The likelihood of her calling for him after her earlier gaff was slim to none.

❧⁓⁓⁂⁓⁓❧

Zane paused by the dining table and studied his boots, wishing his shoulder didn't feel like it had a glowing-hot blade stuck in it. He glanced toward the stairs and swallowed. Of all the irony, Jacinda had obviously thought he was Wade. And hang it if he didn't wish it were true. Well, not that he was Wade, but her husband.

Doc set his bag on the table and snapped it open, offering a stern look. "You ought to be resting." He reached inside and withdrew a vial of powders. "I know I gave you some earlier, but between the two of you, you might need some extra in the next day or two."

Zane took the vial with a nod of thanks. He decided it was probably the better part of wisdom not to tell Doc that he didn't plan to take any more pain meds. They made him tired and knocked his guard down. And he couldn't have that with a group of outlaws on the loose.

He was done waiting around to see what they might do next. It was time to put Joe's and his plan into action. But first they had to get through Kastain's memorial.

Speaking of which, he glanced into the parlor where Joe spoke in low tones with Zoe. Now that the pressure of finding Jacinda had dissipated, he was likely asking Zoe for more details about what she saw this morning.

Zane rubbed a hand down his face. Was that all only this morning? He felt like he'd lived two weeks in the last few hours.

Doc dropped a hand onto Zane's good shoulder and gave a gentle squeeze. "I'm glad we got her home safe."

Zane nodded. "Yeah. Likewise. You think she'll get her memory back?" He scrutinized Doc's face for any reaction. But Doc was the king of inscrutability. If he played poker down at Ewan's, he'd clean the place out.

Doc closed up his valise and hefted it into one hand, lifting his hat from its peg by the door. "I hope she will. Usually patients do. But I've read of rare cases where the patients never did recover their memories. I wish I had answers for you, but all I can say is we'll have to wait and see."

Zane held out his good hand. "I appreciate your honesty."

Doc shook his hand and then tipped a nod toward the door. "I'll just mosey on back to the church and let everyone know that she's all right."

Zane knew he needed to get back, but he and Joe needed some answers too. "Mind if I ask you a couple questions before you leave?"

"No. Of course we haven't had a chance to talk since my return. I should have thought."

"It's been a long day." Zane smiled.

Joe and Zoe stepped into the entry and Joe held up a wanted poster. "Not only did Zoe see the outlaws who captured Jacinda this morning, but she's certain the first was Lenny Smith and the second one was this man."

Zane looked to Doc for confirmation. He nodded.

Zane raised a brow. Lightning Jim Roan. Just the mention of the name sent a shudder through him. The man had built quite a reputation as a gunfighter and an hombre no one dared cross. Zane settled a hand against the butt of his pistol and frowned.

"What is it?" Joe asked.

"Nothing... It's simply... He doesn't seem like a man who would take second seat to the likes of Lenny Smith, does he?"

Joe looked at Doc. "You spent time with them. Did there seem to be tension between the two?"

Doc nodded. "Yes. I only overheard one conversation between them, but Jim challenged him at every turn. And I should mention that Lenny's been around these parts for quite some time. He married a woman and was working out at the logging camps about six months ago. But his wife died and I lost track of him after that. Couldn't have been more surprised when he took me captive and I learned he was Lenny Smith. Can't believe I never recognized him sooner. But he was always clean-shaven before and now he has a beard and an eye patch."

"Any idea how many he has following him?"

Doc pondered. "One's injured bad. Likely won't make it. Another is a simpleton. Maybe three or four more? They didn't let me look around."

Joe shook Doc's hand. "Thanks, Flynn. Glad you made it back okay. Try to rest up."

Zane gripped the back of his neck, willing away the throbbing fire in his shoulder. "Yes. In fact, I think it would be best if you stayed in town for a few days until we can get the Smith Gang captured."

Doc frowned. "I have patients out in the camps. Expectant mothers, and a man who just lost his leg in an accident."

Zane exchanged a look with Joe. What were they supposed to do about that? They couldn't deny the people out in the camps access to their doctor. And yet, they couldn't afford any more time lost to rescue missions either. He gave Doc a sympathetic shake of his head. "We'll do our best to get these outlaws taken care of post haste, Doc. We had the beginnings of a plan. But one key piece was missing. I think them taking Jac has just solved that..." He looked at Joe.

Joe nodded. "Yes. I think so too."

Zane returned his focus to Doc. "We just need a day or two to put it into motion. Can your patients live without you for that long?"

Flynn considered. "I suppose, if it's only for a couple days."

Zane dipped his chin. "If we don't have the outlaws arrested by then, we'll put together an escort to go with you out to the camps."

"I can live with that. Can't deny that after the knocks I took I should probably take a couple days to rest anyhow. Won't do the people any good if I come down sick, myself."

Joe opened the front door. "Zoe can accompany you now, and I'll be along shortly."

Doc and Zoe stepped outside and Joe turned to face Zane. "Sure hope this plan doesn't backfire on us. I'd hate for Wash Nolan to get hurt."

Zane loosed a breath, feeling every one of his forty-five years. "Me too." He swept a gesture toward the upstairs. "I can't leave Jacinda here alone, though. Can you bring Wash by after the ceremony so we can talk everything through?"

Joe nodded. "Will do."

As Joe left, Zane headed for the kitchen. If he couldn't take the pain powders, the least he could do was make himself a pot of coffee. And maybe put a warm compress on this shoulder.

Chapter Nineteen

Zoe stepped through the back doors of the church as Doc held them for her. She gave Wash a little nod to let him know that Mrs. Callahan was all right. He gave her a thumbs-up and then returned to his conversation with his brother, Lincoln.

Zoe moved to her seat with a little furrow tightening her brow. Boys could be so confusing.

But what had she expected from him? A whoop and a jig? Certainly not, since they were about to start Pa's funeral. But maybe more than a cursory acknowledgement.

And yet... maybe that was no more than she deserved after the way she'd put him at arm's length earlier, even if she did have good reason for it.

At the front of the room, the parson raised a hand to get everyone's attention and Zoe pushed thoughts of Washington Nolan from her mind.

Parson Clay spoke a little loudly to cover the few remaining voices. "Doc has a quick update about Mrs. Callahan. And then we'll proceed." He gave Ma a questioning look and she nodded.

Doc crimped the brim of his hat as he spoke. "Mrs. Callahan appears to be fine other than... as you all heard earlier, she has suffered such a blow that it has affected her memory." A murmur traversed the room and Doc raised a hand to quiet everyone. "She has some memories of distant occurrences, but for the time being, don't be offended if she doesn't remember who you are. Other than that, in a day or two, it would be fine for visitors to drop by."

Parson Clay took his place behind the pulpit. "And now we will look to our memories of William Gunther Kastain."

Zoe's heart plummeted. Pa gone. She could still hardly fathom it. She reached for Belle's hand and felt the comfort of her warm grasp.

The parson read a summary of Pa's life that Ma must have written up at some point, but to Zoe's way of thinking, it didn't capture the essence of who Pa really was. It had the dates of significance—when Pa was born, married, died. It had a list of jobs he'd done, several before he'd finally moved his family to Wyldhaven to work for Mr. Heath in the woods. It had a list of those of them who'd outlived Pa and said he was a loving father and husband. But then it ended and Zoe was left with an uneasy feeling, like they hadn't done Pa's life justice.

The feeling persisted all through the hymn they sang. Through the scriptures the parson read about how being absent from the body was to be present with the Lord. And through the prayer that followed.

Then Parson Clay offered that anyone who had a memory of Pa could stand and share it.

And before Zoe knew it, she was on her feet and facing the congregation.

Ma's eyes widened a little, and Belle's face turned a little pale. Zoe knew Ma was simply surprised that she'd stood and Belle was aghast at just the thought of speaking in front of a whole church full of people.

But Zoe didn't mind. And Pa deserved to be remembered for so much more than just the significant events in his life.

She gave the congregation a watery smile. By gum! Her tears started to fall now? She swallowed and lifted her chin, dashing away her tears. "Sorry. I simply..."

From the back row, Wash gave her a nod of encouragement.

She took a breath. She could do this. "Pa's obituary spoke of some of the significant events of his life, but it didn't give much detail, and I wanted you to know some of what made our pa so special to us." She swept a motion to her family on the front row. "His obituary said he was born to farmers in Kansas, what it didn't tell you was that when our pa was nine years old and a tornado was coming, he risked his life to fetch the family's sow down into the storm cellar." She smiled. "The way Pa told it, he was more at risk from his father's wrath for subjecting him to hours in a cellar with the smelly pig, than from the storm itself."

Everyone laughed. Including Ma and Belle. Even the twins and Aiden were smiling. And that gave Zoe the courage she needed to keep going. For Pa.

"The obituary gave the date of Pa's marriage to my ma."

She studied Ma's face for a moment, willing her to remember the good times they'd had with Pa and not focus on the worries over what they would do now.

"But what it didn't tell you was that the first time Pa saw my ma, they were at a Christmas church social."

Ma was already chuckling through her tears because she knew what detail was forthcoming.

"Pa was lighting the candles on a food table with holly and such decorating it."

A rumble of humorous expectation swept through the room.

Zoe nodded. "Yes, you probably guessed. Pa dropped his match and caught a clump of holly on fire, which in turn ignited the tablecloth before he could extinguish it."

A full-out chortle filled the sanctuary.

"Pa said the only redeeming thing was that Ma got assigned the job of bandaging the hand he burnt putting out the flames."

Ma nodded, still smiling, though tears tracked down her cheeks.

"It mentioned several of Pa's jobs. But what it didn't tell you was of the many times that Pa gave some of his earnings to buy for families in need. Or of the days he would come home plumb wore out, but still find time to help us kids with our learning—even if it was only to dole out a whupping that Ma told him one of us deserved."

That got a good laugh out of the congregation. Especially when she pointed to her siblings and added, "Well, really that only ever happened to one of them."

Ma shook her head, but a twinkle remained in her eyes as she dabbed at them with her hanky.

Zoe paused, trying to think what else she wanted to say. Memory after memory assailed her. Too many to recount. And with them came real, gripping sorrow. Her face contorted and it took the greatest of effort to pull herself back. She should wind down before she wasn't able to speak for sobbing.

"I'd best stop rambling. Our family thanks you for being here today and please we'd love to hear your memories of our pa."

As she collapsed into her seat, a man at the back stood. "I was one of those who William helped..."

For almost an hour, people shared stories of Pa's kindness, generosity, and humor. And by the time they stepped outside to the graveside, Zoe felt like a wrung-out rag because she'd volleyed between laughter and tears for most of the hour.

But now came the part she'd been dreading. The part where Pa's body was lowered into the cold dark earth. The part where she really had to come to grips with the fact that she would never see Pa again this side of heaven.

The part where she and Ma and Belle and the twins and Aiden had to get on with living—without his guiding wisdom and calming wit.

She simply wasn't ready for that.

Wash stood just outside the cemetery fence, watching Zoe and her family accept the well-wishes from person after person.

He, Jax, and Kin would fill in the hole just as soon as everyone left. Meantime, he wished that he could whisk Zoe away from all this.

He could see that she was forcing herself to be strong. Forcing smiles of thanks to each person. And he could also see that her family looked to her for guidance of what to do next. With every person that stopped, her family waited for her to speak first, and only once Zoe had greeted them did the others follow suit. Especially Zoe's ma wore a blank look and appeared about ready to fall off her feet. He thought back to the wee hours of yesterday when Zoe had collapsed into his arms. Had any of them had time to rest since then?

Zoe bent and said something to Aiden. He hurried to the food table near the church steps and took up one of the crystal punch cups. He carefully carried it across the lawn and passed it to his mother. She guzzled it down thirstily between well-wishers.

Wash lurched into motion. At the food table, he asked Sandy Laurence for a tray. He filled the tray with cups of punch and threaded his way through the crowd.

Zoe gave him such a look of thanks that if he could, he would have repeated the gesture a thousand times over.

She leaned forward. "Do you think you could get Ma and Belle some bread and cheese? They get to quavering if they go too long without eating." Her own hand trembled as she returned her cup to the tray, and he had a feeling she needed food just as badly as they did.

"I'll do better than that." Wash stepped to the head of the line and held up a hand. "Folks, I know there are just a few of you left, and the Kastains sure do appreciate your kindness, but if you don't mind, let's allow them to sit and eat a mite. It's been a very long day for all of them."

Mrs. Griffin stepped in and concurred. "Yes, that's a very thoughtful suggestion, Washington. Thank you. I'm sure the Kastains would be happy to accept more condolences after they've had a bite to eat." She took Mrs. Kastain's arm. "Right this way, Susan. We have a table and food for you and the children."

Zoe smiled her thanks then moved to sit with her family.

Deputy Joe stopped by Wash's side. "You make a decision about being deputized?"

His heart leapt at the reminder. He did his best to nod sedately and not like a kid at Christmas who'd just been asked if he'd like to have a whole plate of fudge. "Yes, sir. I'll do it."

"Good. Glad to hear it. Soon as you're done here, meet me and the marshal at Mrs. Callahan's place."

"Yes, sir. I'll be there."

Parson Clay stopped by then and asked him if he and Jackson would mind helping Kin put the sanctuary to rights for Sunday's services, while they waited for everyone to disburse.

He would have rather stayed where he was to make certain Zoe was being taken care of and wasn't simply doing all the caring, but of course he couldn't deny the parson. And by the time they finished straightening the pews, sweeping up, blacking the stove and making sure all the psalters were stacked neatly in each row, Zoe and her family had left.

Thankfully, that meant that everyone else was leaving also. Only a few minutes later the cemetery lay empty except for the three of them.

Kin handed each of them a shovel and they set to filling in the grave.

It was solemn work. Hearing the dirt thud hollowly against the coffin until even that sound faded away. Mr. Kastain's walk on this earth was done. Such a short time. Wash swallowed, wondering how many years he would have. He leaned on the shovel for a moment and glanced at the church. When he passed, would a whole church full of people come out to say their farewells?

"This hole ain't filling itself," Jax grumbled.

Wash took the hint and set to shoveling again, but he made himself a pledge. He wanted to live his life like Mr. Kastain had done. In service of his family and others, for the good Lord.

At last the grave was filled.

They all stood and looked down at it for a quiet moment and then Wash passed his shovel to Kin. "I need to go. Deputy Joe asked me to meet him and the marshal at Mrs. Callahan's place."

Kin passed both shovels to Jax. "I'll come with you. I'm supposed to deliver a package to a lady in Camp Sixty-Three for Mrs. Callahan tomorrow."

They headed down the hill toward town, leaving Jax to holler after them, "Oh sure! I'll put the tools away! Don't worry about a thing!"

Kin chuckled.

Wash turned to face his brother, walking backwards for a few steps. "I'll make it up to you by doing your chores on Saturday so you can sleep in."

Jax waved him away with a gesture that said he would believe it when he saw it.

Kin clapped him on the shoulder. "One good thing about not having brothers. You don't have to make promises to keep them happy."

Wash elbowed him. "I thought I was your brother."

Kin grinned. "Closest one I've got at any rate."

***

Zane opened Jacinda's door to find Kin Davis and Washington Nolan standing on the step. Of all the crazy things. Why had Nolan brought Davis along? "What's he doing here?"

Before Wash could respond, Kin lifted his hands. "I'm just here because earlier in the week Mrs. Callahan asked me to stop by today. She has a dress she needs delivered out to one of the camps."

Zane grunted and opened the door wide enough to let them both in. He realized he was being a grouse. The pain was getting to him. Well that and maybe his concern for Jacinda had him a bit on edge too. He pointed Wash to the dining table where Joe already sat, then motioned for Kin to wait a moment. "Sorry to be short. I'll see if I can find the dress for you."

Kin gave a deferential nod.

In his room—her sewing room, he corrected himself—a brown dress hung from one of the cabinet handles. It was the only dress in sight. He took it down and strode back into the entry. He held it up. "This it?"

Kin waggled his head. "Not sure. I've never seen it. Was just told to pick it up."

Zane thrust the dress toward him. "Well this is the only one I can find. Must be it."

"She normally wraps them in brown paper."

Zane gripped the bridge of his nose and willed himself to remember that none of this was the kid's fault. "Fine. Brown paper. I'll get it and string and you can wrap it at the table before you go, but after you deliver it, stick around long enough to make sure it's the right dress, aye?"

"Yes, sir."

A moment later, he set the roll of brown paper, scissors and string on the table and then sank into a seat next to Joe with a sigh. Hang fire, he really wanted this day to be over.

Kin set to folding the dress and they all looked at him for a long moment.

Finally, he lifted his gaze. "What?"

Joe blew out a breath. "News is going to be all over town first thing in the morning anyhow."

Zane nodded.

Joe looked back to Wash and thrust a Bible across the table toward him. "Raise your right hand and repeat after Zane."

Wash placed his left hand on the Bible, raised his right hand, and Zane proceeded to swear him in as a deputy.

The moment they finished with the pledge, Kin burst out. "Crimany! Wash deputized?! What's this all about?" He grinned from ear to ear.

Zane only looked at the kid. Joe and Wash held their silence as well.

Kin raised his hands. "Fine. I never asked." He set about cutting a square of paper large enough to wrap a pair of sows. Zane only hoped the woman would be able to find the dress in the midst of all that paper.

Joe leaned across the table to capture Wash's attention. "Right, so here's the plan. Zane and I had already discussed setting a trap for Lenny. We just weren't sure how to get him to take the bait. But he's played right into our hands by taking Jacinda captive."

"How's that?" Wash absently traced a finger over the grain of the wood.

"We figure that Smith and his outlaws are going to come back to the cave to get Jacinda at some point."

"Mightn't they have already done that?"

Zane scooped a hand through his hair and scrubbed at the back of his head. That was his fear as well. "We hope that hasn't happened. If it has, we'll have to come up with another way to get them the information."

"Where do I come in?" Wash leaned forward.

Joe took over explaining again. "We want you to pose as a vagabond traveling through the area. You camp somewhere near the cave. Lenny will be plenty upset to find Jacinda gone, so you'll have to be convincing that you had nothing to do with it. You'll say you saw a couple of lawmen rescue her and that you overheard us discussing how we had to hurry back to town to accept the shipment of gold for the new bank's vault."

Zane tugged the money pouch from his shirt pocket and tossed it across the table to the kid. "After that, you high-tail it to Cle Elum and hire a wagon and a driver. We'll meet you as you leave Cle Elum and, hopefully, we can arrest the whole gang when they attack the wagon. But they'll have seen you at that point, so you'll have to stay out of sight in the back of the wagon, or the whole plan will go bust. That will also give us just a slight edge of surprise when the attack comes, as they won't know we have an extra man."

Wash tipped his head. "What if they recognize me before that, when I'm by the cave?"

Zane exchanged a look with Joe. "Why would they recognize you? They've never seen you, have they?"

Wash shrugged. "If Doc was captured right out there on the street in front this place, then chances are good that they may have been lurking nearby when I was telling Doc about you getting shot, don't you think?"

Zane collapsed against the back of his chair and looked over at Joe. He should have thought of that. If he wasn't in so much pain; so concerned about Jacinda, he would have thought of it. Wash was right. And they couldn't send him to pose as a vagabond if the outlaws would immediately recognize it as a lie. It would cost the kid his life. "Now what?"

"I'll do it."

Every eye in the room fixed on Kin. He was holding a length of string, and the package on the table more resembled the wadded-up leavings from a post-Christmas morning than a dress ready for delivery.

Zane motioned to it. "What about the dress?"

Kin shrugged. "We weren't even certain this was the right dress, and under the circumstances, I'm certain the lady it's destined for will be understanding if it's a day or two late."

Zane looked at Joe.

Joe shrugged as if to say they were out of options.

What was the world coming to? Zane gripped the back of his neck.

Kin Davis was about to become a deputy.

Chapter Twenty

t was the rumbling in Jacinda's stomach that first woke her, but the sun pouring through the lace curtains at the window made her sit up with a start. When was the last time she'd slept this late?!

"Mercy!" She threw back the covers and leapt to her feet, but a wave of dizziness toppled her to her knees.

She remained there, realizing her head ached.

What day was it? Everything seemed a bit foggy but a few things stood out clearly. Zane shot. Doctor Flynn captured. William Kastain dead. Zoe fleeing the livery as she broadened her stance so the outlaws wouldn't shoot her. She frowned, feeling the weight of her worry over each of those situations like an iron cloak.

A knock sounded on the door.

"Jac? You all right, in there?"

She clutched at the front of her nightgown, eyes widening. What was Zane doing upstairs? He should be in bed resting!

And then, with a rush, all the memories of the day before came flooding back.

Her face blazed warm enough to light the bedside lamp. She'd thought he was Wade! Asked him to— Heavens!

"Jac, I'm coming in if you don't answer me in about three seconds." The door handle moved slightly, proving that he was ready to follow through.

"Zane Holloway, don't you dare come through that door!"

The door handle returned to its proper position. "Did you call me Zane?"

She used the bed to help herself stand, snapping, "That's your name, isn't it?" The room swayed and she clutched at the bedpost.

"So...you...got your memory back?"

Indeed. And she wasn't sure if she would ever be able to face the man again. Yet, she had no other choice. "Yes. I'll be down in a minute."

"Get dressed and sit on the bed. Let me know when you're done. I'm not going to let you take a tumble down the stairs on my watch."

She rolled her eyes. Insufferable man! Despite her irritation, she couldn't deny that it felt good to have someone care enough to hover.

After she dressed, she didn't go to sit on the bed. She opened her door instead, and stepped out onto the landing.

He stood at the top of the stairs, one arm in a sling and the other hand propped on his hip. He gave her a once-over from head to toe. "Knew you'd be too stubborn to listen to reason."

She pulled a face. "Good morning to you too."

With a quick step forward, he drew her into an embrace.

Her breath hitched, but then she relaxed into the lovely feel of his arm around her. One hand resting on his chest, she settled her forehead into the crook of his shoulder. She fit perfectly beneath his chin.

He lowered his head and pressed his cheek to hers. There was gravel in the words he spoke softly. "I'm glad to have you back." Easing away, he looked into her face "You sure you remember me, now?"

She smiled, feeling her face blaze anew. "Yes. And about

yesterday... I'm so sorry I..." She swept a gesture toward her bed, unable to voice the impropriety, unable to meet his gaze.

He chuckled. "Don't think I wasn't tempted to take you up on the offer."

A gasp escaped. "Zane Holloway!"

To her surprise, he stepped closer. "One of these days, you'll agree to marry me."

She lifted her chin. "Will I?"

"Then, you can ask me again, and I'll be able to agree in good conscience."

"Oh, Zane. Do go on with you." She hoisted her skirts and made to brush past him.

But he caught her gently by her forearm. "I mean it, Jac. If there was one thing I decided after I got shot, it was that I wanted to be done high-stepping over my feelings for you. You going missing only compounded that resolve. I love you, and I want to spend the rest of my life with you." His thumb swept a warm caress against the inside of her elbow.

She swallowed and looked down at his hand. And for the first time she had no words of rebuttal.

She thought back to the day before. "When I woke in the cave, the first verse that came to mind was about how God would protect me. I had such a peace in my heart. No fear. No worry."

Zane slid his hand down her arm and captured her fingers. "God did protect you. I believe it was His doing that helped us find you."

She frowned. "Yes. But it could have just as easily been my time to go. I used to genuinely believe that God wouldn't let anything bad happen to those who were truly serving Him with all their hearts. Yesterday when I came to and thought Wade was still alive, I had the most peaceful feeling, even though I was chained in that cave. But today I remember how I've felt for...so many years. When Wade was killed, I simply... lost my ability to trust in God's protection."

Zane released her hand to cup her chin and look deep into her eyes. "We aren't supposed to trust in God's protection, but in Him alone."

"I—" She paused. She'd never thought of it from that perspective before.

"If a woman is carrying two babes and the one is born first, does that mean God cares less for the second born?"

She didn't reply. She knew it was a rhetorical question. Yet she couldn't fathom where he might be leading the conversation.

"Jac, this life is only the beginning! We live in the womb of eternity! Wade was birthed into the next world sooner than you, that's all. God doesn't love you any less! He's simply not done with you here on this plain. The question is, are you willing to trust that His ways are perfect? Is your faith strong enough that you can say you will take the good from God as well as the bad if it fits His plan?"

She felt a pinch of pain in her head. Would she? Did she have a faith that big?

"You remember the verses I spoke to you about?"

She nodded. "Consider the lilies..."

He dipped his head in acknowledgement. "Worry is a sin because it's a lack of trust in God's perfect plan. And like I said the other day, all your worrying can't change a thing, because, I hate to break it to you, love, but you aren't God."

She narrowed her eyes at him. "That's not fair."

"Not fair that you aren't God?" He smiled softly.

"That's not what I meant and you know it." She looked away.

Zane nodded. "I know. And you're hurt because you want

to make everything perfect for everyone. Your goal in life is to smooth everyone's path, and protect them from any pain. But God has a perfect plan that we simply can't see because there are too many parts missing from our perspective. What we *can* know is that God loves us and His ways are perfect. So we do what we can, and we trust Him to do the rest. And if He decides it is best that one of us reach paradise a little sooner than another, who are we to complain about it?"

She folded her arms, pulling away from his touch. "You've given me much to ponder, but my head aches. I think I'll make some tea and take some of Doc's powders."

Zane squeezed her hand. "The water's already hot. I'll bring you a tray."

With that, he disappeared down the stairs.

Jacinda returned to her room and sank onto the edge of her bed and propped her hands beside her. A quaver started in the pit of her stomach.

Because for the first time, she realized that, come what may, she wanted to spend the rest of her life with Zane Holloway.

And the thought of loving and maybe losing someone again terrified her.

Kin Davis huddled over his fire, warming his hands near the flames. It had been a long cold night, but the marshal and Deputy Joe had insisted that he come out immediately in case the outlaws decided to return for Mrs. Callahan during the night. He'd found a hollow tree where he'd stashed the money for hiring the wagon and driver in Cle Elum, then set his canvas shelter under a large oak not far from the cave where Mrs. Callahan had been held captive.

The outlaws hadn't come. He'd stayed awake and kept his

fire going all night just to make sure. And now that through the trees he could catch glimpses of a beautiful orange and red sunrise stretching along the eastern horizon, he was having trouble keeping his eyes open.

He fumbled through his pack till he found the tin of coffee. He sloshed some water into the small pan he'd brought with him and set it over the fire.

While it heated, he would just close his eyes...

A moment later, he jolted and scrubbed a hand over his face. The water was already boiling and hopefully a nice strong brew would give him the boost of wakefulness he needed.

Behind him a rifle cocked.

His hands shot into the air, all thoughts of needing coffee gone. He was suddenly wide awake.

"What you doin' here, boy?"

Kin's heart pounded. He hadn't even heard the men approaching! They must have come up behind him when he'd dozed off. Were these the outlaws? Or some other gang of ruffians? He had to proceed as though they were the outlaws. What if he couldn't pull this off? What if they saw through him and discerned he was working for the law? He took a breath. Reminded himself wryly that chances of that were slim to none.

He spoke cautiously. "Just minding my own business. About to have some morning coffee. Care to join me?"

"He's just a kid," another voice said.

"Just a kid camping right here? What are the odds o' that?"

Definitely the outlaws then. He had to speak up before they filled his spine full of lead and he didn't get to lay the trap with mention of the gold. But what was the right response? "Don't know what you boys are so all-fired angsty about, but I'm just traveling through. This seemed a likely spot to pitch my tent is all."

"This far off the road, kid?"

"Always like to move back from the road a ways. Camping right along it invites all sorts o' trouble from anyone passing by."

There was a moment of pause. Kin held his breath. Had they bought it? And if not, would anyone miss him should he turn up dead? Maybe Parson Clay. Though PC was only a couple years older than him, the man had been more a father to him than his own pa since his death several years ago.

The men behind Kin spoke quietly to one another, and he strained to hear their conversation. But with the wind in the trees and the birds still twittering like all get out as they were wont to do at dawn, he couldn't make out what they said. Finally, he heard one of them stalk away.

Kin relaxed, if only slightly. Everything was going according to plan. "Be all right if I make my coffee and get on my way?" He pressed his lips together, praying the man wouldn't simply agree, because he needed to stick around till they discovered the cave was empty.

"Make your coffee, kid, but you ain't going anywhere just yet." The man remained out of sight behind him, but Kin could feel his rifle just as well as if he could see it.

Kin blew out a breath of relief and dumped a couple scoops of coffee into his pot. He set it on a rock off to the side of the fire to let the grounds sink to the bottom. "Nice morning." He gestured to the sunrise that had now faded to a dome of coral through the leaves overhead.

"Might be a nice morning if our prisoner wasn't missing!" Footsteps crashed through the brush and before Kin knew what had hit him, he was on the ground in the dirt with a hand clamping his throat.

"She's gone! What did you do with her?!"

Kin fought for air. Tried to push the man off him, but he was strong, and as big as a bull. He sat on Kin's legs and didn't even budge from any of Kin's blows.

"Bobby, we need him alive if he's gonna tell us anything!"

The man with the wild, dark eyes, and the long black beard didn't release his grip.

Spots floated before Kin's eyes.

There was a loud *thunk* and suddenly the grip on his throat loosened and the weight on his legs lifted as the man tumbled to the side.

"Ow! Why'd you do that, Vic?" His attacker clamped a hand to his head.

Another man, this one just as scruffy but with lighter hair and a smaller frame, loomed over them, his rifle held like a club.

Kin rolled to his hands and knees and gasped for sweet air.

"I told you we need him alive. He may have seen somethin'. You sure she's gone?"

Kin's attacker was still rubbing his temple. "I know an empty cave when I see it, Victor!"

Kin sat and tried to gather his thoughts. He had to keep his wits about him. He should have expected the attack. What would the lawmen want him to do now? He had to play the innocent witness.

The man called Victor squatted before him, his rifle still cradled in his arms.

Kin felt chilled by his eyes and he suddenly realized that this man might be the smaller of the two, but he was by far the more dangerous one.

"So here's the thing, kid. Our boss was keeping a prisoner in a cave just up yonder." He tilted his head toward the crag. "And now we find her missing and you here. That casts you in a mighty suspicious light."

Kin rubbed his throat. "Why would I take your prisoner and then linger around till you showed up?"

The man nodded. "Why, indeed." He started to turn away.

"But I did see some men taking a woman wearing manacles out of these woods just as I got here last night."

The man swiveled back around, all his focus on Kin.

Kin nodded. "I was just coming off the road. And I heard footsteps, so I hid behind some brush because you never know about the friendliness of people." He gave the big brute named Bobby a glower to drive home his point.

"Keep talking, kid."

Kin shrugged, praying he was selling the story well. "I saw two men. Both of them were lawmen by the stars on their vests, so I was none too interested in letting them see me, since well"—he brushed a hand through the air—"that's a tale better left for another time, I suppose. Anyhow, they had a woman with them, and her wrists were bound. I thought she was their prisoner."

Kin was gratified to see the two men look at each other.

He was even more gratified when Victor tilted his head and asked, "You so keen on keeping out of the eyes of the law, why'd you stay?"

Kin offered the shrug of one shoulder. He reminded himself to proceed with caution. "On account of what I heard them discussing. And me trying to decide if the risks of making an attack on my own were worth it."

"The risks of making an attack on your own? What're you talking about kid?"

"Well now," Kin lifted his pot of coffee and poured it carefully into his mug. "I don't mind sharing my coffee with strangers, but that's about where my generosity ends."

Just as he'd suspected, Victor drew his knife and had him

by the throat in an instant. His coffee sloshed over his hand. Blazes! He should have taken that into consideration!

Victor leaned close with a menacing squint of his eyes. "Kid, you better start spilling them beans you're withholding before you find this knife stuck in your gullet."

Kin raised his hands. "All right. All right. All right." He gingerly pressed against Victor's hand that held the knife to his breadbasket. "They were discussing how they had to hurry the woman back to town on account of they had to ride out to guard a shipment of gold slated to arrive for their town's new bank this afternoon."

"We ain't heard nothing about a shipment of gold!"

Kin shrugged. "They seemed to talk like they'd been keeping it under their hats. Even mentioned the shipment will be lightly guarded so as not to draw attention to it."

Victor and Bobby exchanged a look. "And this shipment is supposed to arrive today, you say?"

Kin spread his hands. "Only telling you what I heard them say."

Victor gave him a shake and then started patting him down, feeling all his pockets. "You must have overheard more'n that since you seemed to think you had enough information to make an attack. Bobby check his horse for money."

Kin was thankful he'd thought ahead to hide the money the marshal had given him. Careful to keep his hands in plain view, he shook his head. "I heard them mention the big bend as a place of concern, is all. I was trying to figure out where that might be. I haven't come across any sharp bends in the road coming in from the northwest, so I figure it has to be somewhere southeast of here."

Victor thought for a moment and then he patted Kin's cheek and sheathed his knife. "Kid, I see you again and I won't let you live to take another breath, got it? You just take yourself on outta this area and forget you ever heard about that shipment of gold!"

Kin nodded violently. "Y-yessir. I will. You won't see me again." He held his breath. Had he overplayed the terrified kid?

Apparently not, because Victor strode into the woods and a moment later returned with two horses. "Bobby, let's ride."

Bobby was still rubbing his head and grumbling as he swung into the saddle, but he rode away without another look in Kin's direction.

When they were out of sight, Kin released a breath and sank onto his haunches. He stared into the fire for several seconds and then set to packing his gear.

He needed to ride to Cle Elum for the next step in the plan. And he was going to have to be forceful if he was to keep people from getting hurt.

After that, well maybe he'd get in a couple good licks when it came time to round up the outlaws. He owed those men at least a couple blows.

Chapter Twenty-one

Lenny cussed and kicked at a rock, then paced back and forth along the banks of the small creek they had camped on.

All his plans to trade the woman for gold, up in smoke!

This was what came of sending his lackies to do his bidding instead of going himself. Yet he'd feared that someone might have been able to trail them to the cave because they'd been moving too fast to properly cover their trail, so it had been safer to send Bobby and Victor to fetch the woman. It irritated him that he'd been right. She was gone, yet why hadn't the lawmen stuck around to await their return? "You're certain she was gone?"

"That cave was as empty as Tommy's head."

Lenny spun and glowered. He didn't like it when the men disparaged Tommy like that and Bobby knew it.

Bobby looked down and shuffled his feet. "The woman was gone, I swear. Besides, the drifter said he seen the lawmen take the woman away."

"Drifter? What drifter?" Lenny bounced his focus between Victor and Bobby. Why was he only just now hearing about a drifter? And what were the chances that a drifter just happened to be camping near the cave where their prisoner had gone missing?

Victor shrugged one shoulder, but when the corner of his

mouth lifted, Lenny's attention snapped into sharp focus. "The woman's gone, but we got some news might be more profitable."

Eyes narrowing, Lenny reminded himself to breathe. "What are you talking about?"

Victor explained the whole scenario from Bobby almost killing the drifter to him blabbing about how the law had hurried off to guard a gold shipment set to arrive this afternoon, concluding with, "So if we can capture this shipment of gold, it won't matter that they found the woman. We'll be richer than our wildest dreams."

Lenny rubbed his jaw. A shipment of gold arriving *might* explain why the lawmen hadn't stuck around to set a trap. And it didn't really matter *how* he got his hands on the gold, whether by theft or by trade. "You believed this drifter?"

Victor shrugged. "We had a knife to his throat. Can't see as how he would lie under those circumstances."

"They were worried about an attack near the big bend, you said? I know just where that's at." He grinned, suddenly feeling like all the risks might be worth it. "But I've a better place in mind. Someplace they'll never suspect. Get some rest boys! We ride in two hours."

However, as he settled onto his bedroll by the fire, a niggling doubt of caution raised its head. This all seemed a little bit like it had fallen from the sky, didn't it? Still, if it *was* true...

He'd be able to get out of this area. Maybe buy himself a sweet spread with lots of cowhands to do the work somewhere far enough away from here that his name wouldn't be known and he didn't have to duck the law all the time.

He clasped his hands behind his head and stared up at the dome of blue sky overhead.

They would proceed with caution. But, yes, they would proceed. The potential reward, far outweighed the risks.

Washington stood just inside the edge of the forest looking out on the Kastain house, like the coward he was. He chuckled at himself and rubbed the back of his neck. He didn't have long before he was to meet Deputy Joe and the marshal in town, but he'd told himself he wanted to stop by to give Belle her painting. The truth, however, had hounded him all the way from home. He wanted to chat with Zoe. Hang it. Even just catching a glimpse of her would bolster him through another few hours. He didn't quite understand his recent captivation with her, yet it couldn't be denied.

She'd been a bit distant ever since the morning her pa died, which was to be expected he supposed. But he wanted to make sure she was all right before he rode out on this morning's excursion with the deputy and the marshal.

Footsteps crunched behind him and he spun around, hand dropping to his pistol.

Head down, Zoe strode along the path, a bowl of mushrooms tucked against her side.

Wash relaxed and then immediately tensed up again. She hadn't noticed him and any sound he made was going to startle her. Plus, what was she going to think about him lurking here?

But there was nothing for it. He couldn't just stand here and watch her come. "Zoe?"

She jolted to a stop and clutched the bowl closer, then relaxed upon seeing him. "Wash. You startled me."

"Yeah. Sorry."

He studied her. She looked a little more rested than she had yesterday at her pa's funeral, but there were still dark circles under her eyes and a droop to her shoulders. Was it possible that she'd shed a few pounds too? She'd always been slender, but today her cheekbones seemed more prominent than ever. And though she'd always been pale, her freckles stood out more than usual.

He tilted his head. "You been eating?"

She frowned and scuffed at the trail with the toe of her shoe. "Not been much hungry lately."

"You've gotta eat, Zo."

She plucked one of the mushrooms from the bowl and nibbled a bite from the top. "There. Happy?"

"More than mushrooms."

She smirked, plunked it back into the bowl, and wrinkled her nose. "Not very tasty without garlic and onions, anyhow."

He smiled, more to set her at ease than because he found her attempt at humor amusing. He worried about her always taking care of others and putting herself last.

She searched his face and then looked away to concentrate on the hole she continued to dig with her toe. "You need something?"

Only this. Time with her. But he couldn't say that sentimental gibberish. Instead he blurted. "Joe and Zane have deputized Kin and me. We're going with them to round up the outlaws who captured Mrs. Callahan."

Her eyes widened. "You're a lawman?"

Pride swelled through him, even though he knew it shouldn't. "I wanted to let you know that I plan to give your family the money I make. It's likely only a temporary job, so it might not be much—"

Zoe was already shaking her head. "No, Wash. Ma won't want to take it."

He curled a hand around the back of his neck. "Well, she won't have much say if it just appears in a package on your kitchen porch, I suppose. She won't know who it's from."

Zoe folded her arms. "But I'll know."

"And you won't tell because you'll know what a relief it is to your ma."

Her lips thinned into a hard line, but she apparently chose not to fight him on it any longer. "When do you leave to help catch the outlaws?"

"Soon as I leave here. They think the attack will come near the big bend."

Her gaze softened in a way that had his heart pounding. "Be careful out there, hmmm?"

"We will be."

She tipped a nod to the painting. "What's that?"

He held up the rolled canvas. "The other day, Belle dropped this painting. She was in such a state that I was afraid what she might do if I gave it back to her right away. But... I wanted to return it. She's very good."

Zoe's face lit up. "Oh! She was worried she lost it. We searched all over. Thank you!" She paused, and her expression turned melancholy. "She wanted Pa to see it before... Well, she was bringing it to him that morning. It crushed her that she was one day too late."

He didn't know what to say to that. Yet one more reminder that the days a man had were short and known only to the Almighty.

She stepped closer. "I've been so excited to see it. Do you mind?" She set the bowl of mushrooms on a nearby stump and held her hand out for the canvas.

He handed it to her.

She unrolled and stretched it wide. "Oh..." The word was an exclamation of awe.

Wash nodded. He had looked at the painting often in the last few days. He couldn't fathom how Belle put such lifelike reality into every detail of the piece. Whatever story Zoe's pa was telling was almost palpable. The laughter could almost be heard. The wagon wheels practically rolled the whole scene right out of the canvas.

Wash stepped behind Zoe and peered over her shoulder. "She could make a living doing this."

Zoe nodded. "That's what Pa always told her. But Ma... she wants different for Belle. She feels a woman's place is in the home. I fear she and Belle will never come to terms over Belle's art."

He glanced over at her. "It's not your job to fix things between them though."

She turned her head and started to speak, but something made her stop.

Everything in him stilled. She was so close. He settled a hand against her back before he thought better of it. "Zo..." He leaned forward almost without thought.

Her lashes fluttered and her tongue darted over her lips.

Almost at the same moment they both reeled back from each other.

Wash scooped a hand through his hair and paced a few steps away from her. What was he thinking? Had he been about to kiss her? He'd never even contemplated kissing a girl before! And this was Zoe! The girl who was practically more sibling than anything. He spun to face her.

Her hands trembled as she rolled up the canvas, tucked it beneath one arm, and then scooped up the bowl of mushrooms. "Uh, I should get back to the house. Ma is probably already worried that I've taken so long."

"Zoe, I didn't mean to—"

"Thank you for returning Belle's painting. It means the world to us to have it back. Oh and please thank your pa for sending Lincoln and Grant to chop wood for us. They did a wonderful job and we have wood to last us well into next spring now, I'm sure."

Hang it, this was no good. Now that the thought had lodged in his mind, he couldn't seem to banish it. He strode toward her, studying those moving lips of hers They were the shade of summer watermelon, and her top lip was shaped like Kin Davis's bow, while the bottom one was full and round.

She continued her babbling, her eyes widening with each step he drew nearer. "Anyhow, I'd best be going before Ma sends out a posse to find—"

Words seemed to fail her as he slowly took her by both shoulders and leaned past that blasted bowl of mushrooms. He drew in a breath and pressed his lips to hers. They were as supple and soft as a rose petal. Pliant and responsive and—

She'd just lost her father. What was he thinking? He drew back and cleared his throat, thrusting his hands deep into his pockets so he wouldn't be tempted to touch her again. "Tell Belle I said I really like the painting."

She blinked and nodded, blue eyes wide as saucers.

He gripped the back of his neck and forced himself to walk away. He really oughtn't to have kissed her like that, because now all he could think of was when he might get the chance to do it again.

❧❧❧

Zoe willed her heart to quit battering her ribs as she watched Wash walk away. What had that been about? She lifted a finger to touch her lips, relishing the lingering feeling of contentment that had zipped through her the moment his lips touched hers.

She'd always imagined that a kiss would be something a

wife had to endure out of duty. Never in her wildest dreams had she imagined that it might be something pleasant.

She felt her face flame and spun to hurry toward the house. Wife, indeed. She wasn't Wash's wife or anything even close to it and it was best she remember that, because if there was one thing Ma had always emphasized it was that kisses were only to be shared between a man and his wife. She would be sorely disappointed that Zoe had allowed such an intimacy. In fact, it was better not spoken of. Besides, Wash had looked a little... sorry? disappointed? disillusioned?...afterwards. So it wasn't likely to happen again.

She pushed through the back door and set the bowl of mushrooms on the sideboard. The bowl clattered like Aiden's top when it was about to fall. She quickly reached out to steady it. But too late, it had already caught Ma's attention.

She paused, shoulders hunched over the bread she'd been kneading at the table. She swept Zoe with an assessing glance. "What's the matter?"

"Nothing." Zoe only allowed herself the briefest moment of guilt for the deception. "Is Belle here? I have her painting."

Ma rubbed a wrist over her forehead, leaving a streak of flour before she resumed kneading. "She's sweeping the front porch."

Zoe started past the table. "I'll just go tell her the good news."

"Zoe? Where did you find the painting?"

"Belle dropped it in the yard and Washington"—too late, she realized that Ma had just figured out what had caused her discomposure—"found it and returned it just now."

"I see." Ma whacked the bread with a fist and Zoe got the distinct impression she might be envisioning Washington Nolan's face.

"I'll just..." She pointed toward the front porch and made her escape before Ma could ask any more probing questions.

Belle worked near the far rail with the straw broom in her hands.

Zoe hurried toward her. "Belle, Wash had your painting. He returned it just now and, oh, it's lovely!"

Belle gave a little squeal and chucked the broom against the railing. She clutched the painting to her chest. "Wash had it? How did he get it?"

"You dropped it that morning when you came home. He said to tell you he thinks it's very good."

Belle unrolled it and studied it with a critical eye. "All I can see are all the spots where I could have done better."

"Well stop it. It's amazing!" Zoe took one side of the canvas and draped her arm around Belle's waist. She dropped her head onto Belle's shoulder as they looked at the picture together. "I miss him." Tears blurred her vision.

Belle sniffed. "Me too." She paused for a moment but then hurried to say, "I think I'm going to go to Seattle and enroll in the Territorial University of Washington."

Zoe lifted her gaze to assess Belle's seriousness.

Belle nodded. "I read in the paper that they are building a new campus this year and that they are accepting more female students—even building special dorms for women. Did you know that their first graduate was a woman? Imagine! And they have a degree for artists, but..." She bit her lower lip and squinted her eyes at Zoe. "I think I'm going to need your help to convince Ma."

"Oh Belle!" Zoe drew Belle tighter to her side. "I'll do my best, but she's not going to be happy about it."

Belle eased back and swiped at her cheeks with a nod. "I know. But Pa would have wanted this for me."

"Yes. He would have." Zoe reached out to gently touch Pa's face on the painting. "You should show it to her. Maybe when she sees how good you've become, she'll realize that you have to utilize this talent."

Belle sniffed. "Not likely."

Zoe gave her sister one last squeeze. "Give her a chance. I'd best get inside and help her finish up dinner."

Zoe was truly happy for her sister to go off to fulfill her dreams, but as she walked away from Belle, Zoe felt her emotions deflate.

Because if Belle was going to defy Ma and go off to artistry schooling, then it would even more so fall to Zoe to be the good daughter who didn't cause Ma any heartache.

And that definitely meant no more kissing Washington Nolan.

She gave a little nod. Later she'd walk to the Nolan place and let him know it could never happen again.

Chapter Twenty-two

≈≈≈≈≈≈≈≈≈

Jacinda stood at the window in her room, looking through the lace curtains toward the new bank building. Construction was almost complete now and according to Dixie, who had stopped by a bit earlier to bring food, the new banker, Merle Olann, had arrived in town last evening searching for land to build his young wife and daughter a home. As soon as he got the house built, his wife would bring their baby daughter from back east.

Jacinda glanced over her shoulder toward her door. She'd told Zane she wanted to rest, but the truth was, despite Doc's pain powders, she hadn't been able to get Zane's admonitions out of her head all day.

He was right. She did like to smooth everyone's way. If she could, she would go through life hauling a cart of pillows so she might quickly thrust one under anyone who was about to experience a bump of any sort. And he was also right, that she'd only started that after Wade had passed. She had been torn asunder by his death. By watching Reagan grow up without a father. And she'd done the very best she could to protect him from further pain. And that had, she supposed, spilled into other relationships in her life. And then, in turn, rebounded to protect her own heart.

And he was also right that it was time to let that all go.

To risk again.

Because she didn't want to keep living in the sin of worry.

She'd spent a good deal of time flipping through her Bible this afternoon despite the fact that her head had ached each time she focused on the words. And each passage had confirmed Zane's words. Yes, being a servant and serving others was a good thing, but her attitude and reason for doing it needed to change.

She wasn't sure how she would accomplish a change of heart, but she aimed to try. And maybe with Zane's help and a lot of pleading with God to realign her focus, she could bring her life back into line with God's Word.

But that wasn't the scariest part of the whole thing. Not by a long shot.

She had also realized that Zane was correct about the reasons she'd been keeping him at arm's length. It was the worry not of loving but of losing someone again. So if she wanted to take her newfound resolve all the way, she needed to see whether this attraction between her and Zane could grow into full bloom.

And if she was going to tell him before she lost her nerve, she'd best go and find him right now.

She slipped out her door and carefully held the rail as she made her way down the stairs.

He wasn't in the parlor. Wasn't in her sewing room, nor the dining room. She met him, just as he stepped out of the kitchen with a tea tray in his big hands. The tiny silver handles of the tray looked at odds in his broad muscular grip.

He assessed her from head to toe and back again. "A little soon for you to be below-stairs, isn't it? How's your head?"

Fingers trembling, she laid her hand over the back of his. "A little soon for you to be lifting tea trays, isn't it? How's your shoulder?" She took in his lack of sling with pinched lips, but reminded herself of her newfound determination not to worry.

One corner of his mouth quirked up. "I won't deny that Doc's pain powders tempted me a fair bit last night, but I wanted to be fully alert if I needed to be. I may have slept better had I taken them, but I did get several hours sleep and I feel some better today. Now it's your turn."

She smiled. "I won't deny that I was also tempted to take more of Doc's pain powders, but I wanted to be in my right mind for a discussion I'd like to have with you."

His brows shot upward. He swallowed. His gaze slipped over her features. "Maybe I should set this tray down."

"Yes. Maybe you should."

He strode to the table and slid the tray onto it.

Jacinda followed him and lifted the teapot. "In fact, why don't you fetch yourself a cup and we can both have some tea?"

He glanced at the clock across the room and she immediately recognized his urgency.

"You have to go, don't you?"

"I'm afraid so. I was just bringing this up to you and then was going to head out on some...official business."

Her heart squeezed. Her pulse pattered. Her palms turned clammy. Official business meant he was going after the outlaws who'd chained her. Kidnapped Doc. Shot him.

And then in a blink she realized that she was worrying again. *Consider the Lilies.* Did she trust in God alone? She set the teapot down, pulled in a breath, and forcibly flexed her hands. She shouldn't even ask where he was off to. But she couldn't help herself. "Is this the plan I overheard you and Joe discussing? To set a trap for the outlaws?"

He folded his arms and his eyes narrowed a little. "It is."

"I don't like it, Zane. It's so dangerous." She settled trembling fingers over her heart.

He tilted his head, stepping closer to take her hand in his.

"That's part of the job. But these outlaws will know this run could be a decoy. They won't risk killing us outright because they'll want to see the gold first. They'll keep us alive long enough to see if they need us for information. By the time they figure out the gold isn't real, we'll have captured them. What did you want to discuss?" He thumbed a caress over her knuckles.

Jacinda searched his face. Was he telling her the truth? Or just some made up story to set her mind at ease. He wouldn't do that, would he?

She dropped her focus to their hands. His was broad and brown and sturdy. It engulfed hers with warmth and comfort. Would she ever see him again? Have the opportunity to settle her hand into the strength of his? And if she did, a moment just like this would come again in the future—one where she stood and watched him ride away into danger—because this was who he was. A man who sacrificed his own safety for the good of the community he was sworn to protect.

The risk terrified her, and yet the very characteristics that made him that hero were what made him worth loving. And she was finally ready. Joy bloomed, and she lifted a contented smile. She would tell him. But now was not the time.

"Jac?"

She remembered that he waited for her to state her reason for wanting to speak to him. "We can talk another time if you need to be on your way."

He stepped closer, obviously curious about her smile. "I have a few minutes."

Pressing her lips together, she traced one finger over the stubble of his jaw. "What I have to say would be better unrushed. It will wait till you get back."

He touched her chin, his brows arching with hope. "Tell me

it's something I'll want to hear and I'll do my best to hurry back as quickly as I can."

"It is something you'll want to hear."

"Well, I'll be." His finger stroked a warm trail across her jawline. "Tonight then. And not a moment later."

With a long slow inhale, she willed her heartrate to return to normal. "Lilies are such a beautiful flower, don't you think?"

A soft smile tugged at the corner of his mouth. "That's my girl."

"Be careful out there."

"Always." With that, he let his hand drop, and strode from the room.

Jacinda's eyes fell closed. *Lord, I'm trying to trust in You alone, but there's nothing wrong with praying for the safety of those we love, is there? Please keep Zane and the others safe, and bring these outlaws to justice.*

Kin rode into Cle Elum and reined his mount to a stop at the hitching post by the livery. He'd retrieved the money Marshal Zane had given him for hiring the wagon, and now it weighed heavy in his pocket.

The bawdy music of a mostly out-of-tune piano called to him. He swallowed and didn't even let himself look toward the saloon. The townsfolk of Wyldhaven had been good to him for a lot of years. He wouldn't repay their kindness by stealing their money and spending it on drink.

"Howdy there! What can I do ya for?" The Cle Elum liveryman was even more ancient than old Bill in Wyldhaven.

Kin stuck out his hand. "Afternoon. I'm here to hire a wagon and a driver. Can pay extra if the driver can prove he's a crack shot. Name's Davis. Kin Davis."

That made the old man squint up his eyes as he took Kin's hand. "I charges extry for every last bullet hole I find when you return my wagons." His handshake was as limp as a dead fish. Something Parson Clay would have had a say about. The parson despised tepid handshakes.

Kin nodded. "I'm good for it."

"Are ya now?" The old man assessed him from head to toe. "Well, I suppose I'll havta take yer word for it." He spat a stream of tobacco into one corner and waved a hand for Kin to follow. "I'll show ya the wagons I got back here. But I ain't got no driver for ya. There's a fire out to one o' the nearby ranches and every last man round these parts is off a helpin'."

Kin paused. The marshal had emphasized that he needed to be in the back of the wagon, out of sight so that none of the outlaws recognized him, but he hadn't said what to do if there was no available driver. "Can you drive it? Just to Wyldhaven?"

The old man cackled as if that was the funniest thing he'd heard in a long time. "No sirree, not I. I knows a s'picious job when I hears about it. 'Sides... I cain't see worth a lick no more. You don't want this ol' coot shootin' at whate'er's gonna be shootin' back. These here are the wagons I got."

Kin lifted his hat and scratched at the back of his head.

One of the wagons was exactly what he needed. It even had a large crate nailed into the wagon bed that would make a perfect hiding place and double to make the outlaws think it was where the gold lay hidden.

"I'll take this one." He handed over the payment and waited for the old man to jot his notations in his book. Through the livery doors, Kin studied the buildings along the street, wondering what he should do now. "You sure there's not a driver available in town?"

"Kid, you callin' me a liar?"

Kin shook his head. "No, sir."

"I'm tellin' you, every man jack o' them is out to the Bar M helpin' fight that blaze. Even the saloon is closed."

Kin frowned. "But I heard singing."

The old man waved a hand and tucked Kin's payment into his desk drawer. "That's just Ray's girls, takin' advantage o' the fact that all the men be outta town."

Kin's brows lifted. Saloon girls.

He took up the poke with the remainder of the money and thrust it inside his shirt pocket, then grinned at the old man. "Get the wagon hitched and I'll be back for it."

It only took him a few minutes to walk down to the saloon, and when he pushed through the doors, he could see that the old man had been right. The only occupants of the room were three soiled doves.

One played the piano, while the other two lounged atop it and sang drunkenly off key. They all stopped and stared at him.

After a moment, one of the ones on the piano slid off and sidled his way. At least he presumed she was trying to sidle. In truth, she barely kept her balance as she staggered through the card tables and chairs.

"Well lookee here, girls." She giggled uproariously. "It's a genuine man still about town." She crashed into Kin's chest and blinked up into his face. "Hi, sugar." Her breath wafted over him and he couldn't withhold a grimace. Was this what he was like when he'd been drinking?

Kin set her from him and focused on the piano player—the only one of the three who seemed like she might be mostly sober.

He swallowed. The woman was large. She was taller than

him, and at least two times his weight and he was just over a hundred and seventy pounds. She closed the cover on the piano keys and stood. "Girl's we'd best call it an afternoon. Head up to your rooms and get some sleep, aye?"

"Aw! She wants the lad for herself."

The other two women stumbled up the stairs, lolling all over each other and laughing until they were in tears.

The large woman folded her arms and stepped out from behind the piano. She had a way of moving that made him thankful he wasn't on her bad side...yet. "What can I do for you, lad?"

Kin was already debating the wisdom of his decision, but he didn't really have any other choice, so he plunged ahead. "You know how to drive a wagon?"

She tilted her head and then burst out laughing. "That's just about the last thing I figured you might ask."

Kin only waited.

Finally, she regained her composure and nodded.

"Know how to handle a gun?"

"Honey, Ray didn't hire me to protect his gals because o' my looks."

"It's dangerous work, but you'd be paid."

She offered a condescending grimace. "In my line of work, everything is dangerous. Lead the way."

Kin stepped outside, rolling his eyes at himself. He was likely never going to hear the end of this from the fellas.

***

Zane stepped onto the porch and bent to make sure his holster was tightly tied. Blast the timing of all this. What he really wanted to do was go back in the house and see what Jacinda had to say, but her safety had to come first. He, Joe and Wash needed to get going if they were to meet the wagon that Kin should have headed this way from Cle Elum by now.

As he stalked toward the livery, Zane shook his head, still unable to fathom that circumstances had dictated that Kin Davis become a deputy. He sure hoped they weren't going to regret the need for that decision.

Joe and Wash were already at the livery, and old Bill was just tightening the cinch on his own horse's saddle.

He nodded at the old man. "Thanks, Bill."

Bill slapped a hand to Zane's good shoulder. "Go catch 'em."

"Aim to."

Taking the back way through the hills, they were able to cut several miles off the distance to Cle Elum and they met Kin and the wagon just this side of the town.

All three of them pulled up on the hillside, studied the scene below, and then looked at one another.

A woman—a very large woman—was driving the wagon. And she was singing at the top of her voice. Zane would have sworn it was the wrong wagon, except that was definitely Kin's horse tied to the back of it.

"What has he gotten us into?"

Joe shrugged in his typical silent demeanor and clucked to his horse, angling down the hill.

Zane looked at Wash. "Remember you and Davis are the aces up our sleeves. Stay out of sight. Stay quiet. And whatever you do, don't risk your life if it comes to that. You've still got a whole lot of living to do."

Wash swallowed. "Yes, sir."

Zane followed Joe down to the road and settled in to ride on the opposite side of the wagon from him.

The woman didn't look at either of them, but stopped her

singing long enough to speak. "Howdy, gentlemen. Name's Kitty." She lowered her voice. "Your boy is in the back there."

Kin's voice emerged, muffled from inside the box. "And it's hotter than He...Gehenna under here."

Zane smirked. "Doubt that, kid. Seriously doubt that." He scanned the hills around them as he spoke. "No offense, ma'am. But how is it that you've come to be driving this wagon?"

The woman gave a deep laugh that threatened to jostle her off the seat. "I was the kid's only choice. Don't be too hard on him. 'Sides, I can bark squirrels with the best o' them so I figure I can hit the sorry hide of a good for nothing outlaw."

Zane hoped she could back up her claims.

He and Joe had talked extensively and they assumed that the attack would come just south of Wyldhaven where the wagon would have to slow considerably for the sharp curve in the road. They'd even had Kin mention it to plant the idea. That place would give Wash his best shots from up on the surrounding ridges. It also was tight enough that the outlaws wouldn't be able to spread out too much.

Yet, in reality, the attack could come at any time. Or not at all.

He just hoped that the temptation of a lightly guarded wagon full of gold would be enough to draw the outlaws out. Because he was ready to mete out some justice to the men who had dared to kidnap Jacinda and chain her alone in a dark cave.

Yes, indeed. Some very severe justice.

❦

Lenny lay on his belly in the dirt behind a large boulder. Of all his men, he was in the safest place, which was just the way he liked it.

He just hoped the story the vagabond had told was true and there really was a wagon of gold coming down this road.

Then again, maybe it was simply his greed that had him hoping it was true. Maybe it was just a story that tramp had told to keep them from knowing he'd freed their prisoner.

At any rate they were here. Waiting.

But he'd told his men to let him know at the first sign if all was not as it should be. He'd stayed alive this long because of caution and he wasn't about to toss it into the outhouse now.

He'd set his men up well before the seemingly expected location of the big bend. The bend would be a good place for an attack for only one reason. And that was because the wagon would have to slow. The rest, well everything else would be better for those guarding the wagon.

No, this place suited his needs better. It was a nice wide spot where the wagon could keep up its speed, but the log they'd felled across the road would deal with that issue. And here in this wide flat area his men could spread out but still find enough scrubby junipers and boulders, that they had adequate cover too. The other good thing about this spot was that the hills sort of flattened out here and that meant anyone riding overwatch up on the ridge wouldn't have such a height advantage on them.

Yes. He smiled. This was a good place.

In that moment, he heard the trundle of the wagon wheels and the squeak of a seat's shocks.

He took a breath, willing himself to stay calm.

His men knew what to do and if they pulled this off, he would soon be the richest man in all of Washington State.

He grinned. His men didn't need to know that he didn't plan to share with them. No, sir. They didn't need to know that, at all.

Chapter Twenty-three

Wash rode along the ridge above the road, watching every shadow or flicker of movement down in the canyon closely, and straining his ears to take in every sound.

So far nothing seemed out of the ordinary.

The sun still blazed at a mid-afternoon angle. Bees droned by every once in a while, laden down with pollen so thick they appeared to be flying yellow dandelion puffs. The birds remained quiet in the heat, but a soft breeze had picked up and should soon have things cooled down. Everything normal for this time of day.

He caught sight of the pink buds of a wild sweet pea. The color took his mind to fanciful thoughts of Zoe's lips and her sweet soft kiss, and he rolled his eyes and forced himself to concentrate on the here and now. If he let his mind wander, there might never be the chance for another of those sweet kisses.

But hang it, how his heart had hammered at the way she'd flushed so prettily and swept her tongue over those pink lips after he'd pulled away—

He grimaced. There he went again—

A bird chirped from the bushes ahead.

He sat bolt upright and dropped his hand to his pistol. The ridge he'd been riding on had sloughed slowly toward the valley floor, and though he was back from the road a good way, he was almost level with the wagon now.

But that bird... Something about it hadn't seemed quite right. Another echoed from across the canyon and Wash's pulse spiked into a full-out gallop. Those were no birds.

He shucked his rifle and searched the brush ahead of him, trying to see the man on his side of the road, but he must be well-camouflaged, wherever he was.

Down on the road, he saw the wagon slow and then come to a stop. Zane and Joe pulled up too. They were looking at something ahead.

Wash craned his neck to see around some brush and his heart sank. The outlaws had felled a tree across the road.

This was it, then. There would be a full-out gun battle.

And he and Kin might be the only advantage keeping the lawmen and Miss Kitty from stepping into eternity today!

He swung down from his saddle and propped his shoulder against a tree as he cocked his rifle.

He was ready.

※ ※ ※

Lenny was ready to give the signal for the attack when Victor slid down the hill and landed beside him with a clatter of rock that nearly sent Lenny's heart lurching from his chest. But of course he couldn't reveal his nerves.

He swung a glower at Victor. "What are you doing here? We're just about to take this wagon."

"That's why I'm here, boss." He held out a pair of binoculars and tipped a nod. "You see that horse tied to the back of the wagon?"

Lenny pushed his hand away. His eyes were just fine. "Of course I see it! You think I'm blind?"

"That drifter I told you about? That's his horse."

Lenny came to full attention. "You sure? Give me the glasses." He snatched up the field glasses and studied the wagon. It was still far enough away that it was hard to make out details. But the two riders, he recognized with a growing dread. He'd expected the deputy. But he'd really hoped that the marshal might still be incapacitated by his bullet wounds. Yet there he was.

"I'm certain. That horse was picketed at the vagabond's campsite, just this morning."

Lenny rolled his eyes. His men really weren't the smartest crew around. His anger started to boil until he remembered that their lack of wits would serve him well, soon enough. He studied the faces of the riders. "Which one of these two played the drifter? Neither of you recognized one of Wyldhaven's two lawmen posing as a tramp?"

"That's just it, boss." Victor shook his head. "It weren't neither o' them, and that's God's honest truth."

Heart clambering, Lenny swung the glasses and searched the hills around them. "This is a—" He flapped a hand. "Tell the men! It's a trap!"

Zane searched the low hills around them, turning his horse in a full circle. "You see anything?" he asked Joe.

Joe shook his head.

Kitty now held a Colt Single Action in her meaty hand. "That tree looks fresh-felled. Why haven't they made their attack?"

Zane shook his head, feeling the skin along the back of his neck prickle. "Something isn't right." He looked for Wash, but the kid was doing an admirable job of keeping out of sight.

Joe fiddled with his reins. "What now?"

Zane considered. "If we're to keep up appearances, I say we move the log and keep going."

Joe nodded. "My thoughts too."

"What's going on out there?" Kin's words were low enough to be heard but not carry.

Zane swung down from his horse. "Hold your britches, kid. There's a log in the road we're going to move. Stay alert. They could attack at any minute."

Kin grumbled something, but Zane was already leading his mount toward the log. Joe unhooked the rope strapped to his saddle, and stepped down to loop it around one end of the log. He tossed the other end to Zane.

Both of them kept an eye on the hills as they worked, and Zane was thankful to see that Kitty kept a watchful eye out, also.

Sweat trickled down his forehead and he swiped at it with the back of his hand. His spine kept tingling as he imagined the Smith Gang sighting down on him. A bullet to the shoulder had been bad enough. He didn't want to take one to the back as well. But he forced himself to keep working.

He looped the rope around his saddle horn and clucked to his horse, then led it down the road until the rope was stretched good and tight. For now, all they had to do was move one end of the log far enough that the wagon could get past. They could come back and saw the log to clear the road more fully later.

With the rope tight, he clucked to the horse once more and the muscles along its haunches bunched up as it put all its strength into the pull.

Joe sat on the road behind the log and used his legs to push against it. That gave it the start it needed and after that, Zane's horse was able to keep it moving fairly easily.

All through the whole process, the area around them remained silent and the only movement they saw was the dance of heatwaves along the horizon.

Zane blew out a breath as he swung back into the saddle. Maybe their trap wasn't going to work after all.

❧

Wash remained in his place by the tree, keeping vigilant watch for any movement as Zane and Joe worked on clearing the tree. He was careful to keep back in the shade as he used his glasses to search the surrounding hills just like Pa had taught him. He didn't want to be the cause of the marshal's and Joe's deaths because he carelessly let a glint of reflected sunlight reveal his location.

But even with the glasses, he saw no one.

His chest felt tight and his breaths were shallow.

What was he missing? He had to be missing something.

That was when he felt the cold press of steel against the back of his neck.

Eyes falling closed, he raised his hands.

He had failed.

❧

Lenny paced as he waited in the small canyon away from the road. His men lounged on boulders or in the grass, waiting his instructions. All except Lightning Jim. He'd sent Jim to scout the surrounding area.

Jim may have failed him when it came to killing the deputy, but he was the best tracker they had. The outlaw could move so silently through the forest that it made a man all aquiver with the anxiety of it. More than once, Lenny had thought twice about how he spoke to the man because he knew if Jim wanted him dead, he could make it happen, and likely even before Lenny knew he was there.

They didn't have long to wait before Jim rode into the canyon with a sullen boy riding before him, hands tied to the saddle horn.

Lenny looked at Victor. "This the kid?"

Victor shook his head. "Never seen that one before."

Lenny cursed.

Jim smirked, causing Lenny's irritation to soar.

"What?"

Jim tipped his head toward the bound rider. "Take another look."

Lenny didn't like his tone that seemed to say he was missing something. But when his gaze settled on the kid again, he realized there *was* something familiar about him. He just couldn't pin it down. He returned his focus to Jim.

Jim's smirk ratcheted up another notch as he nudged the kid forward. "This is the kid who was in the alley with the doc before we snatched him. The one who went for the deputy."

Recognition swept through Lenny. "Ah yes. The kid you missed killing along with the deputy." As Jim's smirk fell away, satisfaction spread.

"Yeah."

The kid turned wide eyes on his captor.

Lenny's irritation reared. He swept a motion. "Get him down. We need to find out what he knows." He pointed to a rock. "That rock there will do nicely, gents."

Jim didn't wait for any of the others to rise to his aid. He untied the knots in the rope, then wrapped one fist into the kid's shirt and yanked him from the saddle. He shoved him to a seat on the rock.

Hands still bound, the kid bounced a look between them.

Lenny folded his arms. "What's your name, kid?"

"Washington Nolan." There was a spark of defiance in his eyes.

"You from around here?"

The boy hesitated for only a moment before he answered, "Born and raised."

"Well, Washington Nolan, born and raised in Wyldhaven, what can you tell me about that wagon the lawmen are hauling?

The boy shook his head. "Not a thing."

"What's in it?"

The kid gave a shrug. "I was riding through the woods and heard the wagon. Got curious and went over to take a look. Then your man here put a gun to my head."

Lenny looked to Jim for his assessment of the kid's tale.

Jim shook his head and spat a stream of tobacco. "Overwatch."

Lenny struck hard and fast and with all the fury pent up inside him for the weeks of failure to make this outlaw life pay off.

The kid's head snapped back and a trickle of red seeped down his split cheek. "I don't take kindly to being lied to, boy."

Wiping the blood on his shoulder, the boy narrowed his eyes. "I don't know what you think I'd have to lie about. If you think there's something so all-fired interesting in that wagon, why would they be transporting it with so few men? I only saw the two deputies and whoever that was driving the wagon."

Lenny settled his hands on his hips. That was true enough. But... "What about that horse tied to the back of the wagon. You ever seen that before?"

There was a brief flicker in the kid's eyes. It was only the slightest of nuances, but Lenny noticed it before the kid blinked it away. "Can't say as I have."

Lenny struck him again. "I told you I don't like being lied to."

"No more than I like being suspected of lying!" The kid's jaw bunched. His eye was already swelling shut.

Lenny paced a couple steps and, this time, put his frustration into kicking a rock. It skittered away, bouncing to a stop along the base of the canyon wall. He propped his hands on his hips and considered. The kid obviously had mettle and it wasn't likely to be easy to make him talk. And they didn't have time to be wasting here if they were going to stop that wagon before it reached Wyldhaven. They wouldn't have had a man riding overwatch if they didn't have something to protect. So that strengthened the story they'd heard from the tramp.

The empty horse though... That mystery taunted him. How had the drifter's horse come to be tied to the back of that wagon? And where was he?

He stalked over, took the kid by the front of his shirt, and hauled him to his feet. "All right. We'll try this another way." He swept a gesture toward Jim as he looked deep into the kid's eyes. "Lightning Jim there grew up in Apache country, did you know that? Course you didn't, but that makes no nevermind. But the Apaches, see, they have perfected the art of letting nature take care of their torture."

Jim was already hammering several long, hefty stakes into the ground on four corners of the rock the boy had sat on only moments earlier.

Lenny patted the kid on the cheek. "Don't worry, if you're still alive when we get back with the gold, maybe I'll use a bullet to put you out of your misery."

He nodded to Victor and Bobby, who stepped over to help him. A quick swipe of his knife cut the bonds on the kid's hands. They stripped his shirt off and with Victor on one side and Lenny on the other they held his arms for Jim to cinch loops of rawhide around each wrist. Bobby did the same around his ankles.

Apparently realizing he was outmanned, the kid didn't fight back, but his eyes gave plenty of clues to the anger pumping through him.

Lenny gave the kid credit for taking this like a man. Any fight would have proved futile, anyhow.

They forced the kid to lay back and tightened the long lengths of rawhide until he was stretched backward over the rock and splayed out like an X with wrists and ankles tied to the stakes.

"Th-th-that do-don't look very c-comfortable." Tommy winced.

The kid was already grimacing in anguish. Lenny had to admire the fact that he'd made no sound. But his torture had only just begun. He'd be screaming in pain before thirst, dehydration, and sunburn took him.

Jim cuffed the back of Tommy's head. "Idiot."

"Ow!" Tommy slunk away from Jim with a hurt look on his face.

Lenny clapped Tommy on one shoulder. "We don't want him to be comfortable, Tommy." He swung an arm over his head. "Mount up, men. Our gold awaits."

Chapter Twenty-four

Z ane wasn't sure what to think. Why would the outlaws drop a tree across the road but then not make an attack while the wagon was stopped?

He and Joe rode warily, hands resting on their pistols. Even Kitty had stopped her singing, for which Zane couldn't deny he was thankful.

He considered Wash somewhere in the hills and Kin in the back of the wagon. Both young men just in their prime. And Joe recently married with his whole life ahead. And Kitty was a woman! He didn't want any of their deaths on his conscience, and at this moment the three of them were like fish in a barrel. He didn't like this. Not at all. This whole thing—their plan—had been thrown together too quickly.

He kept an eye on the horses, knowing that they would likely hear anything before either he or Joe did.

Sure enough, only moments later the horses lifted their heads and pricked their ears.

"Joe."

"I see."

A horse trotted from around the curve ahead. It carried a bearded lean man with a pistol held easily in his right hand. "That's far enough, gents," he called out. Lightning Jim Roan sat before them, bold as could be.

Zane and Joe palmed their pistols as they reined to a stop.

Jim stretched for the sky. "Wait. Wait. Wait! We've got your man."

Joe and Zane looked at one another.

A quick assessment of the hills showed glimpses of men in several locations that proved they were surrounded. Zane clenched his teeth.

To give up was almost certain death, but what other choice did they have?

"What man?" he asked, stalling.

Jim shook his head. "No need to play dumb. We found him riding overwatch. I'm afraid he's a bit…tied up, and won't be able to come to your rescue." He leered.

Zane felt all his hopes drain away. Their one remaining card was Kin Davis? The rogue kid who'd only been deputized the evening before—and reluctantly at that? They were all dead men. And yet…if they could get Jim to open the lid of the box, maybe Kin could take him by surprise and they'd all have a fighting chance.

Joe and Kitty looked to him for their lead.

He shook his head, withholding a growl over the fact that their lives were dependent on Kin.

All three of them lifted their hands at the same time.

"Good." Jim nodded. "Toss your weapon's please, gentlemen." He leveled his pistol on them, once more. "I know you've seen you're surrounded."

They all complied, their guns landing in the dirt of the roadbed with a clatter.

"All of them! I know an ankle holster when I see one."

Zane pressed his lips together and withdrew that gun, tossing it as well. He heard Joe do the same.

"That's better. Now"—Jim swung his gun—"ride off and leave that wagon and you can be on your way."

They needed to get him to open that trunk!

Zane tilted the man a look. "Why you all so interested in a trunk full of women's fripperies?"

Jim's eyes narrowed. "Right," he scoffed.

Zane shrugged. He leaned his forearms against his pommel, aiming for a casual stance and trying to ignore the jab of fire in his shoulder. He grinned at Joe and, thankfully, Joe caught on quickly. He grinned back. Good they'd planted some doubt. Now to plant some more. He'd leave them wondering about the contents of the chest.

Jim opened his mouth, but Zane didn't let him get a word in.

He raised his voice so he could be heard by all the outlaws in the hills. "Here's the thing... You men who work for Smith... you honestly think he's going to equally split the contents of this trunk with you?"

"Equal shares!" One of the men called out his assurance.

Joe gave Zane a sideways glance. That told them where one of the outlaws was staked out.

"Shut up, all of you!" Jim bellowed.

Zane pressed his luck. "The rest of you boys actually believe that?"

"I-I-I be-believe it," called out a voice that was deep enough to belong to a man but which carried a childish ring.

Behind a boulder off to the right. Likely they didn't need to worry too much about that one.

To Zane's frustration, the rest of the men remained silent. But they now knew where two of the men were in addition to Lightning Jim. That was a start. How many more of them were there?

That day when he and Jacinda had been attacked on the road, there couldn't have been more than seven or eight of them. And Doc had said when he was taken, the one he treated wasn't likely to make it, and that in addition to Lenny, he'd counted only a handful of others.

If those numbers were accurate, with Jim in the road before them, and known locations for two more, that only left three or four men unaccounted for.

The odds were getting better all the time. But the difference between three and four might mean the difference between a win or a loss. His stomach clenched.

Zane kept his voice loud enough to carry. "This trunk is full of a little bit of nothing. Go ahead and open it. See for yourself."

Jim squirmed in his saddle. "That'll be up to the boss."

"Your boss too scared to come out and face us himself?"

He was disappointed when silence was his only greeting. He'd hoped to goad Smith into a response.

"Or maybe you're really the boss and just don't want us to know it?"

Jim smirked and Zane saw a glimmer of ambition in those depths. But all he said was, "I'm not the boss."

Beside him, Joe growled loudly. "Bad enough we're about to get shot over a trunk that didn't even need guarding, but for it to be done by a coward who won't look us in the eye? I say he's not the leader you seem to think he is!"

Jim's smirk grew. "Maybe he ain't."

There was only a moment before footsteps crunched on the roadbed behind them. Satisfaction curled through Zane. Maybe this plan hadn't gone all to pieces after all.

He turned his head slowly to see Lenny Smith stomping across the gravel. "I'm no coward, Jim, and you know it! You saw what I did to Jango!"

"Jango was just a dumb kid trying to find his place in this world." Jim spat to one side of his horse.

Kitty let out a low whistle. "Dissension in the ranks..."

"Shut up, woman!" Lenny snapped. His gaze honed in on Zane then. "And why do you keep saying this trunk is empty?! Do you take us for fools? We know it has the gold for the Wyldhaven bank in it!" He paused at the rear of the wagon, eyeing the trunk.

Zane considered giving him a nudge, but then decided to hold his silence. He didn't want to give away the ruse by being too insistent.

Lenny stood there for a long moment and Zane feared he wouldn't open the trunk.

But then with a huff of frustration, Lenny leapt into the bed of the wagon. He cursed. "There better be gold in this here box!"

He grasped the hasp and gave it a yank. Then he threw back the lid.

Zane saw dust puff from the front of Lenny's shirt pocket before he even heard the reverberation of Kin's shot.

Lenny staggered backwards, clutching his chest. Blood seeped between the outlaw's fingers, and his mouth gaped as he looked down to see his wound. His legs caved out from under him.

Kin leapt from inside the trunk.

Jim's eyes widened and he lifted his pistol!

Kin spun in their direction, swinging his gun to bear on Lightning Jim.

Zane could see he wasn't going to get his shot off in time! He lurched his horse into Jim's.

Jim's shot rang out!

The horses whinnied and side-stepped.

Kin toppled from the back of the wagon.

Zane closed his eyes in saddened defeat. He hadn't reacted in time.

The kid had done his best. But the reality was, their chances had been barely better than a hare in the claws of an eagle.

He couldn't see the kid from here but Kin made no sound nor did he rise.

Zane hung his head. This was his fault. He'd gotten the kid shot.

Jim glowered at them over the top of his pistol. "None of you move."

Three outlaws descended from the hills. All of them cast looks from the ground behind the wagon toward Lightning Jim at the front.

Jim glowered. "Any of you have a problem with me taking over leadership?"

"L-Lenny's b-been shot." The childish one crushed a felt hat against his chest.

Neither of the other men spoke. They merely held their guns pointed in their direction.

Jim nodded, apparently taking their silence as unstated permission. "Good. Now, you three are coming with me."

Zane frowned at Joe. Why would the man keep them alive?

Jim smirked. "I can see you are wondering what use I might have for you."

Behind them, Lenny moaned. "Jim!" His voice rattled in the back of his throat as he dragged himself partway from behind the wagon where he had fallen. "Help me." His fingers clawed around a handful of dirt.

Jim didn't even glance his way. "You see now that I've heard there is a bank opening in Wyldhaven, I have this hankering to lay my hands on its money. The area's lawmen ought to know information about when and where the real shipment of gold will be arriving. And we'll take all the time we need to get it. As for you..." His gaze turned to Kitty. "I never cottoned to killing women. But I can't let you go to blab what you've seen either. You follow orders, and I'll see you're treated right."

He rode over to Lenny, leaned out of the saddle, and peered down at the man on the ground. "Smith here was a blundering fool without the smarts to make this life profitable."

Lenny reached up a trembling hand.

And Jim shot him through the heart.

Lenny Smith went limp.

Jim lifted his gaze to look Zane right in the eye. "Make no mistake, I'm not like him." There was a hard edge in his tone that left no question to his meaning.

Zoe walked toward the Nolan house with the sun sinking low on the horizon. The grasses here grew waist high and the sunlight reflecting off the golden and purple heads filled her with yearning and comfort. How many times as children had she and the Nolan boys raced through these fields, playing tag or hide and seek? She slowed and lifted her face to the last warmth of the day as she inhaled the sweet loamy scent of the meadow.

She'd tried to practice what she would say to Wash. But everything she thought of made her face blaze anew.

A girl couldn't just out and tell him that while she'd enjoyed his kiss, it couldn't happen again. But if she didn't tell him she'd enjoyed it, he would think she *hadn't*.

Oh! Why had he gone and done such a silly thing as kiss her?

Her already slow pace stilled. Sand crunched beneath her

hesitant feet. She looked ahead to the spot where she could just make out the smoky wisps from the Nolan's kitchen fire painting swirls against the gilded sky.

Maybe she ought to simply keep her distance. After all, if he never spent time with her again, he couldn't very well kiss her, now could he? Yes. That was probably best.

She spun to return home.

Jackson Nolan leapt from the grass with a loud growl, hands curled into bear-like claws above his head.

Zoe squawked. One hand flew to slap him as the other clutched her chest. "Jackson Nolan! I swear you are the most annoying boy!"

He grabbed her hand to prevent her from clouting him a second time as he bent double with laughter. "If it really was a bear, I'm sure your slap would have sent it running right off." He pounded a fist into his thigh.

Zoe snatched her hand from his and gave him a shove. "Oh, do get out of my way."

He stood, folding his arms and leaning into his heels in a way very reminiscent of his older brother. "What are you doing here?"

Just like that, heat blazed through her cheeks. Drat her fair skin! She looked away, flapping a hand toward home. "I was just going home."

Where Wash's eyes were a soft gray-green, Jackson's were vibrant and piercing. They narrowed now in an assessing manner. "If you're looking for Wash, he's not here. In fact, I've just come from town and he's not there either. He must still be off with Deputy Joe and Marshal Zane."

Zoe's heart squeezed. Her focus darted back to Jax. "Shouldn't they have been back by now?"

Jackson shrugged. "That's what Pa figured, but maybe it's

taking a bit longer than expected." His brow ticked into a little furrow that disappeared so quickly she might not have noticed it if she didn't know him so well. He was worried.

Her stomach cramped. "Okay. I'm sure I'll see him around town later in the week."

Jackson lifted a hand. "I'd better let Pa know 'fore he comes after me with a switch for dallying too long."

She nodded. But as he walked away, she closed her eyes and laid her palm to her heart.

Washington had said they'd be near the big bend.

He would kill her for poking her nose into official affairs— especially if it got him in trouble for telling her where he would be, but she couldn't just go back home not knowing what had happened. She'd never sleep tonight.

With determined steps, she started off in the direction of the big bend south of town.

Wash had long since given up the struggle against his bonds. Every movement ground agony into his spine and now one of his arms had cramped so tight it spasmed every time he adjusted his position. His back screamed for relief that he could not give. His tongue, naught but a twig in his mouth, didn't even offer moisture when he moved it and all his exposed skin burned like fire.

Thankfully, the sun was dipping below the tree line now, but soon the frigid mountain air would have him shivering with cold that would cramp his muscles even more.

Of all the ways to die, this was one he'd never even considered. His mind wasn't twisted enough. But die he would, because back here in this little box canyon the chances of someone stumbling across him were nil.

How many days would it take him to die? Too many unless some wild animal got him in the night.

Pa and his brothers would come looking for him. But likely not until tomorrow. And again, the chances of them stumbling on this exact spot...

Humiliation stole through him as a tear trickled from his eye and sank into his hair. It made his scalp itch, but he couldn't scratch it. He tried to rub his temple against his arm, but a cry of anguish escaped as his spine scraped against the stone. The itch would have to stay. It was more tolerable than the pain.

In the distance a wolf howled to welcome the coming of night.

Closer still, another one responded.

Chapter Twenty-five

Zoe took the back way to the big bend and approached the road from above. She kept her eye out for people, outlaws or otherwise, but didn't see or hear anyone.

Slowly, she crept up to the lip of the cliff and peered down to where Wash had said the ambush would likely take place.

The road was empty. In fact, the dust was spread flat like a wind had been the last thing to touch it.

Zoe frowned and sat up. She searched the road in both directions, but couldn't see anyone anywhere. She pinched fingers and thumb to her temples and tried to remember what Wash had told her. Not much. He'd said the wagon would come from Cle Elum. They figured the outlaws would attack here.

She looked at the smooth dust of the roadbed again. No attack had taken place here. Not today. The wind had been still all day. If horses and a wheeled wagon had passed this way, there should still be markings. Even more so had a clash of battle taken place.

She glanced in the direction of Cle Elum. Her conclusions could be threefold—either the lawmen had never made it this far, or she had misunderstood Wash altogether, or he'd given her a false story.

She shook her head. She had not misunderstood him. And he'd never been deceptive with her.

Pushing up from the ground, she dusted her skirts and started along the ridge in the direction of Cle Elum. If she had to, she'd walk all the way to the town to figure out what had happened.

But she didn't have to walk far.

Only about ten minutes later, she saw the bodies.

She rushed behind a large cedar tree growing at the top of the ridge and leaned against it as she peered down into the road. With the falling dusk, it was hard to tell exactly who they were. Both bodies lay still in the dust and wagon tracks led off the road and into the brush on the other side. After a quick scrutiny of the area, Zoe snuck a little closer.

She still couldn't make out the smaller of the two, but the other was—"Kin!" Without thought, she dashed down the ridge.

She collapsed to her knees by his side. "No! No, no, no. Kin?" She brushed his hair back. His face was as pale as the wisps of clouds in the sky. His lips had no color and a pool of blood had spread a good way around his head.

"Oh, Kin, what happened here?" Despair crashed over her. She gripped her head and rocked, glancing at the other body. She froze. It was Lenny Smith.

Her eyes fell closed. This life was short for all. Whether a man appeared to be on top of things for some time or no, his end would surely come, as had Lenny's. And she knew without a doubt that her pa was in a far better place than that man ever would be again.

"Zoe?" A hand grasped her wrist.

Zoe screamed and lurched back.

Kin Davis sat up with a groan.

"Kin Davis, you just about sent me straight into eternity! You're okay!" She surged forward and yanked him into a fierce embrace. "I thought you dead!"

"Ah, Zoe. My head, if you don't mind." Kin pushed her back from him with a wince and a wry grin. He reached to touch the back of his head and his wince turned into a grimace. His fingers came away bloody.

She had to help him! She glanced around for something to wrap around his wound, but saw nothing. She was still wearing the awful black mourning dress, though, and if she could rip off the bottom tier of the skirt... "Do you have a knife?"

He shook his head and swept a gesture toward Lenny Smith.

Zoe scrambled toward him and sure enough, a knife was strapped inside one of his boots. She tried not to think about the fact that she was touching a dead man as she gingerly grasped the hilt. Thankfully, it didn't take her long to extract the blade and soon she was slicing the seam of her skirt. She glanced at Kin. "What happened here?" She held her breath, afraid what his answer would be.

He gave another shake of his head, brow furrowing in puzzlement. "I was in the trunk in the wagon. When it opened I shot"—he swallowed visibly, his gaze darting to Lenny—"him. And then I was swinging around to shoot another man when..." He shook his head. "He must have got me first."

Enough of the seam was loose now. She grabbed both sides of the material and yanked. "Well thank goodness he didn't get you any better than he did!"

Kin nodded.

With the ruffle now loose, Zoe sliced it in half to make one long strip of material. She stretched it out for him to see. "Your bandage. Now let me see that head of yours."

She moved to stand behind him and gently parted the matted clump of hair. She sucked in a breath at the length of the gash. "Wow. There's a furrow here deep enough for planting. If the bullet had been even half an inch closer to your head..."

Kin swallowed. "Wasn't my day to go, I guess. That's what PC will say, anyhow."

Zoe nodded as she worked to gently but firmly wrap the bandage around his head. "And he would be right. God has big plans for your big heart, Kin Davis. I just know it." She tied a knot in the bandage to keep it in place and swallowed her dread over what the answer to her next question might be. "What about Wash? And Deputy Joe? And the marshal? Did you see what happened to them?"

Kin frowned. "The deputy and the marshal were here at the end, but..." His gaze lifted to hers and a deep sorrow filled the depths of his dark eyes. "I never saw Wash. He was supposed to be riding overwatch." His focus drifted to the hills. "If he was able, he would have come for me."

Tears blurred Zoe's vision. "We have to find him, Kin. He could be out there right now, injured like you were. He might need our help."

Kin pierced her with a serious look. "And it might be too late for him."

She took a breath. Nodded. Kin wasn't saying they shouldn't go after him. He was trying to prepare her for the fact that they might not be in time to help. "Where do we start?"

Kin reached up a hand. "First, we start by getting me on my feet."

Jacinda paced from one window to the next, bending to study the street repeatedly. She tucked one fingernail between her teeth, then switched to her thumbnail. All afternoon her concerns had been rising. She'd prayed, she truly had. She'd even gotten out her Bible and reread Zane's verses about the lilies.

But as hour after hour had gone by with no sign of the men's return, her heart had climbed into her throat and threatened to block her very breath.

Forcing herself to work had resulted in needing to undo stitches on two different projects and she'd finally set the dresses aside.

The sun was setting now, casting long shadows against the golden glow on the street. Something was wrong. Something was terribly wrong.

She fell to her knees by the settee, pressing her forehead against her Bible in despair.

"God? Are You going to require this sacrifice of me yet again? Just when I'd decided to risk once more?"

Silence was the only response.

And if she was honest, that was all she'd expected.

Her faith was a bird with tattered wings. Grounded and lame and broken.

※※※

The pain had become a constant companion. Agony seared every limb, and radiated in every direction till it was hard to decipher exactly where it originated—except for his back. The sharp stabbing pain in his back threatened to make him cry out if he moved. Didn't move. Breathed. Didn't breathe.

Wash stared at the first star that twinkled in the dull blue of the sky overhead.

Thirst had dried his mouth to sawdust. That torture was compounded by the fact that he could hear Wyldhaven Creek only a little way off.

He closed his eyes and tried to block out the sound of the water.

So this was to be his end?

He considered what Parson Clay might say to him right now. Had he made his peace with God, the parson would ask.

Yes. He thought so. At least as best he knew how. He believed Jesus was the way, the truth, and the life, and that He was the only way to heaven. He'd confessed his sins. Now all he could do was trust in the Lord to follow through on His Word.

Did he have any regrets, the parson would ask.

His mouth quirked at the corner despite the pain. Only that he hadn't kissed Zoe Kastain sooner. Yeah. Definitely that. He'd have liked to have lived long enough to do that again.

In the brush off to his right, a branch snapped. Leaves crackled.

His pulse quickened. Was it rescue?

He looked over to see a large gray wolf standing just this side of a tree, head down, attention fixed directly on him.

Hopes deflated, Wash swallowed down the terror pounding in his chest. It pulsed pain through every extremity. Panic nipped at his consciousness. But he took a breath. What should he do? What would Pa tell him to do?

Make noise.

"Go!" He yelled. "Get away!" And then he let all the pain he'd been battling pour into a bellow.

If he was going to die, let him go down fighting.

That was something both Pa and the parson would tell him, he felt sure.

Tears trickled down Zoe's cheeks as she and Kin wandered through the woods. After she'd helped Kin to his feet, he'd draped an arm around her shoulders and insisted that she support him while he tried to backtrail the outlaws to wherever they'd been before their ambush.

"They obviously found Wash, otherwise he would have come right down to check on me as soon as it was safe. So if they found him before the attack, maybe they left him tied up somewhere? This trail could lead us back to where they took him. Even if he's—" He bit off the rest of that sentence with a grimace. "We won't leave him out here alone."

Zoe wasn't much good for tracking sign. One horse's hoof-print looked pretty much the same as any other to her, but not to Kin.

Though he had kept shaking his head and scrunching his eyes shut as though his vision might be bothering him, he had studied all the mixed-up swirls of prints in the road and determined that they should follow some that had come in from the north.

Zoe prayed Kin was right about the trail. At least they were headed toward town. If—no *when*—they found Wash, she would be that much closer to getting both him and Kin to Doctor Griffin.

She couldn't see anything other than bushes and grass and trees, but Kin commented on broken branches, bent blades and scuffs on tree bark that she never would have noticed. Each new discovery had led them onward.

But now, Kin stood in one spot turning in circles. He'd searched the ground around them multiple times and couldn't seem to pick up which direction they should take now. One way led up into the mountains behind Wyldhaven. Another led right to the town itself. And a third direction would take them back to the south into the foothills. Kin was debating between the mountains or the foothills, but hadn't found clear indication for which way to go.

Zoe watched him, worried about the way he kept massaging circles at his temples, but even more worried about what she would do if they never found Wash at all, or worse yet, came across his dead body. Just the thought made her take a breath and lodge a fist against the pain in her heart.

Kin tossed up his hands and met her gaze, so much sadness in the depth of his eyes. "I don't know which way to go. If I make the wrong choice, it could mean his life. I mean, he's likely already—"

"Let's not think the worst just yet!"

"Right." He propped his hands on his hips in defeat.

Zoe stepped toward him and reached out a hand. "We're going to pray."

He frowned. "Seriously?" His tone revealed his disbelief that it would do any good.

She waggled her fingers. "Come on. What other options do we have?"

He sighed and finally took her hand.

Zoe bowed her head, not waiting to see if he would do the same. "God. We need to find Wash, so please help us. And thank You for keeping Your hand on Kin's life today."

Kin snorted softly.

"Please touch Kin's immensely hard head and help him to heal quickly from this bullet wound. Amen."

Kin smirked at her. "My immensely hard head likely has a whole lot more to do with my not being dead than anything the good Lord did."

Zoe tilted her head. "But you do believe He's real or you wouldn't have spoken of Him like that just now."

Kin batted the conversation away with a flick of his hand. "Yeah, I believe in God. I just don't think He cares much about us, least wise not like PC says. Anyhow—"

A faint sound floated on the evening air.

They both froze and looked at one another.

"Was that a voice?" Zoe asked.

Kin only tilted his head to listen.

That was when they heard the bellow.

Kin's eyes widened. He pointed toward the mountains. "That was Wash!"

A thrill of joy shot through Zoe. "Wash?!" She surged in the direction the call had come from.

Kin stumbled through the brush behind her.

She pushed quickly through the low-hanging branches of a cedar—and then heard them slap into Kin's chest behind her. She winced. "Sorry."

He grumbled something about girls that she didn't quite catch.

"Wash? We're coming! Where are you?" She stopped running long enough to listen.

Another cry rang out, this one laced with enough terror that it sent a jolt of horror through Zoe. "This way!" She surged ahead.

"Zoe wait!" Kin called, but she wasn't about to stop now. Wash was within the sound of her voice.

"Wash, I'm coming!" She burst past a large outcropping into the mouth of a small canyon. And froze.

Across the way, Washington was staked out, backwards over a rock, like a hide set to dry. He couldn't move.

And he was surrounded by three large wolves!

Chapter Twenty-six

oe didn't even think. She simply surged ahead, snatching up a tree branch on her way. "Get away you lousy beasts!" She swung the branch, connecting solidly with the hind quarters of one of the wolves.

It yelped and tucked its tail, but only trotted a few steps, where it faced her, sinking lower and baring its teeth.

"Off with you!" She swung toward another. She connected with that one's head.

It yelped and staggered back, eliciting growls from the other two.

"Zoe, you're crazy!" Kin waded into the fray, hurling a rock toward the third wolf.

With her back to Wash, Zoe held her branch like a bat, ready to swing should one of them come toward her. "We can't just let them eat him! Is he alive?"

"Haven't had time look yet."

"Yes," Wash croaked. "Thanks to you two."

Zoe's eyes closed for the briefest of seconds. "Thank You, Jesus. Now how do we get rid of these wolves?"

Behind her one of the wolves yipped, and she heard a rock clatter into the brush.

"Ha! Go on, get!" Kin yelled. "Make lots of noise and look strong!"

Zoe bent and beat her club against a rock as she ground out a yell.

With each stone and yell, the wolves scooted a few paces farther until they finally turned and trotted away into the trees.

Zoe tossed her branch aside and collapsed to her knees by Wash's side. "Oh Wash, what did they do to you?" Every inch of his exposed skin was burnt. Blisters already puckered parts of his face and stomach. His gaze was fixed on her, but he didn't seem to have the strength for words.

They had to get him free! But his gun belt and knife sheath were missing.

"Kin, I didn't bring the knife!" Her hands fluttered over him. Where should she start?

Without a word, Kin bent over one of Wash's ankles, working to loosen the knots in the rawhide.

Zoe scrambled to his nearest hand and set to work on it. The knots were stubborn, and twice she heard Wash hiss when she scraped his burnt wrist with her fingers. "Sorry. I'm so sorry." She realized tears streamed down her face. The knots were stubborn. Tight. Too tight.

She stood and tried to haul the stake from the ground, but it was buried too deep. A sob escaped as she bent over the knot again. Finally, she was able to loose the first wrap of the knot and his wrist came free only a moment later. She lurched to start working on the other hand. Kin had already finished with Wash's second ankle.

With only one of his limbs still tied, he rolled off the side of the rock. A groan escaped him, so guttural and deep-felt that it about tore Zoe's heart in two. He curled into a fetal position, his head resting on the one arm that remained tied. A quick glance at his face showed the muscles in his jaw bulging as he gritted his teeth.

Zoe dashed at her tears, trying to see better. "I'm sorry, Wash. Almost done. I just can't..." Her fingers felt like fat, clumsy sausages.

Kin laid a hand over hers, then nudged her aside. She sank against her ankles and smoothed shaking hands over her skirt.

Wash's body trembled. Muscles in his shoulders and arms twitched and spasmed. Fist curled tight and jaw still bunching, he pulled a long slow inhale in through his nose. "Water," he croaked.

Zoe leapt to her feet. She could hear Wyldhaven Creek just through the trees. On the ground not far away lay Wash's leather Stetson. She snatched it up and dashed through the trees. She scrambled down the bank of the creek, and scooped water into the hat, then rushed back.

Kin had gotten Wash's last wrist free, and both of them sat in the evening dusk, without saying a word.

Zoe sank down by Washington and held the hat toward him.

He curved his hands around hers, lowered his mouth to the water and slurped long droughts. Finally, he lifted his head, and gave her a nod of thanks. She took in his split cheek, swollen eye, and blistered skin. He looked terrible and yet never had a sight been more beautiful to her than his battered face.

His gaze roved over her and after a long moment he reached to touch the side of her head. His thumb brushed at the moisture that dampened her cheeks and he offered her a smile followed by a wince when it stretched his lips.

"She didn't rush to get me water," Kin groused, gingerly touching the back of his head.

Face heating, Zoe held the hat out to him.

Kin offered her a rapid-fire wink as he accepted the hat from her and drank his fill. "More?" He offered the hat back to Wash.

He took it, finished off the water, and then slowly settled the hat onto his head. He glanced around. "You see my shirt?"

They found it off to one side, but whichever outlaw had stripped it from him had torn it in several pieces.

Wash grunted.

Kin stood over him and reached down a hand to help him up. "Probably would have hurt like fire to put it on over that burn, anyhow."

After gaining his feet, Wash stood looking at the ground for a moment, hands propped on his hips.

Zoe winced at the stark red line that delineated the burnt flesh of his torso from the bronzed skin of his back.

Kin broke the silence. "Some deputies we turned out to be."

A chuckle escaped Wash before he frowned. "Where are Deputy Joe and Marshal Zane?"

Zoe exchanged a look with Kin. "As far as we know, they've been taken by some of the outlaws. The one named Lenny Smith was dead in the road next to where I found Kin."

"Hole in his chest looked big, probably a .45." Kin's words were spoken low, like maybe he hadn't wanted Zoe to overhear that bit.

Wash flipped him a glance. "You sure?"

"What does that mean?" Zoe frowned, looking between them.

Kin nodded at Wash.

And he blew out a breath. He settled one hand on against Zoe's back. "Deputy Joe and Marshal Zane both carry .32 caliber. It means Smith was shot by one of his own men."

Zoe clutched at the collar of her dress. "We need to go after them."

Wash shook his head and nudged her to start walking. "Not you. And Kin and I are in no shape to take them ourselves.

Plus, we've got no horses. We're not too far from town. We need to return for a posse." He took a step, but immediately leaned a palm against a tree trunk. He grunted in frustration. "We'll be lucky to make it back by morning."

Zoe slipped beneath his arm, careful not to touch the burnt areas any more than she needed to. She started them in the direction of town. "We'll make it. God sent those wolves so you'd yell and we'd find you. And He's not going to abandon us now." She glanced over her shoulder at Kin to make sure he was keeping up, but covered the scrutiny with a cheeky grin. "No matter what Kin Davis believes about God not caring about us."

Kin's only response was a huff and a wave of his hand to assure her he was fine.

Thankfully, by cutting through the woods as they were, town was only a couple miles away.

Providing both Kin and Wash could maintain this pace, they should arrive inside two hours.

Jacinda stayed on her knees. More because she didn't know what else to do than because she felt a peace or a presence by doing so. She had no other options. No other place to go with her concerns.

She curled her fists and pounded on the cushions and cried out asking God why He had let yet one more evil enter her life. For she knew, each time she lifted her gaze to the sky out the window and found it another shade darker with still no relieving knock on the front door, that something terrible had indeed happened.

And then the knock came.

She flew to open it and found Zoe on her porch, hands

wringing in agitation. "Best you come, Mrs. Callahan. There's to be a town meeting in the boardinghouse dining room. Doc has sent me around to fetch everyone."

Jacinda searched her face. "It's the lawmen, isn't it?"

"I'm afraid so, ma'am."

The doorframe pressed cool against her palms and hard against her cheek when she collapsed against it. "Are they dead?"

Zoe shrugged. "We don't rightly know, as yet. Doc wants to talk to everyone at once."

Jacinda released her grip on the wood. "I'll be right there."

After a dip of a curtsy, Zoe gave a wave and started down the steps. "I'm off to fetch Mr. Giddens. I'll meet you there."

As Jacinda reached for her shawl, a thought registered. If they needed to rely on old Bill for protection now, they were in dire straits, indeed.

It only took her a few moments to go the block down to the boardinghouse. She slipped through the back door and could hear voices the moment she stepped inside. The dining room was just off to the left and light spilled through the doorway, creating a golden patch on the floor of the dark hallway.

"Was there blood? Any body parts on the road?" That was the voice of Ben King, the postmaster.

Jacinda froze and pressed a hand to her chest. Her throat threatened to close off at the same moment her stomach seemed ready to empty right here on Dixie's clean floors.

"Oh Ben! For lands sakes!" Ben's wife, Ethel, exclaimed.

"Well! We need details. So far, all these boys have said is the lawmen are missing. We need more!"

Jacinda forced herself forward. When she stepped into the doorway, every eye in the room fixed on her and then immediately dropped away. Flynn, Dixie, and Rose sat at a table. Ewan McGinty had pulled out one of the chairs and propped his foot upon it. He leaned against his folded arms atop his knee. Ben King and his wife sat at the next table over with Kin Davis and Washington Nolan.

Jacinda did a double take of both of them. Their injuries made her worry congeal like a rock in her stomach. Zane was out there with whoever had done this to them. Zane and Joe.

The boys nodded at her and she returned their greetings and then continued her perusal of the room.

Jerry and Priscilla Hines stood between the two tables and several others were scattered about the room. Parson Clay sat at a third table, alone. His worried gaze remained fixed on the back of Kin's head. Jacinda moved toward him.

The parson rose and pulled out a chair for her.

"Thank you." She felt older than she'd ever felt as she sank into the seat. "What do we know?"

His lips thinned into a grim line. "As soon as Zoe returns with Bill, the boys will fill us in so they can tell the story just once. Doc's orders."

She followed his gaze to the large white bandage that Doc had apparently recently applied to Kin's head. She pulled in a tremulous breath. "Has someone gone for Liora?"

He nodded. "David Hines rode out only a few minutes ago."

"And Butch Nolan?"

Parson Clay frowned. "Wash, did anyone go for your family?"

The boy nodded. "David will ride out to let them know as soon as he informs Mrs. Rodante."

Jacinda relaxed a little. That was good. He ought to have his family close at a time like this. She couldn't imagine what the outlaws might have done to him. He looked like he'd withstood the fires of hell.

Zoe returned then with Bill Giddens and the whole room hushed and turned their expectant gazes on the boys.

But it was Doc who stood. "Thank you all for your patient understanding while we waited for those of us who are town residents to arrive. As you can tell by looking at them, the boys there have been through quite an ordeal. And I didn't want them getting overtaxed. If you all can just listen quietly to what they have to say, we'll take time for questions afterwards."

With that, Doc nodded for the boys to proceed.

Kin and Wash looked at each other and it was Kin who finally stood. He shoved his hands deep into his pockets and didn't shy away from eye contact as he told all that had happened as best he knew it. He spoke eloquently, giving plenty of details so the narrative was easy to follow.

And as Jacinda listened, her heart pounded harder and harder. She propped her forehead into the palm of her hand, not caring how unladylike she might look with her elbow on the table.

Zane and Joe and a woman named Kitty, all presumably taken by the outlaws. Outlaws who had gone so far as to shoot one of their own—at least by appearances.

Kin lifted a shoulder as he concluded. "We don't think the lawmen have been killed or they would have been left in the road where I was. The outlaws must want something from them. And that gives us the chance to track them down and bring them home."

For the first time since he'd started speaking, Jacinda lifted her head. That was true! If the lawmen were dead, they would have likely been found by now! Hope bloomed and then immediately deflated as several in the room broke into loud protests. A pain started pounding in her temples.

After a brief moment, everyone quieted except Pricilla Hines. She gasped, "You don't expect the men who are safely tucked away here in town to risk their lives to go after them, do you? Seems to me they got themselves into this situation and they are the best equipped to get themselves out!"

Kin blinked at her.

Jacinda half expected Parson Clay or Doc to stand and intervene, but both of them seemed content to let Kin carry on the dialogue.

He opened his mouth. Shut it. Blinked a couple more times. Met Washington's gaze and then narrowed his eyes on Mrs. Hines. "Way I see it, ma'am, those two men have risked their lives plenty for the rest of us and it would only be the neighborly thing for us to go after them."

Mr. Haversham, the schoolteacher who had taken over after Charlotte married, swiped a hand through the air as though erasing Kin's rebuttal from a chalk board. "But it's not our job to go traipsing about in the wilderness to rescue two men who were careless enough to get themselves captured."

Washington Nolan squirmed in his seat like he might want to say something, but he held his silence.

Ewan McGinty held no such compunctions. He blew a raspberry to show his disdain for Mr. Haversham's words. "They got themselves captured because they were trying to protect this town! I'm with Davis. If we aren't willing to risk our necks for our own, what kind of men are we?"

And then all pandemonium broke loose. Most were for creating a posse to go after Zane and Joe, but those who were against it, were vehemently so. They didn't want everyone with guns riding off and leaving the town unprotected lest the outlaws take advantage of that fact to launch an attack.

Jacinda scrunched her eyes shut. All the shouting was compounding her headache. Before she realized what she was doing, Jacinda stood.

The room fell silent. Everyone looked at her.

And she couldn't for the life of her think why she had stood.

Liora burst into the back of the room just then, out of breath and windblown. Aurora hurried in on her heels. Liora pressed a hand to her chest, searching Jacinda's face and she must have seen the truth revealed there because she suddenly grasped the nearest chair and collapsed into it. She and Jacinda simply looked at one another for a long moment. Then Jacinda transferred her gaze to Dixie and Doc. Rose. Pricilla Hines who still sputtered beneath her breath. Ben and Ethel King. Ewan McGinty. And finally, to Parson Clay.

She swallowed.

Parson Clay was such an eloquent speaker. Each Sunday he brought them truths straight from the Word in easy to understand sermons.

She was no orator, but the battle she'd been fighting with God since the hour of Wade's death had culminated in this moment and she suddenly knew she had to speak or explode.

The peace and the presence she'd been seeking all day, enveloped her in such an overpowering way that she leaned forward to rest her weight on her fingertips.

"Most of you know my husband Wade was killed by outlaws many years ago when Reagan was just a boy." She tapped her fingers against the smoothness of the wood. "Ever since that time, I've lived with worry. A lack of trust in God. He took a person most precious to me, how could I rest, knowing He might do it again?"

Dixie clutched the pendant at her throat. She gave Jacinda a nod of encouragement.

Ewan straightened, frowned, folded his arms, and kicked at a knot on the floor.

"But Zane said something to me this week... I told him I couldn't trust in God's protection. And he told me I wasn't supposed to trust in His *protection* but in Him alone. I could have cheerfully throttled him." She smiled sheepishly and several around the room chuckled.

"He said we do what we can and we trust in God to do the rest. And he's right. We shouldn't fret about the future, because that's a lack of trust that God has our best in mind. And when He doesn't do things just the way we like, we have to learn to accept it and continue to trust Him. That's where I've been stuck. I couldn't accept that losing my husband was God's best for me." She shrugged. "Truth is, I still don't rightly see it, but I'm trying to come to a place where I realize that just because I don't understand, it doesn't change what God's Word says.

"And as I look around this room, I see so many friends— really people who are more like family—who I never would have met if Wade hadn't passed. God has given me many good gifts. So who am I to question Him when He sends a trial or two my way?

"I decided Zane was right. And just this morning I told him that I was through with worrying. That I was ready to move ahead and risk again, because I loved him." Her face blazed heat all along her scalp. Had she truly just said that aloud?

Dixie chuckled. Liora covered her mouth, eyes sparkling above her fingers, despite the fact that Jacinda knew she had to be deeply concerned herself. Ewan and Doc smirked at one another.

Pushing past her embarrassment, Jacinda spread her hands. "And now this evening here we are... The man I love in danger and me once more at the mercy of God's good plan." Fighting back tears, she looked around the room, meeting every eye. "And I don't want to go back to the woman I was yesterday! We can't add one cubit to our height by worrying, the Bible says. The lilies don't toil and fret and yet God arrays them in beauty. I don't know what the future holds for Wyldhaven. If Zane and Joe are still alive or will be so by the time we find them. Or what the outlaws might do. Only God knows. But what I do know is that we can trust Him. That I want to trust Him. And that we have to do our part. To me, that means we go after Zane and Joe and we do our very best to bring them home safely."

A few grumbles arose and she quickly thrust up a hand to silence them. "But *also* some of us stay here to guard the town."

That seemed to appease everyone, and all around the room heads nodded.

Parson Clay smiled, stood and squeezed Jacinda's shoulder gently. "An excellently made point, Mrs. Callahan. But before we do any of that, I say we pray and ask God to guide us and guard us and protect all involved."

Relieved to have said all she felt she'd needed to say, Jacinda sank back into her seat.

She didn't know what everyone else would choose to do, but she was going with the party that went in search of Zane and Joe. She'd never had a chance to try and help Wade because she'd been home watching Reagan.

This time she wasn't going to stand idly by!

Chapter Twenty-seven

❧

The force of another punch crashed Zane's head against the trunk of the tree they'd tied him to.

Not far away, Joe was also tied and receiving similar treatment.

The outlaws had brought them to a small clearing near an overhanging bluff along Wyldhaven Creek. It was a good hideout. Protected from view from above and sheltered by trees all around in a bend of the creek.

The woman, Kitty, had been trussed up and left in the back of the wagon, but thankfully they hadn't hurt her. At least not yet.

Zane spat blood and stretched his jaw from side to side. For the past several minutes, neither he nor Joe had said anything because neither of them had anything more to say. Of course they weren't going to reveal to this lot that the shipment of gold for the bank wasn't set to arrive for nigh on three weeks on the train from Boston. Because then the outlaws would have no more use for them. But neither could they continue taking a beating like this.

It was time for action, as he'd reminded Jacinda—was that only this morning?

But his options for action were pretty slim at this point with his hands tied behind him to a tree. He glanced past the man who'd been tasked with getting him to speak.

Lightning Jim Roan sat near a fire with the simpleton. He held a long piece of a branch and prodded at the coals. Every once in a while, he lifted it from the flames and waved it toward the lad like he might burn him with it. Tommy would surge away and then Jim would demand he sit still. Then he'd go back to staring morosely into the flames.

Apparently, the man Zane had shot the night the outlaws had attacked him and Jacinda had died. He'd heard Bobby, the one who was beating on him, and Victor, the one who was beating on Joe, talking about it a few minutes ago when Jim had stepped into the woods for a bit. Jim had been close to the man and was taking it hard. He seemingly had blamed Lenny for making the man move when he was too weak to do so, thus his coup that had ended up in Lenny's death this morning.

That left only four outlaws in the camp, but none of them would be anything without the leadership of Lightning Jim. He was the man Zane needed to get to. And there was only one way he could think to get through to a man like that.

"Heard you think you are pretty fast with those pistols?" Every outlaw paused what he was doing and turned to stare. Maybe because he had broken his silence. More likely because of the tone of disdain he'd used. If he was going to throw down a challenge, he'd best make it good.

Bobby pulled back a fist, set to hit him again, but Jim lifted a hand, and Bobby stilled. Across from him, Joe arched a brow as though to question his sanity. Everyone in the area had heard of Lightning Jim. His gunfights were the conception of legends.

Jim looked him up and down and then laughed. "I *am* fast with my pistols." He tossed his branch down and patted the handle of one revolver as though it might be his pet.

"I bet I'm faster." Zane spat more blood and prayed the

man's pride wouldn't give way to sense in this moment. He squinted at him through the slits of his swollen eyes, realizing that everyone in the little clearing had looked to Jim for his reaction. "I'm even bum-handed. I'll be shooting with my left hand."

And then his heart started pounding, because truth was, he wasn't certain he could outgun the man. But going down fighting certainly was better than standing here taking a beating for several more hours.

His thoughts flitted to Jacinda and for a moment he frowned. If Jim accepted and he lost? What would that do to her? Would she pine for him the way she'd pined for her husband Wade all these years? He couldn't deny a little melancholy at the thought that he could fail and then he'd be leaving her behind. And yet, he couldn't worry about that.

Like he'd told her, do what you can and leave the rest to God. What he could do right now was challenge Jim Roan to a shootout.

The rest was up to God.

Jim Roan stared at the marshal, caution raising its head. Didn't the man know who he was? How he'd taken out the three Konos brothers before any of them had even cleared leather? And that before that fight they'd been considered the fastest draws around?

Surely he'd heard the story, right? So, if he had and he was still challenging him, what did that say about that man?

Did he really believe he was faster? Or was he simply desperate to get untied from that tree and quit getting punched in the face.

Jim's lips quirked as he considered his options. His focus

flicked to the deputy. That man had been in town longer than the marshal. In fact, it wasn't really the marshal's business to know what went on in the town, now was it? His job was to track men for the federal government, protect judges, that kind of thing, right? Maybe he didn't know about the bank money. But he'd bet his last dollar that the deputy did.

So...if he accepted the marshal's challenge and killed him, the deputy might be a touch more willing to talk. He was getting tired of sitting here anyhow. Bored of tormenting poor dumb Tommy. They needed information so they could start putting a plan together.

Jim rubbed his hands down his pants and stood. He grinned at Victor and Bobby. "What do you think? Think he can take me?"

Both of them laughed and shook their heads.

"No one is faster than you, Jim," Victor said.

Seated on his rock by the fire, Tommy rocked forward and back and curled his arms around his head. "M-maybe faster, Jim. S-seems like he m-might be fast. Best be careful." He rubbed his hands over his hair and rocked harder.

Jim joined in with Victor and Bobby's laughter as he clapped Tommy on one shoulder.

Tommy cringed and leaned away from him.

"Thanks for your concern, Tommy. But I'm not worried about a two-bit marshal taking me out." He nodded at the man. "All right. You got yourself a fight." He motioned for Bobby to cut the man's bonds. "Untie him and let him get his circulation back. Don't want anyone to ever say that Jim Roan won an unfair fight."

Jim couldn't help but laugh at his own joke. Had he ever won a fair one? Maybe once or twice. But there was too much risk in that. The fellas knew what to rig. All would be well.

Zane frowned as he worked his wrists and tried to rub away the fire blazing through his bad shoulder. That had been just a bit too easy. He glanced at Joe, who subtly shook his head. Zane gave him a nod. This had to be a setup of some sort. But he was free. And all he needed was a little blessing from above.

Victor stepped over with his gun belt and held it out to him.

But Zane didn't reach for it. He looked at Jim. "You gonna give me time to put it on?" As long as a man had a gun on his person, questions were rarely asked if he ended up dead. He didn't want to get shot while he was still trying to swing his gun belt around his hips, especially since it might take some time with his bum arm. If he didn't manage to finagle them out of this, Joe wouldn't be around to speak on his behalf.

Jim folded his arms. "What do you take me for? I'm no bushwhacker."

Zane gingerly prodded the swelling beneath his right eye, still not touching the gun. "So it's loaded?"

Victor glanced over at Jim and they both laughed.

Jim held up a finger. "So here's the catch."

Zane waited. He'd known there would be one.

Jim grinned. "You get one bullet."

Victor tugged Zane's revolver from his holster and spun the cylinder for him to see.

Only one cartridge filled the chamber. Victor lifted it between his thumb and forefinger with a leer stretching his face. Then reloaded it, closed the cylinder, and gave it a spin. He put the pistol back into the holster and held the belt out to Zane.

Zane swallowed as he accepted his weapon.

Joe cocked an eyebrow at him.

Zane shrugged a shoulder.

One bullet was a slim blessing indeed.

But it was a blessing.

The posse rode out of town with Kin Davis and Washington Nolan leading the way. Neither boy should be out of bed right now, much less riding off to the prospects of another gun battle, but both of them had refused to be left behind.

Those who had stayed to guard the town were Jerry Hines, Dixie, Liora, Aurora, Bill Giddens, the new banker, Merle Olann, and Mr. Haversham.

The posse riding out consisted of the two boys, Doc, Ewan McGinty, Butch and Jackson Nolan, Parson Clay, and Jacinda.

Zoe Kastain had wanted to ride with them too, but Susan had arrived in town searching for her just before they left and forbidden it, much to Zoe's chagrin.

Eight of them. Eight against how many? Neither of the boys had quite been sure.

Ewan pulled up beside Jacinda and dipped his gaze to the pistol she'd belted around her hips. "You sure you know how to shoot that?"

Jacinda settled her hand comfortably against the grip. "After my husband, Wade, died, it was my job to make sure nothing happened to my boy."

Ewan's eyes narrowed. "That don't mean you can shoot."

Jacinda swallowed. Truth was, it had been too many days since she'd gone out shooting at targets. And none of her targets had ever returned fire. "I promise not to shoot you in the back, if that's what you are worried about."

Ewan grinned. "Guess that's a start." He urged his mount forward, leaving her to ride at the rear.

Just southwest of the big bend, they found the scene of the first attack. Crows had already started to desecrate Lenny Smith's body.

Jacinda looked away from the nauseating sight. Was Zane out there somewhere even now with crows pecking at his body?

While the men scouted for sign and tried to decide which direction they should go, she swung down and shooed the birds away. She hadn't thought to bring a sheet, and they didn't have time to take the body back to town right now. She strode to the side of the road and set to breaking the branches from some salal. If she piled enough on top of the body, maybe it would keep the carnivores at bay until they could return to fetch him.

She was returning with her fifth armload of leafy branches when she found Ewan scrutinizing the mostly covered body. He spat a stream of tobacco to one side. "He don't deserve the trouble."

Jacinda brushed past him and carefully placed the brush on the body. "He bore a soul, Ewan, just like you or me. He may not have chosen a life of love or kindness, but that doesn't mean I have to do the same."

He spat again, then tipped his head to where everyone else was mounted up again. "Found our trail. Riding out."

From where he sat on his horse, Parson Clay gave her a nod of encouragement.

Jacinda dusted her hands and returned her focus to Ewan. "I'm done anyhow."

Despite his surly attitude, Ewan was enough of a gentleman to stand by her horse and help her mount up. She gave his hand a squeeze of thanks.

They rode out, with Kin Davis leading the way. Doc rode beside him, obviously concerned about his head injury. But

Kin was their most experienced tracker. Reagan had once told her the boy could track a fox across a rocky plateau if he needed to. She only hoped that their need of him now wouldn't set back his healing.

The tracking was slow, and with each passing minute Jacinda felt her anxiety ratcheting up another notch. Zane and Joe could—*no.*

God, I trust. Help me to let it go. Help me to remember You are all I need.

⸙

Standing on the grass along the banks of the stream, Zane kept his hands loose at his sides, careful not to touch his gun before it was time. Ten yards downstream, Lightning Jim Roan faced him, a confident tilt to his lips. Victor and Bobby shuffled nervously in their positions across the narrow creek on either side of Joe. Tommy had hidden behind a tree and Zane hadn't seen him for several minutes. That was good. He'd hate for the kid to get shot.

Above them the overhang of the bluff blocked out the heat of the sun. The shade was cool. The sound of the water soothing. The chirping of birds nearby gave the illusion that all was well. Zane pulled in a slow breath. All in all, not a bad place to die if it came to that.

Mentally, Zane went through the steps he'd gone through so many times. Draw the gun. Pull the trigger. Fan the hammer—in this case, as many times as it took for the bullet to fire.

And don't miss.

He studied the square of pocket that rested over Jim's heart. He'd once had a friend challenge him to shoot a playing card—from the side. He hadn't missed the razor thin edge of the card then. He prayed he wouldn't miss Jim's pocket now.

He was fast. He'd been told by many a man that he was the fastest they'd ever seen. But he'd never let that slip since he'd come to Wyldhaven. Anytime he'd practiced, he'd made sure it was in private where no one could spread rumors about his speed. That kind of story only ever drew a bad sort who wanted to make a name for themselves by seeing if they could beat him in a duel. Besides, he wasn't conceited enough to think he couldn't be beat.

He swallowed now as he assessed Jim. He'd never seen the man shoot. How fast was he?

Jim's fingers flexed. "You know you'll never beat me, right? Especially with only one bullet in the cylinder."

Zane kept his concentration on Jim's hand and held his silence. The bullet could very well be in the first chamber, and well Jim knew it. He didn't need to say it. In fact, keeping quiet would only irritate the man. Those who felt the need to talk themselves up, rarely believed their own press.

They came upon the man unexpectedly. One moment they were riding along and the next, Kin Davis shot a hand into the air.

A man burst from the brush, head down, running with great clomping steps, arms flailing.

Kin and Ewan drew their weapons.

Jacinda frowned, there was something—

"Don't shoot!" she called.

The man lurched to a stop, slowly lifting his gaze to take them in. He noted Kin's gun and his eyes widened. He waved his hands haphazardly. "Don't shoot Tommy! D-don't shoot Tommy! Tommy ain't h-hurt no one!"

Kin and Ewan exchanged a look. Neither of them reholstered

their pistols. Instead, they turned to studying the brush behind the man.

Seeing and hearing no one else, they all fanned out and looked at the simpleton.

Doc swung down, taking his canteen with him. "I recognize his voice. He was part of the Smith Gang." He approached, holding out the canteen. "Looks like you've been running for a bit. You thirsty?"

Tommy's eyes narrowed suspiciously on the canteen, then took in Doc's face. His expression contorted in fear and he thrust an arm up over his face. "I d-didn't want them to h-hurt you none! Honest, I didn't. D-don't hit me!"

"Shh, it's all right." Doc's tone was soothing. "None of us are going to hurt you."

Tommy lowered his arm just enough to peer over top it.

"Go on." Doc jostled the canteen. The water inside sloshed. "It's water."

Without another moment's thought, Tommy snatched the canteen and guzzled thirstily. Water drizzled down his chin, soaking into the front of his tattered shirt.

Ewan's horse moved restlessly as he studied the brush all around them. "We don't got time for this, Doc."

Doc accepted the canteen that Tommy thrust back at him. "Did you come from the camp with Lightning Jim?"

Tommy pressed his lips together. He searched Doc's face, and then each of their faces.

Jacinda offered him a smile, hoping that would put him at ease.

Tommy spun on his heel and motioned over his shoulder for them to follow. "C-come on, I'll show ya. J-jim's mean. He d-don't like Tommy none." He disappeared into the brush.

Jacinda met the men's gazes. Ewan shrugged. Doc did the same. Kin and Wash both lifted a hand.

Parson Clay started his horse forward. "I'd say the good Lord sent that lad to guide us."

"I'd have preferred he used a man in his right mind," Jackson groused as he rode past Jacinda.

She grinned and reined her horse into his wake.

Chapter Twenty-eight

Somewhere off in the forest, Zane heard an eagle cry. The creek burbled.

Jim still hadn't moved.

Zane was all right with that. Every moment they stood here gave him another breath. Another moment to think of Jacinda's soft blue eyes, her dark lashes fluttering closed on a laugh.

"They's all r-rightchere!"

The yell came from off to Zane's right. From the corner of his eye, he saw Tommy burst into the clearing.

"What the—" Jim's attention flicked to Tommy, even as his hand slapped his gun.

Zane dropped to one knee. Drew. Fired. Fired. Fired. Fired! The bullet had been in the fourth chamber. All four shots took him less than a second to get off.

Jim's Colt hadn't even cleared leather yet. But the step he had taken when Tommy yelled, combined with the fact that Zane had been a bit distracted himself, caused him to miss Jim's pocket. The bullet went wide and low.

Jim's eyes were wild and his off arm swung out to the side for balance as he raised his gun and fired.

Zane felt the whip of air as the bullet whined past his ear. He dove for the cover of a rock at the creek's edge.

All manner of chaos broke out across the creek.

He cowered behind the rock, taking quick glances as he could, while still trying to keep an eye on what Jim was doing. By last count, he'd only fired once. That meant he still had five bullets in that six-shooter of his.

Horses poured from the trees.

Jim took a step toward him.

Zane angled himself to have better cover behind the less-than-adequate rock.

"You down on your belly!" That was Doc's voice.

A glance showed him leveling his gun on Victor.

Bobby bolted.

Jim was a couple steps closer now. Close enough that Zane could see the froth in the blood of his wound. His lung was nicked. Jim raised his pistol and Zane ducked low again.

A bullet zinged off the rock only inches from his head.

"Ewan, get that one. There through the brush!" Joe yelled and thrust his chin in the direction Bobby had run.

Doc and Butch Nolan wrestled Victor to the ground.

Kin and Jackson worked on cutting Joe loose.

Tommy clutched at his head and paced before Parson Clay. Zane squinted. What was the parson doing? Looked like he was standing guard over someone squatting at the base of a tree.

Another bullet howled overhead.

Down to three.

But Jim was almost on him now. Close enough that Zane could see the determination in his eyes. A driving need to kill Zane if it was the last thing he ever did. Someone needed to shoot the man or Zane was likely never to see another light of day. "Parson!" He pressed himself as close to the small rock as he could. "Parson!" It was no use. The man couldn't hear him for all the chaos happening on his side of the creek. He continued to stand like he was on guard, attention fixed on

Doc and Butch who were still fighting with a kicking, clawing, biting, and gouging Victor Sloan.

Victor lashed out with his powerful legs, sending Butch sprawling. Parson Clay stepped forward to take the man's place. He pointed his gun in Victor's face. The man went still.

And that was when Zane saw her.

Jacinda, crouched by the base of the tree, pistol in hand. She searched the field and the moment her gaze connected with his, her eyes lit up and her mouth tilted into a small smile.

Zane growled. What was she doing here? He was going to kill her, providing she didn't get shot by one of the outlaws first!

Jacinda's gaze transferred to something behind him. Her eyes widened. She lurched to her feet, gun rising...

Cold steel pressed against the back of his neck.

"Everyone freeze!" Jim bellowed. "Or I kill your marshal, here and now!"

Zane's eyes fell closed even as he put his hands in the air.

He'd taken his eyes off of Jim for one second too long.

⌦⸰⸱⸲⸳✦⸳⸲⸱⸰⌫

Jacinda's elation at seeing Zane alive was severed at the sight of the outlaw hauling him to his feet.

Silence fell over the meadow.

The man swayed like a tree out at the logging camps about to topple, but with his gun pressed so tightly to Zane's skull, there wasn't anything any of them could do. Even if they were a good enough shot to take him out from this distance, as he fell he might squeeze the trigger and kill Zane anyway.

Jacinda searched Zane's face.

Why had she kept him at a distance for so long? All the years that she could have spent getting to know him better. Love him more. Wasted. All because of her sin of worry.

Could he see the regret in her eyes? Feel her despair at being this close to saving him and failing?

Zane's gaze softened. His lips parted. *I love you,* he mouthed.

"I love you too."

Parson Clay gave her a look and Jacinda felt her face heat as she realized she'd spoken the words aloud.

Despite the fact that he had a gun to his head, Zane grinned.

Deputy Joe stepped forward. He spoke loudly, commanding everyone's attention. "So what do we do now, Jim? We're at an impasse. Looks like you are wounded pretty good there. Why not put the gun down and let the doc take a look at it?"

Jim shook his head.

Zane took a step closer to the creek.

Jim tensed and growled, "I said not to move!"

"So you kill him, then we kill you? Is that what you want to happen here?" Joe spoke loudly again, and this time Jacinda was paying better attention.

As he spoke, he fluttered his fingers a little.

Zane took another step forward.

Jim hissed and scooted with him. "You move again and it will be the last step you take, Marshal."

"Hey!" Joe spread his hands. "No one is moving! Let's just talk this out!"

Jacinda frowned. What—

A dark shadow hurtled down from above.

Jacinda gasped and took a step back.

Washington Nolan had jumped from the ledge of the overhang! His elbow *crack*ed into Lightning Jim's skull and the man fell as though he may have been a sack of rocks tossed from the ledge.

Zane stumbled to one side at the same moment that she heard Jim's gun fire.

"Zane!" she cried.

But in the next instant he was on his feet. He rushed over to flip Jim onto his stomach. "Someone get me some rope."

From his place on the ground at Doc's feet, one of the outlaws swore.

"Hey," Doc cuffed him. "There's a lady present. Watch your language."

Ewan pushed into the clearing just then, prodding the other man at the point of his pistol.

"Here." Wash was slow to rise. He stayed on the ground, but stretched a length of rope toward Zane.

"You okay?" Zane gave him a once-over as he bound Jim's hands.

Wash winced and sat up slowly. He cradled his arm against his chest. "My arm feels like it's got a red-hot knife shoved in it."

Zane hauled Jim to his feet. The man bellowed in pain, but Zane only pushed him forward to cross the creek. "Doc!" he called. "I think Wash here may have busted his arm. Better take a look." They splashed across the creek and Zane shoved the prisoner toward Joe. "Get his bleeding stopped so we'll have the pleasure of hanging him, would you?"

And then he was walking toward her.

Jacinda rushed forward. She scanned him from head to toe. His face looked like it had taken a beating, but other than that, no holes. She threw herself into his arms!

Zane took a step back to absorb her weight. "Whoa! What's this?" He grinned down at her.

She wrapped her arms around his neck and gazed into his eyes. "This is me considering the lilies!" And then she kissed him.

For a moment, Zane froze and then his arms came around

her and he tugged her close. His lips moved in matched cadence with hers, as though made for this very dance from the beginning of time.

She stood on her tiptoes and relished the silken feel of his hair in her fingers, his stubble against her cheek, his hands against her back.

After a long moment, they pulled apart.

The meadow lay silent.

She and Zane turned as one to find the eyes of all the men on them.

Jacinda giggled, drawing Zane's gaze back to hers.

He leaned close. "I guess our secret is out, ma'am."

She covered her mouth with one hand. "I think I already blurted in a town meeting that I was in love with you."

His brows arched. "Did you now? Well, I think I like the sound of that."

She laughed. "I did too."

He reached out a hand and when she took it, he laced his fingers with hers. "Let's get back to town, everyone."

As the men complied and prodded the prisoners along ahead of them, Zane leaned close to her. "I'm going to buy you a whole flowerbed full of lilies so you won't forget this day."

Jacinda dropped her head against his shoulder. "Oh, I can assure you, this is a day I'll never forget. Not ever."

Epilogue

One month later.

The church was so full of lilies that even Jacinda had to admit it might be a bit much. Yet, the fragrance! From where she stood in the entry behind the partition, she inhaled the scent slowly. It was perfect!

And my how it had thrilled her when Zane had found her in her kitchen yesterday, and insisted she follow him. He'd led her out her front door, and there had been a whole wagon-load of fragrant pink plants. He'd had them delivered special from Seattle.

She closed her eyes and pictured how the church had looked with this morning's sun spilling through the eastern windows. There had been enough lilies to fill each windowsill, line the platform, and grace the end of each pew, creating a path to the front, where even now, Zane waited for her.

Yes, she could hardly wait to walk down the aisle to this man who loved her so well.

Reagan stood before her in the church entry, with Charlotte only a little way off, peering around the partition into the sanctuary. He tugged on the sleeves of his suit and dipped his chin to look right into her face. "I'm happy for you, Ma. He's a good man." He stretched his arms wide.

Jacinda held her bouquet off to the side as she leaned to

accept his embrace. "Yes. He is." She swept a hand down the front of her champagne lace dress. "Do I look all right?"

His eyes sparkled. "You look beautiful. It's time. You ready?"

She'd never felt more ready for anything. "I am."

Reagan crooked his elbow.

Noticing that they were ready, Charlotte jumped up and down, pantomiming claps, and then darted to the spot where Aurora would be able to see her from the piano. She gave a little gesture to indicate they should proceed.

"S-she's c-coming, PC! G-get ready!" Tommy called loudly.

A chuckle rippled through the congregation and Jacinda laughed along with them.

It thrilled her to no end that Parson Clay had decided to take Tommy Crispin under his wing. The young man couldn't be held responsible for the actions of the outlaw gang, and when Lightning Jim Roan had been sentenced to hang and the rest of the gang had been sentenced to jail, the judge had pardoned Tommy on the condition that he go to live with the parson. Tommy had reluctantly agreed, but now, though he'd only lived with Parson Clay for a little while, his personality had bloomed with confidence. Parson Clay was still working on teaching him proper protocols.

"All right, Tommy. I'm ready. You sit down there by Kin and stay quiet for the rest of the ceremony, okay?"

"Sit d-down and be q-quiet. Yes, sir."

Aurora started the music then and silence settled over the people in the church.

Jacinda pulled in a slow breath. She was truly the happiest she'd felt in years. She felt light. Free. Joyful.

The processional rose into a crescendo and Reagan led her around the partition. Behind them, Charlotte quickly smoothed and spread her short train.

Everyone was on their feet and every eye was on her, but Jacinda only had eyes for one as they walked slowly up the aisle.

He stood next to the parson in a black suit with a string-tie smartly snug at his throat. His face had only the barest remains of the cuts he'd received that awful day a month ago. And while his shoulder still pained him some, Doc had him doing special exercises that were returning his strength. He stood tall, and broad, and strong. And he was hers.

He raised a brow at her and she knew what he was asking. She gave him a nod of assurance. Her headaches were fewer and farther between now, and thankfully today was a good day.

Reagan stopped at the head of the aisle.

The music trailed away.

"Who gives this woman to be married to this man?" Parson Clay asked.

"I..." Reagan's voice hitched a little. "I do."

Behind them, townsfolk chuckled.

Reagan smiled sheepishly. "Hey now!" He spoke over his shoulder. "It's not every day a man gets to give away the woman who gave him life." He smiled lovingly at her. "The one who provided for him, and cared for him, and worked hard to give him an amazing upbringing. I'm blessed to have you, Ma." He bent and dropped a kiss on her cheek.

Her heart practically melted. "Thank you, dear." She squeezed his arm.

Reagan led her to Zane, but before he passed her over, he stretched out his hand. The men clasped hands and shook firmly.

Reagan pulled Zane into a hug. "Thanks for loving my ma. I'm honored to give her to a man like you."

"It's my pleasure."

Reagan grinned. "Knew this day would come from the moment you two met in her dining room all those years ago."

Zane smiled and his gaze flicked to hers. "I think I did too. At least I hoped. Took a lot of convincing, though."

The congregation laughed.

And Jacinda wrinkled her nose at him.

Reagan took his seat on the front bench then, and Jacinda stepped a little closer to Zane's side.

She looked up at him, relishing the warmth of him seeping through her lace sleeve, the gentle feel of his hand at her back, the low timbre of his voice as he spoke his vows.

"Till death us do part."

Jacinda sighed.

She could live with that.

Please Review!

If you enjoyed this story, would you take a few minutes to leave your thoughts in a review on your favorite retailer's website? It would mean so much to me, and helps spread the word about the series.

You can quickly link through from my website here: http://www.lynnettebonner.com/books/historical-fiction/the-wyldhaven-series/

Coming Soon...

SHERIFF REAGAN'S
Christmas
Boots

A *Wyldhaven*
NOVELLA

You may read an excerpt on the next page...

Charlotte tossed and turned fretfully for several hours before she heard the thump of Reagan's boots hitting the bedroom floor and felt the dip of the bed as he climbed in. He'd been dealing with a brawl at McGinty's Alehouse, and she'd partly been worried over his safety, but her mind was eased by the knowledge that he had his deputy, Joseph Rodante, and his mother's new husband, Zane Holloway, as backup.

But if she was honest, her main concern these past few days was because December was almost upon them and she didn't yet have a clue what to buy for Reagan's Christmas present.

Reagan reached over and squeezed her hand. "Hope I didn't wake you?"

She shook her head, then realized he couldn't see her in the dark, so said, "No. I've been awake. I'll sleep better now that your home."

Reagan grunted and punched his pillow into a more comfortable position. "If you are going to have a difficult time sleeping every time I'm called out in the night, I'll have to look into making Joe or Zane handle all the late-night calls."

Charlotte socked his arm gently. "You wouldn't do that to Liora or your mother. Especially not your mother."

Reagan yawned loudly and his voice was more muted when

he replied, "Yes, but she's been doing a lot less worrying lately, have you noticed?"

"I have, indeed."

Reagan's response was a soft snore.

Charlotte sighed and flipped over on her back to stare into the darkness.

She, on the other hand, had worrying a lot of late. What did one buy for their husband for Christmas? Last year had been fairly easy. It had been their very first Christmas and so presents had been things they'd needed for their home. Reagan had bought her a new stove for the kitchen, since old man Jonas, the previous owner of their house, had likely purchased his before the start of the Civil War. And she'd bought Reagan a new-fangled pen that stored ink right in the shaft and a new shaving bowl and razor.

But this year... She'd been racking her brain for months and hadn't been able to come up with an idea. Not because she didn't have ideas, but because, since she'd quit her teaching job to stay at home and be a wife, funds were much tighter this year than they had been last.

After a few hours of restless sleep, she woke, heart still weighed down by her predicament. She lay listening to Reagan's snoring until the sun pierced past the thin gap in the bedroom's calico curtains.

Reagan mumbled and turned over.

She threw an arm across her eyes and angled her head away. She needed more sleep, but thoughts of all she had to get done this day refused her the comfort of continued slumber. She eased from beneath the covers, doing her best not to disturb Reagan.

She hadn't taken two steps before she stubbed her toe on something hard and unyielding. Biting back a yelp and a grumble of irritation, she fumbled through the shadows to feel what it was. Reagan's boots. She gritted her teeth. He'd obviously discarded them without too much thought in his weariness.

She grasped the boots by their tops to carry them to their proper place near the bureau. The shaft of light landed on them as she set them on the floor and she felt her concern mount. The boots were worn and aged. The leather had definitely seen better days, but of greatest concern was the large gap where the top of the shoe had separated from the sole.

Reagan had made no complaint, yet the days recently had been bitterly cold. It just wouldn't do for him to keep wearing such shabby shoes. Not only because his feet needed to be warm, but because it simply wasn't a good image for the sheriff to be tromping around in shoes that were barely holding together. It didn't cast Wyldhaven in a good light.

She left the boots in their place by the bureau, but smiled. And as she headed for the kitchen to start breakfast, she felt like a burden had been lifted.

Finally! She knew what her Christmas present this year ought to be. But her relief over knowing *what* to buy was mixed with worry over the *how* of it. They would be cheaper from the Sears and Roebuck catalog, but at this date, it was too late to have them shipped. She would just have to order a more expensive pair from Mr. Giddens at the livery.

Stepping to the cupboard she pulled the teacup from the top shelf and dumped all the money onto the counter.

Two dollars and six bits. She was pleased. She hadn't realized that she'd saved up quite that much. It ought to be enough to buy a pair of boots, oughtn't it?

But in what size? Reagan only had the one pair of boots and they were always on his feet unless he was sleeping, so she couldn't take them by the livery for a size comparison. She frowned as she stared at the scrambled eggs she was cooking. Maybe his mother would know? Yes. That was the solution. She gave a little nod. She would swing by her mother-in-law's later to ask her about the size.

Reagan woke an hour later and entered the kitchen with his boots in one hand. A large yawn stretched his jaw as he sank into one of the chairs at the table. He scrubbed a hand over his head, displacing his hair in all directions before he bent and tugged on the boots.

Charlotte poured a cup of coffee and set it before him. She grinned and scooped her fingers into his hair, combing it into some semblance of order. "Whatever did you do about your unruly locks before I became your wife, dear sheriff?"

"I combed it myself, but now I leave it messy to get you close enough to catch." He caught her wrist and tugged her onto his lap, looking up with a smile. He winked and raised his lips to hers.

Charlotte relished the feel of this strong hands at her back, the soft hair at the nape of his neck between her fingers, and the brush of his lips over hers.

Only a moment later a knock sounded on the kitchen door. "Sheriff? Sheriff you up?"

Reagan sighed and set her away from him. "Looks like my day is off to a rousing start." He opened the door.

Washington Nolan stood on the porch. "Sorry to bother you, sir! But you're needed in town."

Reagan grabbed two biscuits and pressed some eggs between them. Raising the makeshift sandwich, he said, "See you at dinner." Then he snagged his hat from the peg, stepped onto the porch, and pulling the door closed behind him.

Charlotte sighed and served herself a plate, sinking down at the table to eat alone.

Again.

Charlotte hurried through her breakfast and the morning's house chores and then, with her coat tucked close about her neck and her breath fogging the morning, bustled through the cold to feed and water the chickens. She added wood to the banked fire in the old stove that Reagan had repurposed to keep the hen-house warm, and then dashed the mile into town to talk to Jacinda, Reagan's mother.

She felt a little nervous about the timeframe. But if Jacinda knew the size and she got the order put in today, all should be fine.

Jacinda opened her kitchen door, wiping her hands on a towel. "Oh, it's you. Come in. It's colder than Belle's shoulder out here!"

With a chuckle over the reference to Belle Kastain's perpetual snootiness, Charlotte scooted into the warmth of the kitchen and hung her wraps on the hooks by the door.

Jacinda gave her a guilty look as she set a steaming cup of the herbal tea she kept just for Charlotte onto the table and nudged the sugar bowl her way. "Poor Belle. I really shouldn't have said that. She's gone through a lot in the past few years and I'll be the first to admit that she's really stepped up to help her mother after William's passing."

Charlotte pressed her lips together, not wanting to agree that she shouldn't have spoken like that and condemn her mother-in-law, but also not wanting to reassure her, since it was true they shouldn't speak at Belle's expense. Instead she offered, "I think I've figured out what I'm going to get for Reagan, finally!"

Jacinda pulled out a chair and sank down, gesturing for her to do the same. "Do tell."

"Boots!" Charlotte stirred a teaspoon of sugar into her teacup.

"Good luck getting him to give up his 'comfortable' pair." Jacinda grinned over the rim of her cup.

Charlotte tilted her head. "Am I going to have to make those old raggedy ones disappear?"

"Most likely."

"Well, the side of one busted out just the other day, so hopefully I won't have to fight him too passionately. But I came by for a reason. I don't know what size to have Mr. Giddens make."

Jacinda's eyes widened. "Oh, dear. I always just took a tracing of his feet to Bill. I never asked what size it corresponded to."

Willing away her disappointment, Charlotte set down her cup. "I see. Well, maybe Mr. Giddens will remember the right size. I'll pop over to the livery and ask him. What are you getting for Zane?" Since Jacinda and her US Marshal husband had only been married for a few months, this would be their first Christmas together.

With a swipe at some invisible specks on the table, Jacinda grinned and gave a pump of her brows. "Zane's old Morgan isn't as spry as he used to be. So I placed an order for an Appaloosa from the ranch we visited on our wedding tour. He admired both the dam and the sire, so I know he's going to be thrilled."

"That's so exciting! How are you getting it here?"

"It's scheduled to arrive on the train in a few weeks." She

waved a hand. "I just hope everything goes smoothly. Deputy Joe has agreed to keep it in his and Liora's barn until Christmas morning."

Charlotte reached across the table and squeezed her hand. "Well, I can't wait to see it. For now, I'd better get going. I want to get my order in with plenty of time for Mr. Giddens to get them made." She stood and gestured to the cups. "Can I help you wash these?"

Jacinda brushed away the offer. "No, no. It won't take me but a moment. Thanks for stopping by!"

"Thank you for the tea." Charlotte wrapped her scarf around her throat and slipped into her coat before giving Jacinda a hug. "Have a good day. I'll let you know what I find out."

With that she dashed out into the fat flakes that were now falling from the sky. Thankfully Jacinda's house was on the same end of town as the livery.

❧

Bill Giddens sat hunched near the potbellied stove in the livery tack room, cleaning a harness.

Charlotte got right down to business. "Hi Bill. I need you to keep a Christmas secret."

Bill set the harness aside and scratched at his long gray whiskers. "Beg pardon, ma'am?"

Charlotte smiled. "I want to buy the sheriff a pair of boots."

Bill's face lit up. "Oh! Yes'm. That there, I can do. I have all the fixin's just here."

He flipped a canvas cover off the table in the corner. On the table, several pairs of boots were lined up. Charlotte's gaze immediately settled on the pair on the end. Made of a rich brown leather, they had been hand-tooled and decorated with intricate stitching.

"Oh my. These are beautiful." She picked one up. The leather was as fine and soft as it looked, yet felt sturdy enough to last for a good long while. "Would you be able to have a pair of these made by Christmas?"

"Oh yes, ma'am. I can get right to it. That pair there, they would be seven dollars."

Charlotte dropped the boot as though it had just bitten her. Seven dollars! Her heart fell. She thought of the two dollars and six bits in her savings cup. Could she come up with four dollars and two bits before Christmas? She couldn't think how she would be able to do so.

"I didn't realize they would come so dear."

"Lot o' work goes into that pair, ma'am."

"Oh, I'm sure it does. I didn't mean to imply they weren't worth the cost."

Bill nodded. He pointed to a pair in the middle. "That pair there would only run you five dollars."

Charlotte twisted her lips as she studied the pair he'd indicated. They were fine, they just didn't have all the nice details the other pair had. She wanted Reagan to have the best. Her thoughts again flitted to the contents of the teacup on her top shelf and she sighed. Her mother had always said she had champagne taste. The problem was, now that she was no longer teaching, she only had a beer budget.

So not only did she not know Reagan's boot size, but she didn't even have the funds for the ugliest pair of boots on the table. Her shoulders sagged.

At the reminder of the other fly in her ointment, she turned to Bill. "Do you happen to know the size of the sheriff's boots?"

Bill scratched his whiskered chin. "No ma'am. Can't rightly say as I do. Been some time since Reagan ordered hisself a pair. But if you bring me a sketch of his foot, I can make that do just fine."

Charlotte picked up the boot once more and smoothed her thumb across some of the stitches. "How long will it take you to make a pair?"

"Depends on which pair you want. That fancy pair... I need at least four weeks to make those. These others can be done in three."

Charlotte's heart fell a few more degrees. She set the boot down once more. "I see. Well, I hope to order a pair. I have to"—her face flamed at the thought of admitting that she might not have enough money. Never in her life had she had that issue. Papa had always snapped his fingers and given her anything she wanted. But she and Reagan were determined to make a go of things on their own. They'd both determined that they would never ask a loan from anyone.

"Your pardon, ma'am?"

Charlotte came to and realized she'd left Bill hanging in the middle of her sentence. "I'll let you know by Monday if I plan to place the order. Will that give you enough time to get the fancy pair made by Christmas?"

He calculated on his fingers and then nodded. "Just enough time, Ma'am."

"Good. Then I'll let you know."

"Yes'm." Bill hunched onto his stool and took up his harness once more.

Charlotte bade him farewell and tucked her coat close around her throat as she stepped out into the bracing winter wind and snow.

She pressed her lips together in discouragement.

Today was Thursday. She had four more days to come up with the money and a plan. Even if she could figure out how to raise the money, how was she to get a tracing of Reagan's foot without raising his suspicions?

She sighed and headed toward Dixie's Boardinghouse. Maybe Dixie could help her figure this out. At any rate she could use another cup of something hot to warm her up before she walked home.

Find out more about this series here:
http://www.lynnettebonner.com/books/historical-fiction/the-wyldhaven-series/

Want a FREE Story?

If you enjoyed this book...

...sign up for Lynnette's Gazette below! Subscribers get exclusive deals, sneak peeks, and lots of other fun content.

(The gazette is only sent out about once a month or when there's a new release to announce, so you won't be getting a lot of spam messages, and your email is never shared with anyone else.)

Sign up link: https://www.lynnettebonner.com/newsletter/

ABOUT THE AUTHOR

Born and raised in Malawi, Africa. Lynnette Bonner spent the first years of her life reveling in warm equatorial sunshine and the late evening duets of cicadas and hyenas. The year she turned eight she was off to Rift Valley Academy, a boarding school in Kenya where she spent many joy-filled years, and graduated in 1990.

That fall, she traded to a new duet—one of traffic and rain—when she moved to Kirkland, Washington to attend Northwest University. It was there that she met her husband and a few years later they moved to the small town of Pierce, Idaho.

During the time they lived in Idaho, while studying the history of their little town, Lynnette was inspired to begin the Shepherd's Heart Series with Rocky Mountain Oasis.

Marty and Lynnette have four children, and currently live in Washington where Marty pastors a church.

Made in the USA
Monee, IL
15 February 2023

27337469R00187